914·13
4

D1458205

£1.50

# The Library of

## Crosby Hall

KA 0416880 1

BFWG

Sybil Campbell Collection
Formerly Crosby Hall Library

# PORTRAIT OF THE SEVERN

# THE **PORTRAIT** SERIES

*Portrait of the Broads*
J. Wentworth Day

*Portrait of the Burns Country*
Hugh Douglas

*Portrait of Cambridge*
C. R. Benstead

*Portrait of the Chilterns*
Annan Dickson

*Portrait of Cornwall*
Claude Berry

*Portrait of the Cotswolds*
Edith Brill

*Portrait of Dartmoor*
Vian Smith

*Portrait of Devon*
St. Leger-Gordon

*Portrait of Dorset*
Ralph Wightman

*Portrait of County Durham*
Peter A. White

*Portrait of Gloucestershire*
T. A. Ryder

*Portrait of the Highlands*
W. Douglas Simpson

*Portrait of the Isle of Man*
E. H. Stenning

*Portrait of the Isle of Wight*
Lawrence Wilson

*Portrait of the Isles of Scilly*
Clive Mumford

*Portrait of the Lakes*
Norman Nicholson

*Portrait of Lancashire*
Jessica Lofthouse

*Portrait of London River*
Basil E. Cracknell

*Portrait of the New Forest*
Brian Vesey-Fitzgerald

*Portrait of Northumberland*
Nancy Ridley

*Portrait of Peakland*
Crichton Porteous

*Portrait of the Quantocks*
Vincent Waite

*Portrait of the Scott Country*
Marion Lochhead

*Portrait of the Shires*
Bernard Newman

*Portrait of Skye and the Outer Hebrides*
W. Douglas Simpson

*Portrait of Snowdonia*
Cledwyn Hughes

*Portrait of the Thames*
J. H. B. Peel

*Portrait of the Trent*
Peter Lord

*Portrait of the Wye Valley*
H. L. V. Fletcher

*Portrait of Yorkshire*
Harry J. Scott

## ALSO BY J. H. B. PEEL

POETRY
*Time To Go*
*In The Country*
*Mere England*
*Frost At Midnight*

ESSAYS
*To Be Brief*

NOVELS
*A Man's Life*
*Sea Drift*
*The Young Rector*
*The Gallant Story*

COUNTRY BOOKS
*Buckinghamshire Footpaths*
*Small Calendars*
*The Chilterns: A Vision of England*
*Portrait of the Thames*
*Discovering the Chilterns*

# *Portrait of*
# THE SEVERN

J. H. B. PEEL

PHOTOGRAPHS BY THE AUTHOR
AND MAPS

ROBERT HALE · LONDON

© J. H. B. Peel 1968
*First published in Great Britain* 1968

SBN 7091 0432 4

Robert Hale Limited
63 Old Brompton Road
London S.W.7

PRINTED IN GREAT BRITAIN
BY EBENEZER BAYLIS AND SON, LTD.
THE TRINITY PRESS, WORCESTER, AND LONDON

Blessed is the eye
That is between Severn and Wye.

Thomas Fuller, *Gnomologia*

# CONTENTS

1  Inland Bound                                                    11

2  The Lower Estuary: Newport to Chepstow                          15

3  The Upper Estuary: Chepstow to Gloucester                       30

4  Cotswold Country: Gloucester to Upton-on-Severn                 55

5  Walking on the Water: an interlude                              73

6  The Coloured Counties: Upton-on-Severn to
      Stourport-on-Severn                                          77

7  The Industrial Midlands: Stourport-on-Severn to
      Buildwas                                                     99

8  Light and Shade: an interlude                                   119

9  Marcher Country: Buildwas to Shrewsbury                         123

10 Crossing the Border: an interlude                               148

11 The Welsh River: Shrewsbury to Newtown                          156

12 The Heart of Cymry: Newtown to Llanidloes                       179

13 In the Mountains: Llanidloes to Plynlimon                       191

   *Index*                                                         197

# ILLUSTRATIONS

*facing page*

At Berkeley: founded 1490                                      32

Drake's House, Gatcombe                                        33

Awre Church                                                    48

Medieval barn at Ashleworth                                    49

Beware of floods: near Quay                                    64

Tewkesbury Abbey                                               65

Parish church, Upton-on-Severn                                80

Freshwater sailors, Upton-on-Severn                           81

Near the Malverns                                             96

Worcester: Berkeley's Almshouse                              97

The Compleat Angler: near Hanley Castle                     112

Getting acquainted: above Arley        *between pages* 112 *and* 113

The way to the river: near Bridgnorth    *between pages* 112 *and* 113

*facing page*

Yachtsmen at Holt                                           113

The Wrekin: winter floods                                   128

Daffodil-time near Leighton                                 129

Welshpool: Grace Evans' Cottage                             144

At Berriew                                                  145

Powis Castle                                                160

Montgomery: Broad Street                                    161

## ILLUSTRATIONS

The Severn near Montgomery                176
Llanidloes: the Market Hall               177
My favourite Severn bridge                192
The source of the Severn                  193


## Maps

                                          *page*
The Severn: Estuary to Worcester           16
The Severn: Worcester to Source           86–7

*All photographs by the author*

# I

# INLAND BOUND

A GALE careened from the north-east, gaining strength as the light failed. Waves were breaking over the bows. The propeller began to race. Long experience of narrow waters had taught me never to take a strange fairway for granted, so I consulted the chart, which warned me that my ship, like Sir Thomas Wyatt's long ago,

> Thorough sharp seas in winter nights doth pass
> 'Tween rock and rock. . . .

I therefore steered to port, closed the throttle, let-go an anchor, hoisted a riding light, lowered a second anchor, checked against drift, and then returned into the cabin, by whose metronomic lamp I write these words.

Astern I see a twilight of sky and waves. Somewhere ahead, in the gloom, green fields wait, and quiet lanes, and a river leading to its source among mountains. Meanwhile, it may be asked, what has a storm-tossed boat to do with a pastoral riverscape? The question is valid, its answer direct: the pastoral riverscape flows into the Severn Sea. This portrait, in short, begins from a very exposed site, though where that site exactly is, remains a matter of opinion. The Ordnance Survey map bears the words *Mouth of the Severn*, which it emphasizes by marking a lightship and several shallows . . . Middle Ground, Welsh Hook, Usk Patch. The Admiralty chart is even more vivid, for it utters fathoms and other maritime mysteries. Yet not even the Hydrographer of the Royal Navy can precisely separate the river from the estuary, the estuary from the sea. One fact, however, is indisputable; the estuary to-night looks very much as it did when a Severn schoolmaster, T. E. Brown, described it a century ago: "The sulky old gray brute . . ."

And so, from a swaying cabin, I look forward, through time

and space, over the course of Britain's longest river, more than
200 miles northward to the Marcher country, that land of little
ease, wedged between Cymry and the Sais; so compounded of
each that it often failed to dwell peaceably with either; disliking
London as heartily as it mistrusted Wales.

Then the saucepan boiled, and I ate my beans, and afterwards
went on deck to check anchors and lights. The wind had chased
away so many clouds that the moon appeared . . . full, aloof, revealing. To port lay the hills of Gwent, hump-backed like ebony
whales on an indigo sea; starboard, the Cotswolds. Upon the one
side, Englishmen were saying with John Drinkwater:

> . . . I watch the host
> Of the slow stars lit over Gloucester plain,
> And drowsily the habit of these most
> Beloved English lands moves in my brain . . .

Upon the other, Welshmen were saying with Islwyn:

> Gwyllt Walia ydwyt tithau, Mynwy gu'
> Dy enw'n unig a newidiaist ti.

Once more I looked up-river, to a landscape which offered
something to Everyman's every mood. There was geology . . .
that traumatic drama shaping men's homes, crafts, creeds, customs,
clothes. There was excitement . . . a youth escaping by night from
Worcester, thence to hide among Severnside forests, thence to
reach France, and thence to come back into his own as King of
England. There was architecture . . . cathedrals, abbeys, castles,
cottages, manors. There was mystery, awe (call it what you please)
. . . as G. M. Trevelyan said: "Places where the fairies might still
dwell lie for the most part west of the Avon." There was a
kaleidoscope of Englishry . . . the flat solitudes of Aust, the Cotswolds at Tewkesbury, the Malverns at Upton, the orchards and
hopfields in Housman's "coloured counties", the Wyre Forest, the
Wrekin. There was foreign travel . . . into Wales where still some
of the old people cannot speak English. There was craftsmanship
. . . estuary fishing, Gloucestershire mining, Worcestershire glove-
making. There was humanity . . . the countryfolk both great and
small who had shaped the past and were moulding the future.
There was fame . . . old battles, classic schools, kings whose deeds

outlived their dynasty. And there was a yet greater fame . . . the music of Elgar and the Three Choirs, with poetry of many kinds —Langland, Tyndale, George Herbert, Mary Webb, A. E. Housman, W. H. Davies, Robert Frost, John Masefield—all gathered into that company whom Robert Bridges saluted:

> Rejoice, ye dead, where'er your spirits dwell,
> Rejoice that yet on earth your fame is bright;
> And that your names, remembered day and night,
> Live on the lips of them that love you well.

And with that benediction I turned-in, finding it strange that a river which was to grow slim as a brook, was here so plump that I could sleep on it, and still leave room for steamers creeping warily among the shallows.

Next morning I awoke to clear skies, calm water, and a frost so keen that the shrouds gleamed like sugar icing. In that new light I issued four sailing orders.

First: we shall explore from the estuary to the source because a mysterious destination is more exciting than the familiar landfall.

Second: we shall travel amphibiously and at leisure; sometimes on the water, at other times beside it, always willing to venture inland when occasion invites.

Third: we shall not compile a gazetteer. Many books narrate the history and topography of Gloucester, Tewkesbury, Worcester, Bewdley, Shrewsbury. Others analyse the Severn Bore, recite the river's tonnage and poundage, reveal the Roman sites. Certainly those are important features of the portrait. Certainly I may say of them what Carlyle remarked in another context: "I have read diligently what books and documents about them I could come at." But we shall follow also the advice of William of Occam: "Particulars must not be multiplied unnecessarily." In short, we shall try for the unfamiliar aspects of the portrait, its intimate history. Why, for example, did the birthday of a Severn doctor become a national festival in Germany? Whose name was raised by Stanley Baldwin from the dead? Did King Charles II really hide in the branches of Boscobel Oak? Who among the Severn poets offered tenpence-ha'penny to the world's greatest surgeon if he would *not* amputate his foot? How wide is the river at Endmore Wood? How deep at Llanidloes?

Fourth: to praise times past solely because they *are* past, is as childish as to worship everything new.

Portraiture sets quality before quantity, and is concerned rather to evoke than to define. It transcends its own statement of facts. A man can track a river to its source, litanizing the buildings along its banks, the commerce on its water, the great names in its graveyards; and still his understanding may be slighter than that of the man who, though he observed less, has loved more. What the medieval mystic said of the Source of all rivers, is true of this river also: "By love may He be gotten and holden; but by thought never."

# THE LOWER ESTUARY:
# NEWPORT TO CHEPSTOW

PLACES are never gay, never melancholy. Men project their own moods onto an environment. The appearance of a place, however, is not simply a mood projected; it is a matter of fact. And the fact is, the lower estuary does wear a lean look. It is flat. Sometimes it is flooded. Often a wind cuts it. Always it seems to echo Swinburne's reminder:

> That no life lives for ever;
> That dead men rise up never;
> That even the weariest river
> Winds somewhere safe to sea

Yet it is also a fact that the lower estuary has nothing of Tilbury's level horizon. The Quantocks and the hills of Monmouthshire look down upon it. Moreover it breeds its own amphibious race of men, who take a salmon with as much skill as they shoot a wildfowl; soft-footed and muffled-oared folk, reared on a diet of smugglers' tales, of once-in-a-lifetime storms, of solitude and silence. It may be argued that both the lower and the upper estuaries, since they lie so close to Bristol and Gloucester, cannot nowadays be passed-off as a numinous no-man's-land. In summer, admittedly, you will see at Slimbridge the wild fowl which you cannot hear above the cars, aircraft, transistors; Berkeley on a fine Sunday changes from a pleasant village into an unlikeable carpark; even the forgotten lanes of Summerleaze are remembered by Newport's Saturday citizens. Yet out of season—which is to say, on every working day between October and April—the lower estuary is so lonely that two strangers, meeting there by chance, salute each other as latter-day Livingstones.

At its lowest point—say, between Newport and Clevedon—

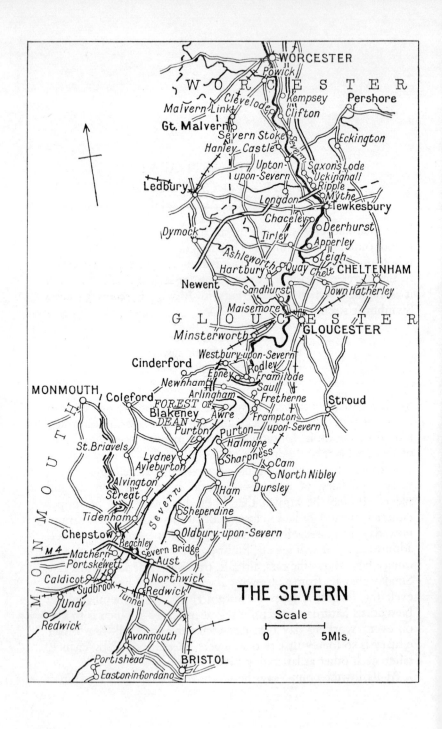

THE SEVERN

Scale

0            5 Mls.

the estuary is an inland sea, nearly ten miles wide, lit by a lightship west of Middle Grounds. Such lights are relatively modern. Even in 1834 the Port of Bristol lacked any official lighting for vessels. It is true that Queen Elizabeth had empowered Trinity House to erect "beacons, marks, and signs for the sea", but these were few and therefore far between. Most British lighthouses existed by courtesy of the Crown, which, in return for a fixed payment, allowed the owners to tax all vessels that passed those lights. A seventeenth-century ship paid to each light an average of one penny per registered ton (the Royal Navy being exempt, though foreign ships paid double).

A century ago these waters bristled with masts. Even fifty years ago many sailing ships and coastal steamers entered Bristol and Cardiff; serving the industrial Midlands via canals to the salt works of Droitwich, the furnaces of Broseley, the factories of Ironbridge, the farmlands of Shrewsbury. Barges travelled from the Severn to the Port of London via the Thames and Severn, and the Kennet and the Avon, Canals. They sailed above Worcester, and crossed the border into Wales. Riding here three centuries ago, Celia Fiennes observed: "The Severn . . . beares shipps and barges . . . carrying coales and all sorts of commodityes to other parts." Two centuries ago Defoe noted the merchants' prosperity: ". . . by the navigation of two great rivers, the Wye, and the Severn, they have the whole trade of South-Wales, as it were, to themselves, and the greatest part of North-Wales; and as to their trade to Ireland, it is not only great in itself, but is prodigiously encreas'd in these last thirty years. . . ." Defoe might have added what the squire of Anthony said of his own Cornish sea: "In passing along, your eyes shall be called away from guarding your fleet to descry . . . the vast ocean, sparkled with ships, that continually this way trade forth and back to most quarters of the world." Those were the days when England not only ruled the waves but also co-opted them. Louis XVIII's Foreign Minister, Chateaubriand, wrote: "If you are born on board any ship, provided she is under sail, you are English born. By virtue of the age-old custom of London, the waves are regarded as English soil." That "age-old custom" owes much to the lower estuary, and especially to the Bristol ship *Matthew*, whose crew of eighteen men, led by the Genoese navigator, John

Cabot, sighted Nova Scotia; and went there again in 1498, and finally launched the Company Adventurers to the New Found Land.

Men still alive can remember the years when the little ships flowed like music round the English coast . . . Humber keel, Norfolk wherry, Hastings lugger, Bristol cutter, Mersey flat, Morecambe nobby, Langstone ketch, Brighton hoggy, Falmouth punt, Thames bawley, Plymouth hooker, Brixham trawler, Severn coracle. "Gone, gone," cried elegiac Elia, "the old familiar faces"; but not yet wholly out of sight, for on the lower estuary you may still see a converted Bristol Channel pilot-cutter, graceful handmaid of the pilots whom John Masefield praised because they

> . . . held up half England's shipping in their hands,
> Both up and down, and saved it from the sands.

The pilot-cutter of the Severn estuary was built to ride the open sea and to skim the inland shallows so nimbly that, when her pilots had boarded the incoming vessels, one man could sail her home single-handed. She was fifty feet long, with mast stepped well back from the stern. Her mainsail was reefed by being rolled round the boom, which rotated on a worm-wheel at the mast. A few had transom sterns; but in most the stern was designed especially against a pooping sea. These vessels remained on active service until after the 1914 War. One of them, the *Jolie Brise*, launched in 1913, became an ocean racer famous in both English and American waters. Reaching up the Hamoaze at Devonport, she once overhauled two naval steam picket boats belching smoke and sparks as their stokers shovelled against defeat. Another pilot-cutter, the *Pet*, was fitted with an engine, and thereafter served as a harbour pilot-boat until 1931. It is difficult to discover when a large sailing ship last plied for hire on the Severn. Certainly the *Haldon*, a three-masted schooner, was working between Ireland and the Severn in 1944, when she was sold for £2,500 (or £1,300 more than she had fetched second-hand in 1923). Nor were those tall ships slow. In 1875 the *Cutty Sark* averaged fifteen knots on six consecutive days, which was faster than a medium-sized cargo steamer in 1968.

The lower estuary is a steep waterscape. Northward the Welsh hills lead to the Welsh mountains; southward the Quantocks etch the sky. Yet even a slight mist will obliterate all sight of land, making a sailor feel like the ancient Mariner:

> As idle as a painted ship
> Upon a painted sea.

At such a moment it becomes difficult to believe that these waters have indeed flowed from Plynlimon. To discover any sign of humanity is impossible. Yet the estuary was the homeland of a very famous piece of humanity. W. H. Davies, whom it marked indelibly:

> Can I forget the sweet days that have been,
> When poetry first began to warm my blood;
> When from the hills of Gwent I saw the earth
> Burned into two by Severn's silver flood.

William Henry Davies was born in Newport on 3rd July 1871, of an English father whose parents (they came from Somerset and Cornwall) kept a tavern, 'The Church House', near Holy Trinity Church. Davies was justly proud of his grandfather, "a retired sea captain", as he called him, "whose pride it was, drunk or sober, to inform all strangers that he had been master of his own ship". In 'The Church House' Davies was born, and from it he attended his first school, which whipped him for shoplifting. As Coleridge had failed to become a successful cavalry trooper, so Davies did not succeed in the window-framing business (though Newport Museum possesses his apprentice indenture as a carver and gilder). Having inherited from his grandmother an annuity of ten shillings a week, he sailed for America, became a tramp there, lost a leg while hitch-hiking by train, returned to England, half-starved in London, wrote poems which no one would publish, and then printed them at his own cost, hawking them from door to door.

In 1908 he produced a prose book, *The Autobiography Of A Super-Tramp*, for which Bernard Shaw wrote a preface: "In making him a poet, Fortune gave him her supremest gift." The preface so boosted the book that, though he never grew rich, Davies no longer had to grow lean. In Newport he was able to rent, for 9s. 6d. weekly, a house which stood, as he said, "at the top of a hilly road, from where one could see, on a clear and mistless day, the meeting of the Severn and the Bristol Channel".

When he was past fifty years old, Davies married the young nurse who had tended him during an illness:

> I thought when I was thirty years
> My marrying time had come;
> But in that year the girl I love
> Was in her mother's womb.

John Masefield once told me that Mr. and Mrs. Davies were "like a pair of lovebirds". They settled at Nailsworth, within sight of the Severn. Having tried several houses, they finally chose 'Glendower', on a steep lane above the town; and there, in 1940, Davies died.

> Let us lie close, as lovers should,
> And count our breaths, as some count sheep;
> Until we say 'Good night' at last,
> And with one kiss prepare for sleep.

According to his lawyer, Davies preferred to live in England because "he did not altogether find the Welsh, except in the humbler valleys, too friendly". Another acquaintance described him as "an ancient Briton in whom the tribal character of the Silurian stock has persisted until the present century". Sir John Squire said of Davies's poems: "A school has arisen which says that the sun, the moon, love, birds, green fields, and flowers have been overdone, and poetry ought to be written about other things. That school is wrong." Fashions in verse will change, but the nature of poetry is immutable, and never was a respecter either of persons or of cliques. Lack of formal education inhibited Davies's critical faculty, prompting him to write, and then permitting him to publish, a number of banal verses. Yet the best of his lyrics are perdurable:

> Sing for the sun your lyric, lark,
> Of twice ten thousand notes;
> Sing for the moon, you nightingales,
> Whose light shall kiss your throats.

Although Newport stands on the Usk, it enjoys a memorable prospect of the Severn. From the famous Double View you may see Wales and Somerset. The town grew up beside a Norman castle on the Roman site of Caerleon—whence the prefix New—

and was razed by Owain Glyn Dwr, but arose again, reached its
zenith during the 1930s, and thereafter declined. At the beginning
of the last century its population was less than 1000; in 1968 it
exceeded 100,000. Clearly something horrible had happened; it
had indeed . . . the Industrial Revolution and the ironworks at
Pontypool, Machen, Abercarn, Bassaleg. In 1945 Newport was
still the chief harbour for the transport of iron on the estuary;
since that time it has lost ground to Cardiff and Avonmouth.
However, it remains the county's administrative capital, and has
moreover a cathedral on the site of a predecessor that was older
than Canterbury's. Newport Cathedral was dedicated to St.
Woolos, that being a Norman corruption of Gwynllws, whose
Saxon hermitage preceded the first cathedral. The present building, though scarcely larger than a parish church, was described by
A. E. Freeman as "a Norman jewel in a Gothic casket". East of
the tower is the Galilee Chapel of St. Mary, made partly of stones
from the Saxon church.

Most of modern Newport looks much the same as most of any
other industrial city, but is redeemed by the splendour of the hills
above it.

Facing Newport from the Somerset coast, Portishead has a tide
of forty-five feet. The Romans fortified Portishead; and the
Saxons raised an earthwork which ends there, the Wansdyke.
Some scholars believe that Wansdyke was built to prevent a Celtic
invasion and to control the Fosse Way; others, that it was simply
a frontier or Wodensdyke (Woden being the god of boundaries).
The Tudor manor house at Portishead was long ago hemmed-in
by docks and housing estates. The church and its lofty tower mark
the site of a vanished village whose market cross, twenty feet high,
stands in the churchyard. The church itself contains a medieval
ring which held the veil that was drawn across the sanctuary
during Lent.

Nearby, the village of Weston-in-Gordano is an interesting
place. Its first name means "the westerly settlement". Its second
name comes either from the Old English gar-denu, meaning 'tri-
angular valley', or from gor-denu, meaning 'dirty valley'. The
natives assure me that the former is the only true meaning. Here
was buried the fifteenth-century Sir Richard Perceval who rebuilt
a church which his Norman ancestor, Ascelin Perceval, had

founded. A twentieth-century member of the family, Miss
Perceval, designed the churchyard cross.

Easton-in-Gordano has a Victorian church with Norman font
and fifteenth-century tower. Every year at this church a sermon is
preached in memory of a local man, Samuel Sturmy, author of a
mariner's manual containing *inter alia* a description of a gale, part
of which was used by Swift, almost verbatim, in *Gulliver's Travels*.

This is the busiest sector of the estuary, with vessels entering
Avonmouth and Bristol. The phrase "Shipshape and Bristol-
fashion" is at least as famous as another local saying, "Paying on
the nail", recalling the four short columns or 'nails' near Bristol
Exchange, on which the merchants paid for their purchases. And
long before the Exchange was built, Severn merchants were trading with Iceland. An anonymous poem, written in or about the
year 1435, tells of voyages to those cold coasts or "costes";

> Of Yseland to wryte is lytill nede
> Save of stokfische; yit for sothe in dede
> Out of Bristow and costis many one
> Men have practiced by nedle and stone
> Thitherwardes wythine a lytel whylle,
> Within xij yeres, and without parille,
> Gone and comen . . . unto the costes colde.

In 1968 Avonmouth Docks handled nearly one-fifth of the
sterling value of the kingdom's annual imports. Although Avonmouth lies some six miles from Bristol, it is nowadays within the
city limits; and new quays have been planned at Avonmouth and
Portishead. This prosperity seems to be contradicted by the relatively small number of vessels on the estuary; but it must be remembered that, until a century ago, the greater part of the world's
maritime commerce was borne by ships of less than 500 tons. At
least twenty such vessels would be needed to carry the cargo of
one modern medium-sized merchantman. Moreover the armada
of coastal craft has almost disappeared. Many of those little ships
were designed, built, owned, and manned by country people.
They were a part of rural England, indigenous as the church, the
mill, the manor. Even today there are men at Minehead who can
remember when their coal and groceries arrived by sea from
Bristol. Long ago Defoe had described England's coastal coal

trade as "the great Nursery for our best Seamen". Less than a century ago these small sailing ships taught Joseph Conrad how to speak English and when to pipe-down. In 1878 he served before the mast of a 200-ton coaster, and his tribute to the east coast sailors is also a description of the Severn seamen: "Tan and pink-gold hair and blue eyes, each built as though to last forever . . .".

Inevitably, meanwhile, one asks: "Which bank of the estuary is the pleasanter?" The swiftest answer comes from the native: "The bank whereon I was born and bred." In fact, both banks are served by a railway, and each admires the other's hills; but whereas the northern hinterland is deeply rural, the southern shores are over-shadowed by Bristol and Gloucester. My own preference is for Monmouthshire. Its unspoiled villages outshine any to be found on the Gloucestershire side. Even the spoiled ones contain relics of an historic past: Caldicot, for example, a *calde cot* or 'cold hut', which may itself be a synonym for Coldharbour, meaning 'shelter for travellers' (in this instance, for travellers by sea as well as for overlanders).

Caldicot Castle stands at the end of a drive, and is admirably maintained by the local Council. During the reigns of the Empress Matilda and King Stephen it was occupied by Milo FitzWalter. Four centuries later it became the seat of the Kemeys family, one of whom—Sir Nicholas Kemeys—died defending Chepstow Castle for King Charles I against the rebels. In 1935 the Kemeys family set a memorial at the place where their ancestor fell.

The village inn at Caldicot is called 'Ye Olde Tippling Philo-sopher', but nobody there could tell me why. I drank a half-pint of cider in the Philosopher's Lounge, and another half-pint in the Tippling Bar.

Caldicot Pill is reached via a lane which, having crossed the railway, ends at a decrepit factory and an old cottage. Beyond, a few hundred yards of cart-track lead to the Severn. This is a nostalgic shore, immersed in memories of ships that no longer pass, of longshoremen who no longer live.

Portskewett, the next village, seems even more oppressed by departed glories, for this wilderness of bungalows and villas was one of the three chief Welsh harbours. Its name is anglicized Welsh; *porth* or 'harbour' and *ysgaw* or 'elder wood'. The mini-ature Norman church is perched on a knoll, and at first sight resembles a model of itself. It has a tympanum and some Tudor modifications to the nave and tower. The village stocks are at Chepstow.

If Portishead is famous for its tide, then Portskewett is noted for its tunnel, the longest in Britain, with a shaft 200 feet deep. Designed by Charles Richardson for the Great Western Railway, the Severn Tunnel—fourteen years in the making—was built by Sir John Hawkshaw. Often the work had to be abandoned because of floods, and always the workmen were in danger. Although only 400 yards of it are permanently under water, the tunnel is nearly four and a half miles long, rising to a height of twenty-four feet and a width of twenty-six. The estuary at this point has a minimum depth of fifty-eight feet at low water, so, for safety's sake, the tunnel roof was set thirty feet underneath the lowest part of the river bed. A row of railway cottages marks the pumping and ventilation plant, from which air can be driven through the tunnel at a rate of 800,000 cubic feet per minute. The pumps are able to raise 12,000,000 gallons of spring-water every day.

Sudbrook, a hamlet of Portskewett, contains a modern pulping factory whose ugliness is emphasized by a terrace of neat Victorian cottages overlooking the estuary. Here too is an Iron Age earthwork, Sudbrook Camp, which was probably occupied until *c.* A.D. 100.

An hour's rambling along the riverside railway will take you into Mathern; but if you approach the village from the Gloucester highway, you may never reach it at all, being discouraged by the contemporary bungalows. A venerable cottage-cum-Post Office warns you that you are half a century too late. Yet the warning is only half justified, for the real village stands near the estuary. That is Mathern. The rest is Modern.

Mathern church is dedicated to a Welsh warrior-princeling, St. Tewdric, who, after the Hindu fashion, spent the last phase of his life as a hermit. Then came the Saxons, burning and looting. News of their incursion reached Tewdric at Tintern, six miles away. And at that point the Saint eschewed his oriental pose. He hurried home to his people, and once again led them to victory over the barbarians. In that victory he was killed, though not before he had asked to be buried at Mathern. So, they buried him there, and built a church to his memory. Long afterwards, when the grave was opened, his skull showed its fatal wound. Tewdric's church decayed, and in the thirteenth century was replaced by the present building (on my last visit I noticed that the verger kept his broom on the stairway to the rood screen). The tall tower was added by Bishop Marshall five centuries ago. Mathern church then became a Court House for the Bishops of Llandaff, of whom four were buried there during the sixteenth century.

The lane continues past Mathern church, into the grounds of what is now a private residence, but was for many years the Bishops' Palace. Above its walls and through a gateway you can see the Palace; a small yet stately building with a tower, oriel windows, Tudor chapel.

Moynes Court, with a fourteenth-century gatehouse and two towers, was rebuilt during the seventeenth century by that Bishop Godwin who discovered the dent in Tewdric's skull. The coat-of-arms of Bishop Godwin appears above the doorway.

The Innage is a Tudor house with an archway of Caernarvon stone.

Mathern is in Monmouthshire, but its neighbour, Beachley, is in Gloucestershire because at this point that county claims both banks of the estuary. Beachley is a nondescript place in flatly uninteresting country. For several decades it was deafened by motorists racing to catch the Aust ferry. Nowadays those nuisances commit themselves to the Severn Road Bridge that was opened during the 1960s.

In 1828 Eleanor Ormerod was born near Beachley, at the mansion of Sedbury Park. This remarkable woman, daughter of a Cheshire antiquary, taught herself to become a naturalist. In 1877 her booklet, *Notes For Observations Of Injurious Insects*, invited farmers and fruit-growers to submit their own observations. Many foreign governments sought Miss Ormerod's advice; and it is impossible to estimate how many millions of human lives were saved by her campaign against the pests that cause famine.

A little below Beachley is an islet named after St. Tecla—another of those uncountably canonized Celts—who was said to have been murdered during the fifth century. Her islet contains a holy well, a hermitage, and some remains of a chapel that became obsolete at the Reformation.

The estuary's function as a national frontier is emphasized by two shallows; the Welsh Grounds (nearly ten miles long) and the English Stones (a relatively small shoal) whereon floats a tale of the Civil Wars. The Welsh ferryman has rowed some Royalists to England, and on his return he meets a party of rebels in pursuit. They order him to row them across. What shall he do? On the one hand, he is a loyalist; on the other, he has no wish to speed his own meeting with Charon. So, at the point of a sword, he compromises by landing the rebels on the English Stones, assuring them that they can easily paddle ashore. Having (one assumes) collected his fare, he hastens home, well knowing that the rebels never will paddle ashore, because the tide has turned and will soon drown them; which it does. Since Mars and Venus share a law of the jungle, the ferryman must be accounted a good soldier. Cromwell, a far more brutal warrior, retaliated by closing the ferry; and closed it remained, for a hundred years.

Facing Beachley across the water, Aust is nothing much to look at, having been for too long a motorway to the ferry. Yet here, as at Beachley, a chapter of science was begun, among the clay and limestone that hold the remains of ichthyosauri, pleisoauri, and other venerable dead-ends. Hither one day came William Buckland, who was born at Tiverton in 1784, son of the vicar of Axminster (a cripple whose crutches were engraven on his headstone). At Axminster young Buckland began to collect fossils; he continued to collect them at Winchester; and when he became the first Reader in Geology at the University of Oxford, his collection went some way towards balancing the University's lack of any collection at all. Being a sound classic, Buckland named his inaugural lecture "*Vindicae Geologicae*". In 1829 he ventured to describe the extinct *Pterodactylus macronyx*. He was the first to suggest that the Earth had passed through an Ice Age; he refuted the fallacy that toads can be embalmed alive within rocks; he uncovered the remains of creatures which had travelled overland from Africa to England; he became President of the British Association and of the Geological Society, Canon of Christchurch, Dean of Westminster. All this scientific method was carried into his domestic life, for in order to prove that his firstborn was not wanting, the Dean weighed him in the balance, against a leg of mutton. Buckland, at all events, believing that Aust Passage contained deposits of nitrogenous materials, collected some fossils, which he sent to Lord Playfair's laboratory in Manchester, where analysis confirmed that the specimens were rich in phosphates. Thus it may be said that the fertilizer industry was born beside the Severn.

Aust's second claim to fame rests upon the opening sentence of the second chapter of the second book of Bede's *A History Of The English Church and People*: "Meantime, helped by King Ethelbert, Augustine summoned the bishops . . . to a conference at a place which the English still call Augustine's Oak, on the border between the Hwiccas and the West Saxons." Aust's claim to be the site of that meeting is disputed by several other places. Whether near the Severn or far, this is what happened: having landed in Kent, Augustine was appointed Archbishop of Canterbury, with instructions to create dioceses and to enforce conformity. The Celtic bishops did not conform, notably in their dating of Easter. Augustine therefore summoned them to a conference, at which he emphasized the errors of their ways. His perorations failed to move them. At a second meeting the bishops decided to put Augustine to the test. If he arose from his chair to greet them, they would again listen to his arguments; but if he received them sitting, they would hear no more from a haughty foreigner. In no sense did Augustine rise to the occasion, but rather descended to threats.

There is one aspect of the portrait which the literature of the Severn has overlooked, the Royal Navy. Although the estuary never vied with Scapa Flow, it did achieve a naval tradition, especially when the Royal Naval Reserve was founded in 1859, manned by fishermen and merchant seamen. There were no R.N.R. officers until 1861, and none could rise above the rank of Lieutenant. By 1914, however, they could become Captain; and in 1918 several had become Commodore. An R.N.R. seaman at the beginning of the twentieth century retired with either a gratuity or a pension. When pounds really were sterling, "Life begins at sixty" came true for many a Severn reservist who had bought a new fishing boat with his long-service reward. The Severn Division of the Royal Naval Volunteer Reserve included the Cardiff Division until 1947. It was an officer of the Severn Division, Commander F. Pollinger, R.N.V.R., who became

Director of Combined Operations Signal Schools during the late war, and the first R.N.V.R. officer to achieve the rank of Commodore.

I have heard many a landsman's yarn about seafaring on the lower estuary; of a swell surging forward at prodigious speed; of waves whipped by a gale. But the truth is, a swell seldom flows fast enough to win the Boat Race; and the highest waves may occur when a gale is slackening. There is nothing unusual about white-capped waves at Beachley. Every wave wears white when its height from trough to crest becomes one-seventh of its distance from the next wave. The real hazards of navigation on the lower estuary are caused not by waves but by shallows and races and rocks. Given a Force 8 wind and a spring tide, the unskilled cabin-cruiser may soon find himself out of control.

Drake himself walked and sailed along the estuary, as we shall soon discover; and so also did another famous Englishman, William Gilbert Grace—W.G. of immortal memory—who was born at Downend, in 1848, at a house called The Chestnuts. By felling part of the orchard, his father, a doctor, was able to make a cricket pitch; and there, with his four brothers and four sisters (not forgetting a dog fielding on the boundary) W.G. learned to play a straight bat. When he was only fifteen years old he opened for his county; scoring 170 in the first innings, and 56 in the second. When he was seventeen he played for All England. When he was eighteen he scored 224 for England against Surrey at the Oval; and on the second day of the match he was allowed to leave the field in order to compete in the National Olympian Association meeting, where he won the quarter-mile hurdles. Many years later, as an elderly man, he was still hitting and skittling in first-class cricket. Those indeed were the days

> When Worcestershire was Fostershire
> And Gloucestershire was Grace.

W.G.'s most memorable achievement was to score 839 in three successive innings, on wickets which a modern public schoolboy would regard as an unkempt outfield. But that was before the playing of games had become a battleground of broken bottles, and the livelihood of men who could not afford to lose. W. G. Grace, by contrast, transmuted a trivial accomplishment into a symbol of chivalry. Even today, and despite the Test Match, some people still say, of a dirty trick: "It isn't cricket."

And yet, in the last resort, it is not the works of men but the wonders of the deep that prevail throughout the lower estuary. To cite Celia Fiennes again, the Severn here "begins to swell into a vast river of seven mile over, before it enters the sea". Wind, water, solitude; those are the first and the last impressions. The lower estuary echoes the wind-woven astringency of Britten's *Peter Grimes*.

And suddenly, between Aust and Beachley, the potential sea becomes an actual river, scarcely a mile wide, joined by its twin, the Wye, flowing down from Chepstow.

# THE UPPER ESTUARY:
## CHEPSTOW TO GLOUCESTER

ALTHOUGH Chepstow stands on the Wye, it provides two notable features of the Severn, which flows nearby, and was the source of local prosperity.

The first feature is shipping and trade, as revealed in the medieval name, *ciepestow* or 'market-place'. The modern Welsh name is Cas Gwent. Until Henry VIII abolished the Lords Marchers, Chepstow merchants paid no duty on exports and imports, so that their harbour became a clearing house for South Wales and the West of England, outstripping Cardiff and Newport. Unlike those two towns, however, Chepstow never became a large industrial zone. On the contrary, in 1881 it ceased to be a Customs port. Defoe found the place ". . . a town of very good trade . . . to this town ships of a good burthen may come up, and the tide here runs with the same impetuous current at Bristol; the flood rising from six fathom, to six and a half at Chepstow Bridge."

The second feature is the bridge itself, which formerly marked a boundary of the Forest of Dean. The oldest extant draft of *The Miners' Laws and Privileges*, printed from a manuscript copy in 1627, states that the Forest bounds extended ". . . between Chepstowe Bridge and Gloucester Bridge, the halfe deale of Newent, Ross, Ash, Monmouth Bridge, and soe farr in the Seassoames as the blast of a horne or the voice of a man may bee heard".

Immediately above Chepstow the estuary makes formidable reading for mariners. From being a river scarcely one mile wide, it expands into an apparent sea several miles broad: never again, it is true, so vast as at Avonmouth, yet at Oldbury-upon-Severn not far short of three miles across. Off Tidenham the fairway swerves to starboard, passes Sheperdine Sands, and leaves a narrow passage into Lydney. Large vessels, however, must hug the right bank

until, above Sharpness, the fairway steers to port. These are the
waters whose pilots Masefield praised:

> The Brig-Men, studying the hourly change
> Of depth, of current-speed, of current-range,
> Of shoals becoming deeps; of deeps that filled
> (No warning given), as the River willed;
> Of sands engulfing any ship that struck;
> In depthless unplumbed squotulence of muck. . . .

Near Oldbury-upon-Severn they have built a dam to feed the
power house and its gawky pylons striding across the landscape.
Oldbury church stands apart from the village, on a knoll called
Cowhill because, says the legend, its original site, near the river,
was so often flooded that a wise woman advised the natives to
tether a brace of heifers and then to rebuild at the spot where the
heifers halted. The present church of St. Arilda was rebuilt after a
fire, but the north porch and fifteenth-century tower are intact.
From the knoll you can see the Welsh hills, and Tyndale's monument nine miles away at Nibley. This is not the loneliest reach
below Gloucester, but sometimes I feel that it is the most solitary.
No road follows the shore. You may walk for half a day, sighting
only three or four houses and the hamlet of Sheperdine whose
New Inn is old and known locally as 'The Windbound'. A row of
stone cottages marks the site of a chapel which became a farmhouse and was then converted into several dwellings. I once met a
Sheperdine lightkeeper whose task was to maintain the fairway
lights down-river to Beachley, including a light on St. Tecla's
Island.

Dr. Johnson believed that a biography, or written portrait,
ought to be revised every century, for even if no new facts were
found, the perspective would have changed. Had this portrait been
written fifty years ago—even thirty years—some of the old people
would have been leading much the same life as their grandparents
led; untroubled by traffic, reading the local newspaper once a
week; freer than their fathers from physical pain, and less likely to
enter a workhouse; yet at heart the same farmfolk, the same fishermen, the same sailors. To them a car would have seemed as useless
as a dukedom to the man who could not afford the price of his
coronet. They walked, or cycled, or rowed; and when a motor

vehicle did shatter their peacefulness, it was likely young Ted's belt-driven Douglas, which he had bought second-hand for fifteen shillings (a fair price in those unjust days). Nearly everyone believed in Heaven, and not a few made some effort to avoid Hell. Adultery never had been unknown, but divorce was a rich man's sin. To fight for King and Country seemed neither criminal nor comic, but rather a mixture of self-interest and self-sacrifice. Rare as exhibits at a circus, black men or brown were regarded with kindly albeit condescending amusement; and foreigners looked best when they stayed where they belonged. Admittedly there was much amiss in the world—for example, the squire ought never to have blocked that footpath—yet the birds sang; and times had been worse; and all good neighbours rallied to another in his need.

These features of the portrait are obsolescent but not yet obsolete. There are still a few cottages hereabouts into which the news of the world is not invited every day. Several have no car, and are therefore doubly concerned not to drive on the French-hand side of the road. Nothing imaginable can restore the quietness and the freedom from scurry which bred this dwindling band; and only a catastrophe could restore the hardship which whetted their courage, carved their faces, and lit some of them with serenity.

The left bank, meanwhile, comes within sight of the Forest of Dean, that ancient home of miners and charcoal-burners. Like the Cornish tinners and the New Foresters, the men of Dean achieved a local Parliament, perhaps the oldest of its kind in England, dating from 1018, having a charter from King Canute, written in Danish. The free miners could dig anywhere within the Forest, except among graveyards and private gardens. The Court of Mine Laws lapsed in 1745, but a seventeenth-century Court House, now a hotel, is still used by the Verderers who grant licences to a few private enterprisers digging for iron, stone, and coal in the Royal Forest. The Dean towns of Cinderford and Coleford are respectively ugly and plain, yet the Forest glades remain vivid in spring, sedate in summer, flamboyant in autumn, and throughout the winter austerely splendid.

St. Briavels is a Forest village with a Norman church and parts of a castle that became a debtors' prison, of which the 1832 Commissioners of Inquiry reported: "There is only one window, which

is one foot wide . . . and does not open." A native of St. Briavels, having worked in a mine for a year and a day, may become a Free Miner, with the right to mine on his own within the Forest. This privilege is said to have been granted in recognition of the Dean miners' services during the medieval Scottish wars, when they undermined the walls of Berwick-upon-Tweed.

Dean miners were at least as wild as Cornish tinners. Tewkesbury men complained to King Henry VI that the Foresters had pillaged their ". . . boats and trowes conveying all manner of merchandise down to the Severn to Bristol". The King at once caused letters of the Privy Seal to be proclaimed throughout the Forest: ". . . that no man of the said Forest should be so hardy to inquiet or disturb the people passing the said river with merchandise, upon pain of treason". This proclamation was ignored, and Tewkesbury again petitioned the King, saying: ". . . the said trespassers came to the said river with greater routs and riots than ever they did before, there despoiling at divers times eight trowes of wheat, rye, flour, and divers other goods and chattels". Parliament thereupon imprisoned the offenders, and ordered them to make a full restitution.

At the foot of the Forest a railway and the south Wales highroad screech within a few hundred yards of the river: not so the remains of a Roman road, about eight feet wide, moving quietly through the Forest from Lydney to Weston-under-Penyard in Herefordshire. The modern highroad defaces Lydney, many of whose houses are bleak and brickish. Lydney church, on the other hand, is of local reddish sandstone, with a graceful seventeenth-century spire. In the churchyard I found an epitaph worthy of Herrick's elegy for Prudence Baldwin:

> Here a pretty baby lies
> Sung asleep with lullabies,
> Pray be silent and not stir
> The easy earth that covers her.

Lydney Trading Estate, whose buildings cover 300,000 square feet, may be good for business but is bad for beauty.

At Lydney lived Sir John Winter, secretary and chancellor to Henrietta Maria, Queen Dowager. In 1640 the Crown sold to Sir John ". . . all the mines, minerals, and stone quarries within the

3

*Drake's House, Gatcombe*

limits of the Forest (of Dean), to work and use the same, together
with all the timber, trees, woods, underwood growing in any part
thereof . . .". His home, White Cross, shared with Berkeley Castle
the honour of defying the rebels when all other royalists in
Gloucestershire had been subdued. While Sir John was away from
home, a rebel force under Colonel Massey planned to capture
White Cross; but having studied its fortifications, they exchanged
valour for discretion, and were content to send a message, calling
on Lady Winter to surrender. Her reply was:

Sir,
   Mr. Winter's unalterable allegiance to his King and Sovereign,
and his particular interest to this place, hath by his Majesty's commission put it into this condition, which cannot be pernicious to any
but to such as oppose the one and invade the other; wherefore rest
assured that in these relations we are, by God's assistance, resolved
to maintain it, all extremities notwithstanding. Thus much in Mr.
Winter's absence you shall receive from
                                                    Mary Winter.

Stung by such courageous contempt, the rebels withdrew to
Gloucester, having destroyed Sir John's iron mills.

   Next year the rebels returned to White Cross, and this time
they besieged it, but retreated when Prince Maurice entered the
Forest with 3,500 troops. Knowing that he could not resist a re-
newed assault, Sir John burned his house to the ground, rather than
allow it to be captured. The master was not unmindful of his
servant. Employed by the King as courier to the Queen in France,
Sir John found himself mentioned in the despatches which he
carried: "This bearer, Sir John Winter, as thy knowledge of it
makes it needless to recommend him to thee, soe I should injure
him if I did not beare him the true witness of having served me
with as much fidelity and courage as any. . . ." The rebels felt
otherwise. On 29th September 1645, the Commons resolved
". . . that Major-General Massy, in consideration of his good and
faithful service which he hath done for the kingdom, shall have
allowed to him the estate of Sir John Winter . . ." less 40,000 trees
which the rebels felled for money.

   A lane from Lydney crosses the railway, follows a few hundred
yards of canal serving a timber mill, and so enters the ghost of

Lydney Harbour. It is a strange experience, to stand on the deserted jetty, in the presence of a few crumbling buildings, one of which has been preserved as a sailing club. Men still alive can remember when the queasy canal sparkled with the bow-waves of bustling barges; derricks and drays worked day and night; seaward the sails outnumbered the clouds. Then indeed Lydney lived up to its Old English name, Lidaneg, "the sailor's island". Now all has changed. I have come here half-a-dozen times without sighting any kind of craft. Yet there must be craft, because Sharpness Docks, across the water, contains a tidal basin 540 feet long, with twenty acres of floating dock, and 12,000 feet of quays. From Sharpness to Gloucester is thirty miles by river, but only sixteen via the ship canal, which carries vessels of 1,000 tons into Gloucester.

This pervasive loneliness extends even to the opposite shore. Above Sheperdine the world seems deserted except for a few elderly fishermen whose skill was once practised by many; notably the Stopping Boats and their salmon nets. But boats are used, too, by Severn wild-fowlers. In 1908 the Court of Chancery decided that all such boats must be afloat, and that if the wild-fowler is aground, or standing on the bottom, he becomes a poacher.

The Severn lampreys are famous. Medieval Gloucester was required to send a gift of them to the Sovereign on his accession and at Christmas. King John, in fact, fined the citizens forty marks for failing to make their gift large enough. To the Empress Catherine of Russia the Severn lampreys seemed so delicious that she ordered them to be sent regularly to St. Petersburg. Celia Fiennes declared: "... here are fine Lamprys taken in great quantertys in their season of which they makes pyes and potts and convey them to London or else where, such a present being fitt for a king. . . ." In 1835, however, Gloucester ceased to supply the Sovereign, pleading that the gift was an anchronism, not required by the Municipal Corporation Act. Since then, I understand, Gloucester has become both willing and able to send fish pie to Buckingham Palace.

And what of the famous Severn coracles that are still to be seen on the river? These flat-bottomed craft are five feet long, three feet wide, and one foot deep; having a board as seat, and around the seat a carrying-strap. Even a winner of the Diamond Sculls would find it difficult to manœuvre these fragile craft, which draw only a few inches of water. Up-river the Welsh build their own type of coracle, and observe a yearly Coracle Festival at Cilgerran. King Edward II's French expeditionary force was equipped with Severn coracles for catching fish in Lent. During the nineteenth century the Severn coracle became especially popular among riverfolk who could not or would not pay tolls to the new bridge-builders.

Meantime, on the right bank, Berkeley is waiting to tell some stories. Unlike many settlements near a river, this village stands on a hill, which is one reason why they built a castle there. Berkeley used to be a pleasant place; now it often becomes unpleasant, partly because of traffic to and from the nuclear power station, partly because its castle has been opened to the public. Necessity decrees that when hordes of people visit a place, the place ceases to be worth visiting. Come here early on a summer morning, or on a wintry afternoon; then you will discover things worth finding.

The main street of Berkeley is flanked by many weathered houses climbing to what must have been a market place. The oldest inhabited building, 'The Mariner's Arms' (formerly 'The Bush') announces that it was built c. 1490, yet it contains two windows c. 1390. In 1086 the manor was held by the King's provost, Roger Berkeley, whose family had taken their name from the place, *beorc-leah* or 'birch wood'. King Henry II, distrusting the Berkeleys, took away their manor, and gave it to a Bristol merchant, Robert Fitzhardinge, who softened the blow by allowing his son to marry a Berkeley. From that day to this the castle has remained with the Fitzhardinge family, except for the period 1485–1553, when William Fitzhardinge, in return for a marquisate, granted the castle and twelve of his manors to Henry VIII and his male heirs. The King's female heir, Mary Tudor, returned the gift. At Berkeley Castle Edward II was imprisoned and murdered, by command of his wife and her lover, Mortimer. In captivity the King composed an elegy:

> On my devoted head
> Her bitterest showers
> All from a wintry cloud
> Stern Fortune pours.

There was a time when Berkeley tried to co-opt Edward II without as it were killing him. " 'Tis true," says Defoe, "they show the apartments where they say the King was kept a prisoner: but they do not admit that he was kill'd there." During the Civil War the castle was among the last Gloucestershire strongholds to fall to the rebels. The damage then done can be seen between the two gate houses.

Berkeley's Early English church stands near the castle; perhaps that is why the church tower was built at some distance from the church itself, lest an enemy used it as a sniping post during a siege.

The most illustrious vicar of Berkeley was a Cornishman, John de Trevisa, who in 1362 became a Fellow of Exeter College, Oxford, and then of the Queen's College; but was ejected with several other scholars for his part in an academic feud. When the recalcitrants left, they took with them the College keys, charters, plate, books, and cash. Having travelled in Germany, Trevisa returned to Oxford, patched a truce with his College, and became chaplain to a fellow-Wyclifite, Lord Berkeley, who encouraged him to translate several Latin works: notably *Polychronicon*, a treatise of nineteen volumes on theology and natural science, which opens with a dialogue between Lord Berkeley and Trevisa. Sometimes the translator inserted his own opinions; for example, disapproval of a decadent monasticism: ". . . and nowe for the most partie monkes beeth worst of all, for they beeth to riche, and that maketh hem to take more hede about secular besynesse than gostely devociouns . . .". Caxton hinted that Trevisa had translated the Bible. Certainly the first Earl of Berkeley gave to King James II a manuscript "of some part of the Bible", which (so he said) had been in Berkeley Castle "neare 400 years". No one knows what became of this manuscript. Perhaps it was the copy that was reputed to have been recorded in the Vatican catalogue, but thereafter vanished without trace. It is interesting to recall some of the words which Trevisa used: *orped* or 'brave', *magel* or 'absurd', *malshave* or 'caterpillar'. These and much else in Trevisa's vocabulary are obsolete, yet he did use one word (to describe the chatter of peasants) which the twentieth century revived: Trevisa spelled it *wlafferynge*; we pronounce it 'waffling'. Trevisa was altogether a doughty man—he rebuked one topographer for omitting Cornwall from the list of English counties—yet he was not Berkeley's greatest son. That honour belongs to Jenner.

Edward Jenner, born at Berkeley in 1749, was the brother, son and grandson of a vicar of the parish. When he was six years old his parents died. Their places were taken by his eldest brother, Rev. Stephen Jenner, who, having succeeded his father as vicar, apprenticed Edward to a Chipping Sodbury surgeon, and later sent him to London, to study under John Hunter, Britain's foremost surgeon. Jenner, too, might have become a fashionable doctor, but he preferred to live near the brother who had been *in loco parentis*. He therefore returned to Berkeley, married a Cotswold girl (one of the Kingscotes of Kingscote), and practised as a country doctor. Berkeley, after all, was his home. There he had learned the names of the plants that heal sickness; there he had studied geology and archaeology; there he had written verses, including *Berkeley Fair*:

> The rosy milkmaid grabs her pail,
> The thresher now puts by his flail. . . .

Jenner's "rosy milkmaid" was more than a poetical cliché, for a Berkeley milkmaid had once assured him that the best defence against smallpox was cowpox. Jenner's London colleagues dismissed the dairymaid as a teller of old wives' tales; but Jenner, a rustic, knew that some rural fictions are less strange than the truths which they enshrine.

At Berkeley, meanwhile, he spent much time studying smallpox, a disease which usually disfigured and often killed its victims. On 14th May 1796, in a thatched summer-house beside the church wall, Jenner took his reputation and a child's life into his own hands and those of a "rosy milkmaid". He inoculated a boy, James Phipps, with a vaccine of cowpox taken from the fingers of a milkmaid, Sarah Nelmes. Six weeks later he inoculated the lad with smallpox. Thereafter he waited, knowing that he had acted unethically and perhaps criminally. But James Phipps did not develop smallpox. On the contrary, he lived to celebrate his hundredth birthday. Jenner himself knew that the child's immunity was not due to chance. It was a genuine example of *post ergo propter*, proving that a vaccine of cowpox could indeed prevent smallpox. Within a few months the London sceptics were clamouring to be vaccinated.

Jenner might have made a fortune from his discovery. Instead, he shared it without thought of personal gain. The vaccine travelled throughout Britain, across Europe, into America. On a single day Jenner vaccinated two hundred people at Petworth in Sussex. Yet seldom was a prophet so dishonoured in his own land. Jenner's first paper on vaccination was declined by every English learned society to which he submitted it. The Royal College of Physicians withheld its fellowship from him until he should have passed the customary examination in Latin, which he declined to do; adding that he never would do it ". . . not even for the whole of John Hunter's museum". Jealousy and ridicule harried him long after his vaccine had saved tens of thousands of lives. Six years passed before he could persuade Parliament to grant £10,000 towards the founding of a National Vaccine Institution, and when the Institute was founded, an envious clique soon manœuvred him out of it. But other nations regarded him otherwise. He was elected to membership of almost every scientific society on the Continent. Foreign monarchs were proud to bestow their Orders on him. Several Roman Catholic countries honoured him with religious processions. In Germany the anniversary of his birthday became a national festival.

Stricken by the death of his wife, and weary of malicious colleagues, Jenner retired from public life though never from private practice. He remained a magistrate, an adept with the Severn lavenet, an ornithologist so well-esteemed that his paper on bird migration was read posthumously before the Royal Society. Nor did he forget his 'guinea-pig', James Phipps; for when the boy became a man, and contracted tuberculosis, Jenner had a cottage built for him, and with his own hands helped to plant the garden with flowers. At the age of seventy-two, Jenner suffered a stroke, but spent the next two years so actively that he killed himself by walking through a blizzard in order to supervise gifts of fuel to the poor. Next morning he was found lying on the floor of his study, unconscious and paralysed. He died within twenty-four hours. By all accounts—and there are many of them—Edward Jenner was indeed a beloved physician. Ten years after Jenner's death, Landor wrote to his own sister: ". . . every child ought to be inoculated with the vaccine at three months by order of the magistrate, and every parent who resists it to be imprisoned. . . ."

Beyond Berkeley the river becomes much narrower, and at Sharpness is scarcely a mile wide. Sharpness itself confirms a description which appeared in a Statute of 1430, declaring this to be 'The King's Highway of Severn'. Though narrow, the highway is not straight, for reefs and shoals between Sharpness and Gloucester make low-water navigation impossible for large vessels, and hazardous for small ones. It was these hazards, at least as much as Bristol's jealousy, which quashed Gloucester's claim to be a port, until the Sharpness Canal bypassed the river. In 1791 a Portuguese captain sailed his ship into Gloucester, which so impressed the citizens that they rang the church bells.

Slimbridge, inland a little from Sharpness, retains traces of old beauty despite the ugliness of new houses. The church is especially handsome, overlooking a farm across the lane. The name Slimbridge, by the way, does not connote a place with a slim bridge; 'slim' means 'slime' from an overflowing river.

Slimbridge produced a couple of Tudor rectors who became bishops. The first was Henry Stokesley, Bishop of London in 1536; the second was Owen Oglethorpe, who, as Bishop of Carlisle, crowned Queen Elizabeth I. One likes to think that his lordship invited some of his Slimbridge flock to witness the Coronation and the four great pageants on the day preceding it, when the young Sovereign, coming by water into the heart of her kingdom, won that heart by declaring: "I will stand ye a good Queen."

Yet those bishops were outshone by a chaplain who was born on this reach . . . was, indeed, thrice-born insofar as three Severn villages claimed to be his birthplace; Slimbridge, Cam, North Nibley. If greatness be defined as the most perdurable influence for good, upon the largest number of beneficiaries, then William Tyndale was among the greatest of all Severn men.

In 1510, from some village hereabouts, William Tyndale or Tindale went up to Oxford, where he graduated under the name of Hichyns. After a period of study at Cambridge, he returned to Gloucestershire, as tutor to the sons of Sir John Walsh of Little Sodbury Manor, which contains a notice: "From the attic of this old house came the inspiration of the noblest thing that England has, our English Bible." In that house, so the story goes, Tyndale told Lady Walsh that, if God spared his life, he would enable any ploughboy ". . . to know more of the scriptures than thou dost". In short, he would translate the Bible into English.

A London alderman, Humphrey Monmouth, gave Tyndale shelter and encouragement, but the Church declined to sponsor his translation of the Bible. Tyndale therefore went to Germany, where he translated the New, and parts of the Old, Testament. As Thomas Campion was to print Romish tracts from a secret press in the Chiltern Hills, so from a secret German press Tyndale sent into England his Bible, financed by English merchants. It cost half a crown or rather less than a mason's weekly wage. To the Papacy, however, a translation of the Bible was heresy. Copies of Tyndale's Bible were therefore publicly burned at St. Paul's Cross; and although many thousands of his New Testaments reached England between 1525 and 1534, the Church tracked-down and destroyed such a vast quantity of them that only two have survived—at St. Paul's Cathedral and at the Bristol Baptist College —together with a fragment of the first quarto edition at the British Museum.

Tyndale's was not the first of such translations. Wyclif had produced his own version in 1380 (and all who read it were liable to forfeit their "land, cattle, life, and goods"). Yet even a cursory comparison reveals the skill with which, by polishing the prose of Trevisa's generation, Tyndale sharpened the quills that were to create King James's Bible: "Though I spake with the tongues of men and angels, and yet had not love, I were even as soundynge brasse: or as a tynklynge Cymball." Sir Thomas More, Lord High Chancellor of England—himself to become a martyr— arraigned Tyndale as "a devilish drunken soul" who had misrendered the Scriptures in order to defame the Church; to which Tyndale replied: ". . . I have never altered one syllable of God's word against my conscience."

The Church meanwhile was eager to discover the secret press and to kill the known heretic. Tyndale, an unworldly churchman, wholly dedicated to his task, consorted with publishers and others whose motives were less exalted. It was only a matter of time before he was kidnapped and handed to the Emperor Charles V by a man whom he had befriended. For eighteen months he languished in a Brussels cell so damp that it nearly killed him. From that cell, remembering perhaps the Severn apple orchards on

a May morning, Tyndale wrote his only surviving letter, appeal-
ing for a warmer cap: "... for I suffer extremely from cold in the
head, being afflicted with a perpetual catarrh, which is consider-
ably increased in the cell; also a piece of cloth, to patch my leg-
gings. My over-coat has been worn out. My shirts are also worn
out. I wish also ... permission to have a candle in the evening; for
it is wearisome to sit alone in the dark."

On 6th October 1536, Tyndale was strangled and then burned
at the stake. *Tantum religio*, cried Lucretius, *potuit suadere malorum*.
But Tyndale's last words were more hopeful: "Lord, open the
King of England's eyes." That hope was well-founded. By his
own labours Tyndale had opened the eyes not only of the King
but also of a kingdom, and was to sharpen the ears of the forty-
seven scholars who created the incomparable simplicity and
majesty of the Authorized Version. The Bible can be assessed apart
from dogma. Its stories are a child's joy; upon English literature its
cadence has set an imprimatur deeper than Shakespeare's; its
message has brought comfort and courage to more people than the
mind can imagine. "If every other English book should perish,"
said Macaulay, "the Bible alone would show to the world
the beauty and power of the English language." That is why
William Tyndale's was among the greatest of all Severnborn
achievements.

Beyond Slimbridge the estuary grows wider, and at Frampton-
on-Severn it changes course from north-east to north-west. The
name Frampton is a corruption of Frome, a local tributary (Welsh
*ffraw*, meaning 'fair' or 'fast-flowing'). The village lies nearer to
the Gloucester–Berkeley Canal than to the estuary. It is an attractive place, set around two sides of the largest village green in
Gloucestershire, with pond and cricket pitch nearby.

Frampton Court was the seat of Richard Clutterbuck, who
transformed an ancient swamp into the present green.

The half-timbered Manor House, now a farm, was the birthplace of Fair Rosamund, daughter of Walter, Lord Clifford. Although part of the house is still called Rosamund's Bower, the
lady's real name was Jane, as Dryden observed:

> Jane Clifford was her name, as books aver,
> Fair Rosamund was but her 'nom de guerre'.

By any name this Rose was so fair that Henry III chose her as his mistress. Anthony à Wood stated: "We rede that in Englonde was a king that had a concubine whose name was Rose, and for her great bewty he cleped her Rose a monde, that is to saye, the Rose of the world." Her summer, however, was brief; and she retired to Godstow Nunnery beside the Thames near Oxford. Her father bequeathed to the Nunnery "The mill of Franton in Gloucestershire and a little meade laying neare it, called Lechton, and a salt pit at Wyche for the health of his soule and for the soules of Margaret his sometime wife, and Rosamund his daughter".

Meanwhile, what does this part of the river look like? The answer is . . . like no other river in rural England. Still nearly two miles wide, the Severn resembles an inland sea. By comparison the Thames is dwarfed, the Tweed is dwarfed, and so are the Tyne and the Tees and the Avon. Looking down from the hills, you suppose that the upper estuary might carry an Armada, and still leave room for manœuvre. And although at first glance both shores appear lonely, each supports several villages: Saul, for example, taking its name from *salh-leah*, the Old English name for sallow wood, which they still call 'salley'. During a recent flood nearly fifty houses were swamped at Saul, and hundreds of acres lay under water. Rainfall at the source of the Severn was 28·4 inches. Even in Bewdley the average December norm of 3·5 rose to 8·21 inches.

Fretherne, the next village, is marred by some bad Victorian architecture; notably the church, which had the misfortune to be rebuilt (1851) by the Rev. Sir William Lionel Darell Bt., whose seat, Fretherne Court, is as ugly as the church. However, from the summit of Barrow Hill you can see nearly forty churches that are worth looking at. Fretherne might have had its own railway station because Brunel wished to span the river at this point, but the Admiralty objected, and the line was diverted via Gloucester. Not everyone in those years welcomed the new roads and railways. Brunel's line from Oxford to Cheltenham was obstructed by the Thames and Severn Canal Company and by Squire Gordon of Kemble; the former because it feared competition; the latter because he valued privacy. In the end each objector received £7,000 as compensation for inconvenience, and the railway had to build a tunnel lest Kemble House were disturbed by the passing trains.

The hamlet of Wick or 'dairy farm' was the birthplace of an eighteenth-century 'card' named John Gully, son of the local publican. He became champion heavyweight boxer of England, M.P. for Pontefract, and the owner of three Derby winners.

Framilode was From-gelad or 'ferry near the Frome'. This pleasantly Victorian village, looking to the Severn for its livelihood, is the hub of the elver fishing, with Epney as its collecting station, the only one of its kind in the world, or so they told me. Born in the Sargasso Sea, elvers or young eels cross the Atlantic leisurely—two years is an average time—reaching the Severn in April. There they are caught in gauze nets on a timber frame. Some elvers elude the nets, proceed up-river, and explore the fields in search of ponds. But they never spawn in England. The surviving adults return to the Sargasso.

The elver trade is controlled by the Ministry of Agriculture and Fisheries, which has stocked the upper Thames with half a million elvers from the Severn. In 1965 the Polish government sent an air liner to collect four million Epney elvers. The medieval Abbots of Gloucester leased their Framilode fishing to the Abbots of Winchcombe at £4 yearly. Today that fishing is worth a fortune.

Whenever I do pass this way I never fail to meet someone carrying fishing tackle, as though to emphasize that the Severn supports almost every kind of British freshwater fish (trout and barbel were introduced in 1956). The estuary is visited also by whales, sharks, eels, dolphins, sturgeons, lampreys, lamperns, and many of the common saltwater fish. As one would expect, the fishing is not a public right. In the words of the Severn River Authority: "It is necessary to obtain a licence from the Severn River Authority before fishing for freshwater fish or salmon."

This reach has just enough villages to seem companionable, yet few people walk beside it, for it lacks a well-defined public footpath.

The opposite shore is a deeper countryside. Even in summer I have walked north from Lydney's deserted harbour without meeting anyone between noon and teatime. On the right bank all roads lead to Gloucester, and at holiday time all roads seem to lead *from* Gloucester; but on the left bank several green lanes climb a country quiet as Clun.

One feature of this sector is defined by the two Purtons, facing each other across the estuary, both in Gloucestershire, and each taking its name from the Old English *pirige* or 'pear tree'. Even today the left bank is studded with orchards; and among them Sir Walter Raleigh stayed, at Purton Manor, now a farmhouse. To the next hamlet, Gatcombe, came Sir Francis Drake.

Gatcombe offers a vivid example of the steep hinterland hereabouts. Less than fifty yards from the estuary, the lane out of Gatcombe begins to climb and soon becomes too steep for cycling. This place is a favourite of mine. You approach it via the steep lane through woods, and when you arrive you find only four (or is it five?) small houses sheltered by a seawall carrying the railway and concealing the estuary. Drake lodged here, at a house which became 'The Sloop Inn' when the railway was built, and is now a private residence, Drake's House. Gatcombe was once a port, handling food and other supplies for the Forest of Dean. Later it built a dry dock for the Severn stopping boats.

But perhaps you are still puzzling over the visits of Raleigh and Drake. Why did two famous sailors come to these remote hamlets? They came to buy timber for the Fleet. Nowadays officers of flag rank do not scour the countryside seeking materials for their ships. That and much else belongs to the Admiralty; but there was a time when the Royal Navy looked to the private enterprise of its senior officers, who in any event were eager to obtain the best timber for their own squadrons. But Drake and Raleigh did not visit the estuary solely in search of quality; quantity had become an urgent challenge. In 1610, for example, there were in Sussex alone 140 forges using 1,800 trees a week, or about 80,000 every year. This so alarmed King James I that he ordered the royal forests to be surveyed; they were found to contain only 350,000 trees, of which less than half were fit for shipbuilding. Mammon as usual was myopic. Having razed the Sussex Weald and many other woodlands, the ironmasters still refused to use coal for smelting, because of the price. Fortunately for England, the industrialists in 1651 devised a coke burning furnace. But centuries of havoc were not to be mended overnight. Long after Drake and Raleigh had died, Samuel Pepys was turning to the Severn for naval timber. On 20th June 1661 his diary stated: "Up by four or five o'clock, and to the office (the Admiralty), and there drew up the agreement between the King and Sir John Winter about the

Forrest of Deane. . . ." Pepys and Winter then consulted the map: ". . . I turned to the Forrest of Deane in Speede's Mapps, and there he showed me how it lies . . . with the great charge of carrying it to Lydney." Two months later Pepys and Winter met again, at 'The Mitre' in Fenchurch Street, where they enjoyed ". . . a venison pasty . . . and good discourse, most of which was concerning the Forrest of Deane, and the timber there, and the iron-workes with their great antiquity, and the vast heaps of cinders which they find, and are now of great value, being necessary for the making of iron at this day; and without which they cannot work . . .". Shortly after this, a captured Dutch ship, the *Elias*, was converted especially to carry timber from the Forest of Dean to the royal shipyards at Woolwich. She must have called at Gatcombe many times. And England's enemies many times plotted to destroy the source of her cargo, for John Evelyn's *Sylva* declared: "I have heard that in the great expedition of 1588 it was expressly enjoined the Spanish Armada that if, when landed, they should not be able to subdue our nation, and make good their conquest, they should yet be sure not to leave a tree standing in the Forest of Dean." Fuller's *Worthies*, which appeared two years before *Sylva*, emphasized the Spanish eagerness to destroy Dean Forest: ". . . a Spanish ambassador was to get it done by private practice and cunning contrivances." The Armada certainly compelled the politicians to look to their moat. Writing a century after Drake, Samuel Hartlib in his *Legacy Of Husbandry* reported: ". . . the State hath done well to pull down divers iron-works in the Forest of Dean, that the timber might be preserved for shipping, which is accounted the toughest in England, and, when it is dry, as hard as iron."

From Gatcombe a green lane meanders to Awre, a village of almost tangible quietude. There are handsome old houses here, an hospitable inn, and a church not far from the river. Domesday Book mentions a salt-works at Awre (probably for curing fish) and a village priest (which suggests that the present church was built on the site of an earlier one). Awre has its place in English literature, for an entry in the church register says: "Let it be remembered for the honour of this parish, that from it first sounded out the Psalms of David in English metre, by Thomas Sternhold and John Hopkins . . ." Sternhold (*obiit* 1549) may have been born at Awre; certainly he lived here, on an estate called Hay Field. He was sometime Master of St. Bartholomew's Hospital—not the London hospital but an almshouse in Lower Westgate Street, Gloucester. Hopkins, who died in 1570, as rector of Great Waldinfield, Suffolk, owned an estate in Awre parish, called Wood End. He wrote some verses for Foxe's *Acts and Monuments*, and is said to have composed the old 'One Hundredth'. Together at Awre these two men translated their metrical version of the Psalms. In the complete edition (1562) sixty psalms were signed by Hopkins, forty by Sternhold.

I visit Awre at least twice a year, and always I come away the better for my visitation. The hostess at 'The Red Hart' provides the sort of beef-and-pickle sandwiches that elsewhere would cost thrice as much. In the tap room they told me that in 1943 a whale was sighted at Awre. The unfortunate creature died of exhaustion, on Church Rocks, and somebody stole two tons of its flesh. On another of my visits to the inn, I found the entire company—hostess and five elderly villagers—listening raptly to a radio programme entitled *Listen With Mother*. "Now," said the voice, "are you all sitting comfortably? That's right. Once upon a time there was a dear little rabbit called Bunny. . . ."

Etloe, which is a tithing of Awre, was the birthplace of William Wickenden, a farmer's son, who, by the generosity of Dr. Edward Jenner and other local gentlemen, was sent to read theology at Cambridge; but illness unfitted him for the priesthood, and he took to writing verses instead. Some of his louder lines shall introduce a remarkable feature of the portrait, the Severn Bore:

> And see, hoarse Boreas shakes the craggy shore,
> And circling eddies mark the whitening bore,
> And wave impelled by wave, tremendous sound,
> And like a deluge whelms the hissing ground.

Wickenden was not the only poet who described the Bore. Michael Drayton called it by its Tudor name, Hygre:

> . . . the Hygre wildly raves;
> And frights the straggling flocks . . .

Camden's prose is less vague and more vivid: ". . . rage and boisterousness of waters, which I know not whether I may call a gulph or whirlpool, casting up the sands from the bottom, and rowling them in heaps, it floweth with a great torrent . . .". Yet even in Camden's day the Severn fishermen ruled the waves: "The watermen us'd to it, when they see this Hygre coming do turn the vessel, and cutting through the midst of it avoid its violence. . . ." Two centuries later Defoe watched the Bore ". . . rolling forward like a mighty wave: so that the stern of a vessel shall in a sudden be lifted up six or seven feet upon the water . . .".

What, then, is the Severn Bore? A full answer lies deep in the physics of local geology. A simple definition goes somewhat as follows: the Severn Bore is a tide which, meeting a residue of slack or ebbing water, becomes a wave. The Bore occurs every month, just before and soon after a spring tide; and the most impressive Bores occur during the spring tide nearest the vernal and the autumnal equinox. Starting near Sheerness, the Bore reaches its maximum height between Framilode and Stonebench, sometimes thirty-three feet high. Above Gloucester it subsides, though an aftermath has been known to ruffle the tideless waters of Worcester, where a man was killed by a swordfish. At Fretherne, as the river becomes suddenly narrow, the Bore rears up like a wall, and is followed by a second and a third wave, and after that by the tide itself, seething and soaring.

Some people assume that the Severn Bore is unique, but they are mistaken. There is a Bore—a far more impressive one—at Duncansby near John o' Groat's in Caithness. The modern *North Sea Pilot* contains a verbatim description which it printed in 1875: "Before entering Pentland Firth all vessels should be prepared to batten down, and the hatches of small vessels ought to be secured even in the finest weather . . . the transition from smooth water to broken sea is so sudden that no time is given for making arrangements." Duncansby Bore has its counterpart at the west end of the Firth, known to mariners as the Merry Men of Mey, and when these two wage war, even the *Pilot* breaks into seamanlike poetry: ". . . a sea is raised which cannot be imagined by those who have never experienced it." And that is what a landsman will say when for the first time he sees the Severn Bore surging through Stonebench.

A different sort of surging occurs on the left bank, where cars

*Awre Church*

and lorries thunder along a highway linking industrial Wales with
the industrial Midlands. All the more remarkable, therefore, is the
beauty of Newnham-on-Severn. A green bank bisects part of the
main street, and on it the villagers have planted flowers, so that
snowdrop, crocus, primrose and daffodil each in season tells a new
time of year. If you come here early in the morning, you will find
yourself in a quiet place, formerly a borough, with a lane called
Severn Street, dipping to the water. And if you go down to that
water, you will find there a boat or two, and some hulks, and
much mud, and a tide flowing so fast that it swirls the logs and
litter out of Gloucester. But you will seldom see a human being
there, and scarcely ever a ship. Yet this was once a busy port, from
which Richard Strongbow, Earl of Pembroke, sailed to conquer
Ireland, taking with him miners and smiths from the Forest of
Dean.

Newnham church—the third on that site—bestrides a hill of red
marl, overlooking the estuary's lordly curve past Arlingham;
overlooking, too, the roofs of Fretherne, Frampton, the Cotswolds, the Malverns and faraway Exmoor.

In 1775 a girl was murdered in a meadow near Nass church-
yard; and men said that grass never again grew on the spot where
she had died. The bereaved father, Ronyon Jones, moved from
Nass to Newnham-on-Severn, and built a house there, called 'The
Hay', in which is preserved a sword that King John presented to
Newnham Corporation.

They made glass at Newnham; and during the seventeenth
century some of it was used by Sir Edward Mansell, to build
Britain's first greenhouse, which he heated with coal from the
Forest of Dean.

Coal of another sort—'sea coal'—was harvested on this reach,
having been cast overboard in order to lighten ship while riding
the shallows. Samuel Rudder described the harvest two centuries
ago: "They sink a net with mouth extended by an iron hoop with
a long pole just before the net, by which means and by the assistance of the current the coals roll in."

Above Newnham-on-Severn the estuary turns from north-east
to south-east, leaving Westbury-on-Severn a mile or more inland.
At Westbury, as at Berkeley, the church stands apart from its
tower; the lower part of the tower (c. 1270) was used as a look-out

4

*Medieval barn at Ashleworth*

post against marauding Welshmen. The spire, 160 feet tall, was added during the seventeenth century. In 1644 it once again became a look-out post when some rebels climbed it in order to snipe at a party of King's men sheltering in the church. Inside the church a glass case contains a book which is sometimes mistaken for a chained Bible. In fact, it is Foxe's *Book of Martyrs*, a copy of which was given, by the printer, to the birthplace of every person whom the book mentions: in this instance a lawyer, John Baynham of Westbury Court, who in 1531 was charged with Protestantism. There is an irony in the date, for in that same year Henry VIII compelled Convocation to recognize him as "Protector and Only Supreme Head of the Church and Clergy in England" (Archbishop Warham being allowed to insert a vague *caveat*: "so far as the laws of Christ permit"). Yet this same King had already written an orthodox tract, *De Septibus Sacramentis*, for which Rome awarded him a title that is still borne by his successors, *Fidei Defendor* or 'Defender of the Faith'.

John Baynham, at all events, was taken from his chambers to the Chancellor's house at Chelsea, where they flogged him and hauled him thence to be racked in the Tower. His wife was sent to the Fleet Prison. Under torture Baynham recanted. He was fined, made to do public penance at Paul's Cross, and then released. Within a month he recanted his recantation, and was again tortured in the Tower: but this time he stood fast, and on May Day 1532, was burned alive above a barrel of pitch. His dying words were: "O ye Papists, behold, ye look for miracles and here now ye may see a miracle, for in this fire I feel no more pain than if I were in a bed of down. . . ."

Adjoining the church, Westbury Court contains parts of an earlier house, seat of the Baynham family between the reigns of Edward III and Henry VIII. In 1574 the Court was purchased by Sir Duncombe Colchester; in 1694 Colonel Maynard Colchester designed the gardens that can be seen from the main road.

The Severn hereabouts often breaks its banks, which is one reason why they bear much fruit, notably around Minsterworth, the Saxon Mortune, or 'place beside the water'. In 1086 it became Menstrelie, and in 1154 Minstreworth, 'the place belonging to the minster' (that is, to St. Peter's, Gloucester). Deafened by a main road, Minsterworth is not attractive, though in years past its riverside orchards must have made a brave sight at blossom time. Minsterworth boatmen were exempt from harbour dues and market tolls, a privilege which they acquired when their village became part of the royal Duchy of Lancaster.

Minsterworth looks across the river to Elmore, where at low tide it is possible to ford the river via a shelf known as Church Rock. A cottage, called 'The Shark', recalls the surprise of a Severn man who caught such a fish in his long-net. During the 1930s a school of dolphins was sighted on this reach.

Elmore Court, incorporating part of a thirteenth-century house, is the seat of the Guise family, who still possess the document with which John, son of Hubert de Burgh, conveyed the lands to Sir Anselm de Gyse in 1274.

Nearby, at Hardwick, Britain's first reformatory for boys was founded in 1854 by Thomas Barwick Lloyd Baker. Soon after Hardwick the river catches sight of Gloucester, and at once sheers away, as though disliking what it saw.

Gloucester was recognized as a port by Queen Elizabeth in 1580, but the Bristol merchants protested so strongly that within two years Gloucester had lost its right to collect customs dues. Three centuries later the new canal enabled Gloucester once again to become a port. In 1968 its docks covered an area of fourteen acres containing 10,000 feet of quays, from which mixed cargoes were carried to Worcester in vessels up to 400 tons and to Stourport in vessels up to 150 tons.

Gloucester has scarcely anything to show that it was once a type of Cheltenham for retired soldiers of the Roman army. During the Civil Wars a large part of the city was either burned or bombarded. Some eighteenth-century businessmen tried to create a Gloucester spa, by building a pump room and other fashionable amenities, and joining three springs via a pipe. But their efforts failed. Gloucester never did challenge Cheltenham; and in 1962 two of its three springs were declared unfit for drinking.

The less said about modern Gloucester, the better. Of all the Severnside towns it is the largest and the ugliest ... miles of arc-lit carriageways, factories, housing estates ... deafened day and night by lorries and other commercial travellers ... a pimple blotching the Cotswold complexion. Gerard Manley Hopkins diagnosed the earlier stages of the disease:

... all is smeared with trade; bleared, smeared with toil,
And wears man's smudge ...

Whenever I enter Gloucester, I practise the preaching of another
poet, Stephen Spender:

Never to allow the traffic to smother
With noise and fog the flowering of the spirit.

The substance of that spirit is Gloucester Cathedral and the
tower that prevails above the chimneys. Robert Louis Stevenson
was right when he said: "Mankind is never so happily inspired as
when it made a cathedral." And Defoe also was right when he
described Gloucester's cathedral and bridge as ". . . all I see
worth recording of this place".

Although Gloucester is prosperously null and void, it does have
three good tales to tell, about two good poets and a bad one. The
bad one, John Taylor, left Gloucester because its Crypt Grammar
School had (as he put it) "mired him in Latin". After some seafaring, Taylor became a Thames waterman, writing and hiking
through Britain and the Continent.

The second poet, William Ernest Henley, was born at Number
2, Eastgate Street, in 1849. He too attended the Crypt Grammar
School, but was never "mired". When he was sixteen he lost one
of his feet from tuberculosis of the bone, and nine years later, while
starving as a journalist in London, he was told that he must lose
the other foot. He thereupon sailed to Edinburgh—that being then
the cheapest way of getting there—and presented himself to
Lister, who was practising at Edinburgh Hospital. Henley offered
the surgeon all his money—tenpence ha'penny—if he would save
his foot. Lister agreed and succeeded. That was in 1873. Two years
later Henley was still in hospital, but not ineffectually, for Leslie
Stephen, editor of *The Cornhill*, had published one of his poems,
about life in a hospital ward; and in February of that year, while
lecturing at Edinburgh, he visited the bed-ridden poet, and afterwards introduced him to Robert Louis Stevenson. The two men
became friends. Stevenson, indeed, used his influence to secure for
Henley the editorship of *London*. Later, as editor of *The Scots
Observer*, Henley published some verses of a promising youngster:
*Barrack Room Ballads* by Rudyard Kipling. When Joseph Conrad,

middle aged and poor, was wondering how he could support his family, Henley accepted his *The Nigger of Narcissus*, and published it in *New Review*, between July and December, 1897. Greatly encouraged, Conrad wrote to Edward Garnett: "Now I have conquered Henley, I ain't 'fraid of the divvle himself." Henley's own poems have fallen out of fashion, yet some of them span the generations, as when he confesses that he loves the blackbird above all others:

> For his song is all of the joy of life,
> And we in the mad, spring weather,
> We two have listened till he sang
> Our hearts and lips together.

The third poet, Thomas Edward Brown, was Henley's head-master at the Crypt Grammar School. Born in 1830 at Douglas on the Isle of Man, Brown took a double first at Christchurch and a fellowship at Oriel. From Oriel he went to Gloucester and then to Clifton College. As with Emily Bronte and Haworth, so with Thomas Brown and Man; he pined for home. What he called "the Gloucester episode" remained an unhappy memory. However, before retiring to his well-beloved Island, Brown lived awhile at Clevedon, on the lower estuary, where he felt more kindly toward the Severn, and was able to praise its seascape:

> A grassy field, the lambs, the nibbling sheep,
> A blackbird and a thorn, the April smile
> Of brooding peace, the gentle airs that wile
> The Channel of its moodiness . . . .

As Sir Arthur Quiller-Couch remarked, Brown attracts ". . . a band of readers to whom his name is more than that of many an acknowledged classic".

And there was a fourth Gloucester notable, Robert Raikes, son of and successor to the proprietor and editor of *The Gloucester Journal*. In 1780, at a timbered cottage in St. Catherine's Street, Raikes opened a Sunday School which is commonly regarded as the first, though in fact it had been preceded in 1777 by the Rev. Thomas Stock's Sunday School at Ashbury in Berkshire. Yet neither Berkshire nor Gloucester held the first Sunday School, for in 1769 Hannah Ball founded a School at High Wycombe.

Seven years previously, at the age of twenty-nine, Miss Ball had experienced a mystical trance, and was deeply moved by a sermon which Wesley preached at High Wycombe. Wesley himself said that she possessed a "... peculiar love for children and a talent for assisting them". Nevertheless, Robert Raikes was among the pioneers of Sunday Schools. His statue is in the park near Southgate Street; another stands on the Thames embankment.

The Severn meanwhile is about to pluck a surprise from the nettle of Gloucester's industrial desert.

## COTSWOLD COUNTRY:
## GLOUCESTER TO UPTON-ON-SEVERN

HAVING shaken off the soot of Gloucester, the Severn not only recovers its spirits but also changes its appearance; and this surprise it springs while still within sight of the factories, at a place called Over (Old English *ofer*, meaning 'ridge' or 'slope'). Now at last and for the first time the Severn is a rural river, tree-lined on the left bank, and slender enough for a schoolboy to swim across it. Over Bridge—designed by Telford with a single arch of 150 feet—was opened in 1828 to replace a thirteenth-century bridge of eight arches.

Presently comes Maisemore, a village with several thatched, timbered, and redbrick cottages. The name emphasizes its nearness to Wales, being a Saxon version of *maes mawr* or 'large field'. Canon Isaac Taylor reckoned that the prefix *Llan*, meaning 'a church', occurs in eleven place-names near the Severn in Gloucestershire and Shropshire. Maisemore's concrete bridge (1956) replaced a stone bridge (1785). A Cross at the east end of the new bridge bears this inscription: "This Cross was taken from St. Michael's Church Gloucester in 1956. A Cross which stood on a bridge built about A.D. 1200 carried this inscription in Latin and Norman-French: In honour of Our Lord Jesus Christ Who was crucified for us William Fitz Ankertil of Lilton made this Cross and the same William Fitz Ankertil Began this Bridge of Maisemore."

Natives call this The Long Reach, perhaps because the river meanders for miles without sighting a village. You must walk inland a mile, on the right bank, before you catch a glimpse of Sandhurst, whose church contains a Norman lead font. In all England there are only sixteen such fonts, and six of them are in Gloucestershire.

East of Sandhurst a lane leads to Down Hatherley. The rectory (now demolished) was the birthplace of Button Gwinnett, the rector's son. Having failed as a businessman in Wolverhampton, Gwinnett sailed to America, where he so prospered that he became President of the State of Savannah and in 1776 a signatory of the Declaration of American Independence. Gwinnett's church was rebuilt, but the lead font at which he was baptized has survived; the smallest of its kind in Gloucestershire.

Many people would choose Deerhurst as the showpiece of this reach, but I prefer Ashleworth, a hamlet of ancient cottages, set around a green and the base of a medieval Cross. The old vicarage must be among the loveliest Tudor houses in Gloucestershire, shaped like the letter E, with a storeyed porch in the middle.

Parsonages are a feature of the Severn, and since we shall meet many of them, this seems the moment at which to consider the domesticities of a vocation that began as the professions of poor and often unlettered men, then ranked next after the squire, and is now the occupation of graduates with less pocket-money than a village constable. In the Severn countryside, as throughout England, the parson has from time immemorial suffered what we now call a housing problem. Thus, in 1280 the vicar of the Gloucestershire parish of Churcham had nowhere to lay his head; so, Bishop Thomas de Cantilupe ordered the Abbot and Convent of Gloucester to give him the wood wherewith he might build a vicarage. In 1671 the rector of Hempsted had no home; so, Viscount Scudamore of Holme Lacy in the county of Hereford built a rectory at Hempsted; on the doorway of which, the second occupant, Archdeacon Gregory, wrote a secular *Te Deum*:

> Who'er doth dwell within this door
> Thank God for Viscount Scudamore
> A.D. 1671
> *Sciant posteri.*

*Posteri sciunt.* In 1830 or thereabouts the Bishop of Gloucester reported that one hundred of his parishes lacked any kind of building which could be converted into a parsonage; and although the Bishop did build or enlarge 100 clergy houses, his successor's first visitation revealed that 114 benefices were still without a parsonage. These facts suggest that pluralism was sometimes a necessary evil.

From Ashleworth a lane leads to the river half a mile away, past a house, a church, and a barn that once belonged to St. Peter's, Gloucester.

The church, almost touching the house, offers a cross-section of architecture from Norman to Tudor, and of geology from limestone to Dursley tuff-stone.

The house (they call it Ashleworth Court nowadays) is a fortified medieval dwelling which the Tudor owners made more comfortable. The present owners, who are farmers, have made the place even more comfortable.

The barn has scarcely changed since Abbot Newbury built it four centuries ago. According to my pacing, it is 125 feet long by 25 feet wide.

There are on the Severn many groups of buildings which linger in the memory; some because of their history; others because of the beauty of their appearance; and it is difficult indeed to choose one group that outshines all others. This group, certainly, stands high among my own favourites. And beyond it, a few hundred yards away, the lane ends at my favourite Cotswold Severnscape. Perched on a knoll, a short stone's throw from the river, The Boat Inn resembles rather a cottage than a pub. Its paved terrace is just small enough to contain two chairs and one table. Below, the river glides and glistens and sometimes gurgles. Above, the Cotswolds mount up like unweary eagles. This remote place was once a quay-of-call for bargemen; and on the signpost it still is Quay. If you do come hither, come on foot, leaving your vehicle by the road at Ashleworth Court, for this lane is so narrow, its destination so delicate, that even one car will create an inelegant concourse.

Set a man in a meadow beside a river, and then challenge him to name it. What does he look for first? If he is wise, he looks at the horizon. Are there hills on it? Or mountains? Or only sky? Then he scans the middle distance. Is it fertile? Barren? Arable? Woodland? Does it bear oats? Apples? Hops? Heather? And the houses . . . are they of grey stone or red? Brick-and-flint maybe? Thatched, slated, tiled? A countryman will not undertake to name a river by its buildings alone—unless they are weatherboarded, or oast-houses—but he will cite a county via its speech. The speech hereabouts has lost its western lilt. Among old people the vowels may still echo the softer sound of Awre and Aust, but already a Midland timbre is heard. By such katabolism a region is broken down and forced to reveal its identity.

Quay is the place at which, for me, the Severn confirms an identity that will abide until, above Llanidloes, the mountains impose a transformation. "Rivers," said the Latin poet, "are roads that move." And movement, since it implies change, may seem to destroy identity. Even so, all rivers contain a part which distils the whole . . . the Duddon at Seathwaite, cascading a narrow gorge . . . the Stour at Honington, which Shakespeare may have forded on a truant holiday . . . The Fal at King Harry . . . the Thames above Cliveden . . . the Esk below Langholm, speckled with salmon . . . the Lune as it baptizes Kirkby Lonsdale, with the fells for godfather . . . and at Quay the Severn, red-banked, cattle-cropped, hill-swept, sinuous. Quay is the place to be when

> . . . whoever wakes in England
> Sees, some morning unaware,
> That the lowest boughs and the brushwood sheaf
> Round the elm-tree bole are in tiny leaf.

And not only the elm tree, for here the river enters a countryside long renowned for its orchards. Daniel Defoe passed this way: ". . . all the while on the banks of the Severn; and here we had the pleasing sight of the hedgerows being fill'd with apple trees and pear trees". In one respect, however, the past differed from the present: ". . . and passengers as they travel the road may gather and eat what they please". Contemporary capitalism does not invite such *laissez-faire*. As a result of this fruitfulness, said Defoe: ". . . you meet with cyder in the publick-houses sold as beer and ale in other parts of England". Again past and present differ. Hops have supplanted apples because beer is more profitable than cider.

A second local harvest was the famous Gloucester cheese, a by-product of the riverside herbage. Celia Fiennes noted that many farmers used a communal technique: ". . . I find the custom of the country to joyn their milking together of a whole village and so make their great Cheeses." Gloucester cheese-makers were among the first to produce a red or coloured cheese, which they did by adding the pigment of saffron (*Crocus sativus*). Farmers who grew this crop were dubbed Crokers.

Severn cheese is still remembered by the annual Ceremony of the Christmas Cheeses at the Royal Hospital in Chelsea, where the pensioners or veteran soldiers receive a gift which began in 1691, when the Hospital ordered: "... cheese from Gloucester at 3d. per lb". This reference to the price identifies the cheese, for in these parts any curd remaining after the vats had been filled was made into small cheese, to be sold for 3d. per lb at three weeks old or (as the farmers expressed it) 'in a recent state'. Nowadays the Chelsea pensioners receive their gift from the English Country Cheese Council.

As a dog recognizes the bone which it cannot analyse, so our unscientific fathers understood that cheese helped to balance their lack of meat in winter. Thomas Parr, a Severn character who awaits us at the Welsh border, was a great cheeseman. To mark his hundredth birthday in 1635, somebody composed a jingle, stating Parr's belief

> That cheese was most wholesome (with an onion)
> Coarse Meslin bread, and for his daily swig
> Milk, buttermilk and water, whey and whig.

Both Defoe and Celia Fiennes had much to say about the roads, and little of it was pleasant, for the difficulty of travel is as old as the departure of the Romans who had simplified it. Throughout the middle ages all roads were rougher than any cart-track today. Many became impassable when rain had filled their vast ruts; and, as a precaution against robbers, undergrowth had to be cut back from either side of the way, to a distance of 200 feet. Crosses were raised in remote places, as landmarks. Lanterns burned from church towers at night. Bells were rung, to guide travellers. And at Tewkesbury 'The Bell' was built and maintained by charitable guilds expressly to receive pilgrims. Only three classes of travellers went alone: lepers, felons on their way to exile overseas, and the King's messengers. Roads, in fact, were so perilous that the Church in her prayers joined travellers with captives, sick persons, and pregnant women. This state of affairs outlived the middle ages. Only some two centuries ago Defoe reported: "I saw an ancient lady ... drawn to church in her coach with six oxen; nor was it done in frolic or humour, but meer necessity, the way being so stiff and deep, that no horses could go on it." Even today many of these Severnside lanes carry posts to show the level of water during a flood. Some have timber causeways; a feature which Celia Fiennes noticed: ". . . on the banckes of the Severn . . . its a low moist place therefore one must travel on Causseys . . .".

Now the river changes course, from north-east to north; and at Haw Bridge (built in 1961 to replace the bridge damaged by a runaway barge) the course changes again, from north to south-east, passing Tirley on the left bank, where Rev. Joseph Frederick Hone served as parish priest from the reign of George IV until the Jubilee of Queen Victoria. The fourteenth-century church tower contains a clock made from harrows, plough-shares, scythes, and other fragments of farm implements.

Apperley, on the right bank, emphasizes its own fruitfulness, for the name comes from the Old English *apuldor-leah*, meaning 'apple tree wood'. But apples are not the only harvest. Sturgeon also are taken—and salmon, too—with a net ninety yards long.

The vanished Apperley Court was the seat of the Strickland family who in 1550 received a grant of arms with a turkey as its crest. Tradition says that William Strickland had sailed with Sebastian Cabot, first importer of turkeys into England from North America. A more recent tradition says that turkeys were so-named because they first reached England in a Turkish ship.

Few folk know that this reach of the river—bounded, that is, by Gloucester, Herefordshire, and the Forest of Dean—was once a nest of poets. In 1912, when he was nearly forty years old, Robert Frost sailed with his family to England, having failed to sell his wares in America. On the advice of a retired London policeman, he went to live at a farm in the Chilterns. Later he rented a house near Dymock, north of the Forest of Dean, which Gibson and Abercrombie had found for him. There he wrote *North Of Boston*, the book which at last made his name. There, too, he deepened his friendship with Edward Thomas, whom he urged to return with him to America in 1914. Thomas's widow, Helen, once told me that her children and the Frosts' produced their own magazine. Frost, Thomas, Drinkwater, Gibson, Brooke, de la Mare, Masefield, Abercrombie; all lived here, or near here, or spent much time here; and together they created a quarterly magazine, *New Numbers*, printed at Gloucester. Wilfred Gibson described the scene, in the conversational tone which Frost himself had set:

Our neighbours from The Gallows, Catherine
And Lascelles Abercrombie; Rupert Brooke;
Eleanor and Robert Frost, living a while
At Little Iddens, who'd brought over with them
Helen and Edward Thomas

Near Apperley the Severn is joined by the Coombe Hill Canal,
the shortest in Gloucestershire, less than three miles long. Opened
in 1802, it was built in order to convey coal and other heavy cargo
into Cheltenham; the roads at that time being worse than cart
tracks at this time. The canal prospered until railways arrived. In
1876 it was closed, but found a new use again many years later
as an unofficial nature reserve for the botanists and zoologists
who now study the plants and creatures thriving on its stagnant
waters. I remember coming here in August, when the brown-
ribbed bulrush stood eight feet high. At one time the countryfolk
would have coveted such a crop for thatching their roofs, seating
their chairs, stuffing their hassocks, reinforcing their pack-saddles.
Coombe Canal, by the way, crossed a country so level that no
locks were needed; yet at Wainlode Hill, where the canal joins the
river, the bank rises one hundred feet above the water.

Leigh church, within sight of the canal, introduces Dick
Whittington, whose sister-in-law was baptized there. The story of
Dick Whittington and his Cat is at least as old as the Caroline
journalist who hawked it in a ballad—*London's glory and Whittington's renown*—which told ". . . how Sir Richard Whittington . . .
came to be three times Lord Mayor of London, and how his rise
was by a cat". Whittington may indeed have been fond of cats,
but he never became Lord Mayor of London, nor ever a pauper
nor a knight. His father was Sir William Whittington, Lord of the
manor of Pauntley, a few miles west of the Severn; his mother
was Joan, widow of Thomas Berkeley, a kinsman of the Lords of
Berkeley; his wife was Alice, daughter of Sir Ivo Fitzwaryn, a
Dorset knight. Whittington himself reached London with ample
money and sufficient influence. He became the richest member of
the Mercers' Company, and thrice Mayor of London—in 1397,
1406, 1419. Among his good deeds were the rebuilding of New-
gate Prison, the repairing of St. Bartholomew's Church, the enlarging of the Guildhall, and the endowing of an almshouse which
the Mercers' Company still administers.

The Severn meanwhile pursues a secluded way toward the village of Deerhurst, which is dominated by a church, a chapel, and a saint.

The church stands on the site of an abbey that was old when William conquered England. Its flat-topped tower, seventy feet tall, is partly Saxon, partly Norman. The Saxon font stood for centuries in the Worcestershire church of Longdon; but a pious lady happening to find the base of a font in a riverside garden at Deerhurst, noticed that its carvings resembled those on Longdon font. Enquiry proved that Longdon had in fact received its font from Deerhurst. The Worcestershire parish thereupon returned it thither; and there it now rests, on its rightful base, in its proper home.

A signboard at the church gate points across the lane to Odda's Chapel, and states where the key to it may be had. At first glance this chapel appears to be a stone barn, joined to the timbered Abbot's Farm. I once gave a broadcast talk from that farmhouse, and what I said then I shall paraphrase now. For centuries the chapel had been used as a byre of Abbot's Farm. In 1885, while the farmhouse was being converted into two cottages, the vicar of Deerhurst, who had come across to talk with the workmen, was so impressed by the thickness of the byre walls that he consulted a Tewkesbury antiquary, named Collins, himself a builder. The two men discovered that the byre was a Saxon chapel whose nave and chancel, separated by a semi-circular arch, were only forty-six feet long. On the outside of the wall, obscured by trees, they found a Latin inscription: "This altar was dedicated in honour of the Holy Trinity." One wonders why Odda's Chapel lay so long undetected, for in 1675 a stone (it is now with the Ashmolean Museum) had been found in an orchard near the chapel, and on it another Latin inscription: "Earl Odda had this royal hall built and dedicated in honour of the Holy Trinity for the good of the soul of his brother Elfric, which here quitted his body. Bishop Ealdred dedicated it on 12th April, in the fourteenth year of the reign of Edward, King of the English." Earl Odda is mentioned in the *Worcester Chronicle*, which states that "Odda, lover of churches, helper of the poor, defender of widows and orphans, guardian of chastity, received the monastic habit from Bishop Aldred, and died at Deerhurst a month later, but was buried in the monastery at Pershore".

So much for the church and the chapel; now what of the saint? His name was Alphege, and he was born in 954, heir to an ancient name and large estates. These things he set aside, preferring instead to become a monk at Deerhurst. But his lineage and his talents he could not discard; on the contrary, they soon attracted to Deerhurst a number of influential men and women seeking spiritual guidance. Alphege, in short, was marked for advancement. He became Bishop of Winchester while still a young man, and Archbishop of Canterbury when he was fifty-two. Tradition says that he persuaded Olaf, King of the Vikings, to forbid the trade in slaves. Certainly he was captured by a band of Vikings who for seven months held him in their ships at Greenwich. When they offered his freedom in return for a ransom, Alphege declined, saying that the cost would cause hardship to his people. The Vikings then murdered him, and his body was buried by Londoners. Eleven years later King Canute ordered the body to be buried in Canterbury Cathedral, and himself came from Denmark to attend the ceremony.

On, then, through a deeply Cotswold country, to Chaceley and another remote inn, 'The Yew Tree'. When the Industrial Revolution built canals, and linked them with rivers, these waterside inns sprang up throughout England like mushrooms overnight. In 1782 a German visitor, Pastor Moritz, noted in his diary: " . . . I came to another inn with the sign of Navigation Inn, so called because the coal-barges on the River Trent rest here after their work." 'The Yew Tree' is a pleasant place, but at weekends not restful, for a sailing club has made its headquarters nearby. On my last visit I counted twenty-five cars within a few yards of the water.

At Forthampton church—a short walk inland from Chaceley—they buried John Wakeman, last Abbot of Tewkesbury, first Bishop of Gloucester, who translated the Book of Revelation for what is sometimes called Cranmer's Bible because Cranmer wrote its preface. Published in 1540, this was the first English Bible to be authorized for use at public services. Parish priests, in fact, were required to chain a copy of it in their church.

On the opposite bank, Tredington retains many half-timbered houses, but has lost the manor in which King Edward IV spent the eve of the battle of Tewkesbury. The Norman church has two unusual features: a timber tower (rebuilt 1883) and the fossil of an Icthyosaurus on the floor of the porch.

At this point two place-names—Stoke Orchard and Apperley— announce a feature that so far has been only suggested. If you come here in autumn you will see the original of a portrait which Virgil painted: *Strata jacent passim* . . . "The apples lie scattered, each under its own tree." Apples recall the name of John Philips, a minor Augustan versifier whose attempts to revive the art of writing blank verse were reservedly praised when Somerville urged James Thomson to

> Read Philips much, consider Milton more,
> But from their dross extract the purer ore.

Philips was nicknamed 'Pomona's bard' because he had written a poem, *Cyder*, praising the 'Silurian' or Severn vintage:

> To the utmost bounds of this
> Wide universe, Silurian cider born,
> Shall please all tastes, and triump o'er the vine . . .

A pleasant example of early copywriting; but Philips was not the first to advertise cider. In 1685 a Chiltern fruitgrower, William Ellis, published *The Compleat Planter and Ciderist or choice Collections and Observations for the propagating all manner of fruit trees.* Fourteen years later a member of the Royal Society, Nicholas Facio de Quillier, must have caused a deal of bricklaying by writing a paper entitled *Fruit-walls improved—by inclining them to the Horizon: or a way to build walls for fruit trees.*

In this part of England cider remained the *vin du pays* until the nineteenth century. Writing of the Severn scene as he knew it during the 1870s, John Masefield remembered " . . . the matchless orchards for pears and apples, from which the natives make much intoxicating liquor". As cider was supplanted by beer, so in its time cider supplanted mead, which had been England's national drink until the early middle ages. By the thirteenth century, however, the domestic accounts of Bishop Swinfield of Hereford made only one reference to mead. Five centuries later, cider was still so important that John Thorn, a West Country farmer, noted in his diary for 1818: " . . . Cyder the plentiest this year it has Ever been

*Beware of floods: near Quay*

for years sold at £2 hogshead". In 1840 another farmer, noting the effect of climate, complained that the price of cider was half what it had been in 1839. Sometimes the apple harvest was so poor that even the Severnfolk had to drink beer; sometimes the hop harvest was so poor that even the Burton men had to drink cider. Nowadays the National Fruit and Cider Institute offers technical advice to the brewers. Some farmers, however, make their own cider, in the same place and after the same manner as their fathers. I have in mind a Severn barn, and a millstone set above a circular trough, driven by a horse. The juice and pulp (or pomace) are fed into a cistern holding five hogsheads or about six hundred gallons. Part of the liquid is then drained-off, and the pomace is placed in the press. Some farmers spread a cloth between each layer of pomace; others prefer straw; several use only oat straw, claiming that it adds a deeper tinge to the cider. After pressing, the juice is 'tunned' into casks. Welshmen used to season their tunnage with candy, alum, brimstone, and brandy. A fortnight of fine weather will cause fermentation. Having been strained through a cloth, the cider is 'racked' into new casks, and the pomace serves as cattle food. John Drinkwater evoked a still-life from his own memories of the Severn:

> At the top of the house the apples are laid in rows,
> And the skylight lets the moonlight in, and those
> Apples are deep-sea apples of green.

Unfortunately there is another crop, the hedgerow, which has fallen upon hard times. Hedges are not ornaments. They mark boundaries, and succour many sorts of life. Their disappearance disturbs the balance of nature, robs the landscape of a beautiful feature, and spawns a network of barbed wire. Yet any landowner may, without licence, fell 885 cubic feet of timber annually, provided that not more than 150 feet of it are sold. In other words, a landowner may legally destroy about twenty large trees a year, without considering any interest except his own. To put the matter even more plainly, every hedgerow tree along the Gloucestershire Severn might disappear before 1987. A Nature Conservancy report showed that in 1945 a selected area of seven square miles of countryside contained 70·8 miles of hedges. By 1963 the mileage had dropped to forty. In 1965 it was twenty. I repeat, this

5

*Tewkesbury Abbey*

is not a sentimental complaint. When riverside trees are felled and not replaced, the river becomes an open land drain.

But now the tower of Tewkesbury appears, and with it a place that one wishes to praise, and does praise, but not as one could wish.

Come to Tewkesbury at traffictime, and you will be aware only of vehicles thundering through a narrow street disfigured by a multiplicity of road signs. You may, as you enter the town, become aware also of a large church and a timbered hotel. Certainly you will observe people huddled on the pavement; sometimes darting through a gap in the traffic; more often scurrying back again; a contemporary cross between rabbits and sheep. And having emerged from the *mêlee*, you will exclaim: "Thank heaven we've got through that place."

If, however, you arrive at seven o'clock of a summer morning, you will be free to sample whatever is savoury; starting with Tewkesbury Abbey, which Defoe reckoned to be ". . . the largest parish church in England; I mean, that is not a collegiate or cathedral church". Tewkesbury Abbey is said to occupy the site of a seventh-century church built by St. Theoc, who gave his name to the town (Domesday Book spells it as Teodekesberie). The present Abbey was begun in 1102, completed in 1123. Its stone came from Caen in Normandy. The great tower returns a benediction which Robert Bridges bestowed:

> Now blessed be the towers
> That crown England so fair
> That stand up in prayer
> Unto God for our souls . . .

De Clares, Despencers, Beauchamps, Nevilles . . . each played their part in the story of Tewkesbury; and a bloody scene it was, capped by the famous battle of 4th May 1471 between King Edward IV and the armies of Queen Margaret. The Queen's husband, Henry VI, had been a pious pacifist, unfit to rule. The general anarchy persuaded the Duke of York that he possessed a better claim to the throne. He therefore quitted his governorship of Ireland, landed in Wales, and set about creating a Yorkist party. The task was not difficult, for the King had become insane, the Queen aspired to be Protector, and many Englishmen felt no desire to be guarded by a woman. The Duke of York soon made himself King Edward IV. But Queen Margaret was resourceful, niece to the King of France. She had moreover a son, the Prince of Wales. Supported by foreign troops, she continued the Wars of the Roses. Having decimated themselves in battles and skirmishes, the nobility of England and their retainers met at Tewkesbury; or, more precisely, the new king, hurrying from London, caught the Queen at Tewkesbury as she raced toward the Lancastrian stronghold in Wales. Although each side had marched forty miles on the previous day, they lost no time in attacking. Part of the Yorkist army was commanded by the future King Richard III; part of the Lancastrian by the Prince of Wales, a boy of eighteen. The Queen's troops were defeated. Some found sanctuary in the abbey, but were dragged thence to be executed in the Market Place; among them Edmund Beaufort, Duke of Somerset. So ended the sordid Wars of the Roses:

> Once more we sit in England's royal throne,
> Re-purchased with the blood of enemies.
> What valiant foemen like to autumn's corn,
> Have we mow'd down, in tops of all their pride.

I have never counted the Tewkesbury inns, but I do know that twenty of them are on the Ministry's list of notable buildings. 'The Bear' (1308) claims to be the oldest in Gloucestershire.

The black-and-white 'Old Tudor House' (1540) became a Court House during the seventeenth century, but was then converted by Rev. Samuel Jones . . . into a Dissenters' Retreat. Despite those Whigs, there must have been some Jacobites in Tewkesbury, because the 'Old Tudor House' suffered damage when King George I was crowned.

'The Bell', as we have seen, received pilgrims, for the medieval Church found nothing amiss in an orderly ale-house or *eala-hus*. William of Newburgh's *Chronicles of the Reigns of Stephen, Henry II and Richard I* show that potations in an ale-house were commonly tempered by prayers: *Cumque inter potandum preces ex more indicerentur, et nomen salvatoris.* 'The Bell' so impressed a certain Miss Mulock (later Mrs. Craik) that she used it in her fiction. A plaque at the hotel states: "This house is mentioned in *John Halifax, Gentleman* as being the residence of Abel Fletcher, the Tanner."

The black-and-white 'Royal Hop Pole' was honourably mentioned by Dickens. Mr. Pickwick and some of his friends, you may remember, were travelling through the West Country, slaking their thirst *en route*: "At the Hop Pole at Tewkesbury they stopped to dine; upon which occasion there was more bottled ale, with some Madeira and some Port besides; and here the case bottle was replenished for the fourth time."

There is a weir at Tewkesbury, and the Severn's first lock. The liveliest waterscape can be seen beside the flour-mill at the end of a *cul-de-sac* from the High Street, where the River Avon flows down from Bredon, well-laden with cabin-cruisers. These modern features of the portrait help to fill a gap that occurred when steam and petrol submerged the Severn's commercial traffic. Many of the inland sailors regard their boats as slow motor cars, yet all respond to the water's mystical lure, and some use its language. And why not? Better "Hard to port" than "I say, for Heaven's sake mind that thing over there. It looks to me like a weir". On the other hand, few people are more to be avoided than those who break Joseph Conrad's rule: "To take a liberty with technical language is a crime against the clearness, precision, and beauty of perfect speech." It is surprising, how quickly a cabin-cruiser will teach neatness even to the untidiest landsman. On these unhazardous waters many a helmsman has heard—or imagined that he heard—those church bells which the citizens of Gloucester rang for the daring Portuguese captain who took his ship into their city. Myself, I find that freshwater never can slake a thirst for the sea. Anywhere above Aust, and I become aware that charts are a pedant's plaything; that the gulls have gone; that no man ever drowned, except through his own fault, nor needed his sea-legs, unless he were drunk. Nevertheless, these Severn skippers do well when they put their own interpretation on Wordsworth's deeper waters:

> Hence in a season of calm weather
> Though inland far we be,
> Our souls have sight of that immortal sea
> Which brought us hither . . .

Most people regard Tewkesbury as either a place to be passed as quickly as possible or as a place whose traffic must be endured

for the sake of admiring the abbey and the ancient houses. Yet
Tewkesbury is also an industrial town, made prosperous by factories and housing estates that look very much the same as the
housing estates and factories of any other English industrial town.

Mythe, just above Tewkesbury, recalls the Old English *gemythe*
or 'waters meet' . . . the waters, that is, of Severn and Avon. Here
the river passes under one of Telford's bridges, introducing a man
whose *Autobiography* speaks for itself.

Thomas Telford was born in 1757, the son of a Dumfriesshire
shepherd. Like his contemporary, James Brindley, he received no
formal education. Having been apprenticed to a local stone-
mason, he migrated to Edinburgh and thence to London. In
Scotland between 1801 and 1823 he built the Caledonian Canal,
more than 1,000 miles of roads, and 1,200 bridges. He made the
Gotha Canal for the King of Sweden, and the Warsaw frontier
for the Tsar of Russia. Mythe Bridge he built when he was in his
seventieth year. He often carried a book of poetry, and may have
been reading it when he ought to have been costing Mythe Bridge,
for the bill exceeded anyone's expectations, and had to be paid
with borrowed money. On the Severn he built several other
bridges, two churches, and one town. Despite an arduous life, or
perhaps because of it, he lived to be seventy-seven, and was buried
in Westminster Abbey.

There are two curious features of the portrait above Tewkesbury. The first is an outcrop of woad (*isatoris tinctoria*) thriving on
the red sandstone beside the river. When fermented, the plant's
yellow leaves yield a blue dye. Pliny the Elder reported that British
women dyed themselves with woad "while performing their
religious rituals". A great quantity of woad was used by the dyeing trade until recent times. In Lincolnshire, not far from Bourne,
I once discovered an obsolete woad factory and a woman who
had worked there as a girl.

The second curious feature is a rare and unpredictable tide,
known locally as a 'quarry'; bewildering to any stranger who finds
himself rowing down-stream against it. This 'quarry' is not a
true tide but rather an effect of tension between seawater and
freshwater.

At Bushley, on the left bank, the Severn enters Worcestershire.
Payn's Place, a half-timbered house (1460) contains a room called

The Queen's Room because Queen Margaret was said to have escaped thither after the battle of Tewkesbury; more reliable reports, however, state that she was captured on the field, and sent at once to London. After several years' captivity the Queen was ransomed by the King of France, and died eleven years later at her father's court in Anjou.

Beyond Mythe the Severn recovers its seclusion. You must walk the better part of a mile inland before sighting a village, but the journey is worthwhile because at Ripple you enter a place of rare beauty, set around a green. Some of the houses are black-and-white, some are thatched, some are of redbrick.

The Almshouse was built by the Woodwards, Wardens of Malvern Chase, during the sixteenth century, and rebuilt in 1701.

In the church two Woodwards are remembered: "John Woodward, sometime yeoman of the guard unto King Phillipe and allso to Queene Elizabeth, died the fowerteenth of October, 1596, and here lyeth buried" . . . "William Woodward, gent grandson of Sir John Woodward is here laid to sleep with his grandfather in the dust of the same grave."

The chief feature of Ripple church is a month-by-month calendar, in the form of twelve misericord carvings, showing a medieval countryman hedging in February, sowing in March, harvesting in August, and in December sitting by the fire. These carvings remind us that the medieval peasant, though he spent a hard life tilling his lord's demesne, enjoyed six weeks' annual holiday . . . the holy days of the Church. Nor were these holidays simply a respite from toil. On the contrary, they invited every man to share communal junketings and, if he had mind for it, to indulge private meditation. Something of that medieval ethos was restored in 1943 when the Council for the Church and Countryside prepared modern forms of service, to be used on Plough Monday, Rogationtide, Lammas, and Harvest.

Beyond Ripple the river steers north-east, past Saxon's Lode (Old English *lad* or 'water-course'), which some people believe ought to be called Sexton's Lode because, they say, the land here was held during the sixteenth century by the sexton or sacristan of Worcester Priory.

In an off-moment, when love of Sussex had overheated his prejudice—which never was cool—Hilaire Belloc dismissed the

Midlands as "sodden and unkind". Either he did not know, or had chosen to ignore, these northern Cotswolds. In far fields and at the end of alleys you will find mansions and cottages that were built by men who could blend usefulness with comeliness. The sheep, too, are Cotswold; and so are the stone walls dividing the fields that look down upon the river. The tones of voice are Cotswold; no longer West Country, not yet commercial.

The name 'Cotswold' used to be specific, but has grown vague. In 1250 it was Coteswaud or 'the *wald* of forest belonging to Cod'. This Cod was a chieftain, recorded at the Worcestershire village of Cutsdean, formerly *Codestune* or 'Cod's tun'. So, a proper name became an adjectival noun describing parts of Gloucestershire, Worcestershire, Warwickshire, Oxfordshire, and Wiltshire. The word ought really to be used of the local stone, called Oolite, from two Greek words meaning 'egg' and 'stone'; each appropriate because the lumps of calcium carbonate are indeed egg-shaped.

As the river approaches Upton-on-Severn, the Cotswold countryside recedes. Upton itself is a hotch-potch of new ugliness and old beauty. Some neat cottages crouch in the shadow of a hideous cupola on the Norman church-tower (the rest of the church was rebuilt during the eighteenth century). In 1745 the villagers demolished their steeple by means of ropes attached to horses on the far side of the river.

There are some good inns at Upton. 'The White Lion', for example, appears in *Tom Jones* (Augustine Birrell said that Fielding's novels, "like most good ones, are full of inns").

No longer a port-of-call, Upton is a haven for holiday-makers and cabin-cruisers. Yet the old men of my childhood had seen these quays crammed with boats and barges hauled by horses, tugged by tugs, or wafted with oars and a sail. Now and then an astute merchant would obviate the middlemen by selling direct from his own barge. At a time when roads are lethal, and railways a liability, it seems strange that commerce has neglected the Cotswold Severn. At Upton today you overhear the voice of the old Greek poet: "Do not tie-up here, sailor. The harbour, as anyone can see, is dry."

Academic amnesia was displayed by a sixteenth-century rector of Upton, John Dee, who obtained permission to hold the living for ten years in plurality with Leadenham, and might have held it for life, had he not forgotten to see the dispensation formally sealed.

Educated at Cambridge and Louvain, Dee dabbled in alchemy and astrology, and so risked being imprisoned as a colleague of the Devil. In 1554 he *was* imprisoned, for casting a horoscope of King Philip, Queen Mary, and the Princess Elizabeth. However, he was saved by his cloth, by his flair for mathematics, and by the pension that King Edward VI had granted to him. He was commanded to consult with German physicians during the illness of Queen Mary, and to draw a chart (it is in the British Museum) showing all the Crown's lands discovered by Englishmen. His *British Monarchy* advocated a fleet of sixty ships to form ". . . a little Navy Royall". This suggestion was quoted with approval by Captain John Smith, who said: "To get the money to build this navy . . . who would not spare the one hundredth penny of his rents, and the five hundredth penny of his goods . . ."

Now, as though to announce a new landscape, Bredon Hill appears; the same whereon Housman's lovers lay in summertime, listening to the church bells

> In steeples far and near,
> A happy noise to hear.

The Severn has entered the sandstone and pastures and orchards which Housman named "the coloured counties".

# WALKING ON THE WATER: AN INTERLUDE

A CLOCK struck six, but the day slept on. Not for another hour did it open one eye; and even then—as though misliking what it saw—the eye went to sleep again.

Meanwhile I followed the road to the river, through a land which seemed precisely the same as at teatime yesterday . . . silent, starry, and so frozen that lamplight from a cottage revealed icicles thick as candlegrease. The sight of those icicles took my own temperature. Though I had come muffled against it, the cold entered everywhere; not creeping under crevices, but striding through an open door.

Presently I glanced eastward over my shoulder, and there I saw the faint lessening of darkness which precedes the light. Out of it loomed a hayrick, towering like a cathedral; and then one tree, lonely as a lost signpost. And still the silence held, tinged with expectancy because the dawn chorus sleeps as it were with one eye on the horizon.

I could see the river now; or, rather, I could see where it lay, for the surface was covered with ice. In order to reach it, I had to cross a field of furrows ringing like granite underfoot; and when I reached a patch which the plough had missed, each stem of stubble went down with a crack. Probing some waterside reeds, my stick struck the river unaware, with an impact that jarred my wrist. Warily I put one foot forward, testing the ice; and then indeed I walked upon the water. Many times I had walked beside it. Often I had swum in it. Once, on a makeshift raft, I had paddled across it. But now I felt it under my feet.

By this time the east was alight, advancing like a slow fire through lattice hedgerows; setting a scene which Mary Webb had noticed:

No bracken lights the bleak hill-side;
No leaves are on the branches wide;
No lambs across the field have cried
—Not yet.
But whorl by whorl the green fronds climb;
The ewes are patient till their time;
The warm buds swell beneath their rime
—For life does not forget.

Guessing which among the birds would speak first, I won my own wager when a lark sprang up, two fields away, spilling his matins in minims of largess, ever the same, yet with each morning new as the song heard by De Nerval in the Luxembourg Gardens:

*A la bouche un refrain nouveau.*

What unawareness, I wondered, or what faith, had made possible such music as that, in a world so inhospitable as this?

A robin answered my question, from the top of a hayrick; but we spoke each a different language, and neither could understand the other. And after the robin, came a cheeping that might have been sparrows; and after the sparrows a moorhen from his pond beside the cottage; and after that a "darkling thrush" whose kind had led Hardy to ask whether the bird were uttering

Some blessed Hope whereof he knew
And I was unaware.

Certainly I was unaware of the distant mountains until, happening to look up, I saw them come out of the west, catching an easterly fire, and in it revealing their snow-tipped summits. I had quite forgotten the cold, musing beside a frozen river at first light of a February morning.

The river, too, seemed unaware of the mountains, as though nothing should distract from the unfolding of its own comeliness. Holly berries glowed, cordial as Christmas cards. A hoar frost preened twigs, grassblades, cart-ruts. Sheep on the far bank (how silently they must have been grazing) nibbled their own smoke screen; and when one of them coughed, the sound sped quicker than bullets.

Gradually the dawn chorus dwindled and was replaced by the chatter of cold birds scavenging a colder country. Morning had

arrived, and on it the eastern sky became a sunset, flamboyant as
Day Lewis's winterscape:

> Blood-red across the snow our sun
> Still trails his faint retreat.

Presently it did retreat, into its own pallor, and was outshone by a
sky so icily blue that not even my own meditations could any
longer keep me from shivering. Moisture had frozen on my chin.
The left foot was numb. Fingertips began to burn. So I went back,
the way I had come—crackling the stubble, rasping the furrows—
to find that the cottage had extinguished its lamp, and was now
sending up an incense of apple wood.

Noticing snowdrops in the cottage garden, I shared a second
calendar with Mary Webb:

> And see! The northern bank is much more white
> Than frosty grass, for now is snowdrop time.

And among those snowdrops I detected the tip of a daffodil,
prising the frozen soil. Such an early visitor recalled Kipling's envy
of it:

> This season's daffodil,
> That never hears
> What change, what chance, what chill
> Cut down last year's.

True, I thought; yet I thought also of Meredith's recipe for an all-
the-year-round contentment: "We should," he said, "love every
change of weather." This weather, certainly, had changed fill-
dyke to frost-dyke; daubing slate skies with blue, sprinkling old
age on the winter wheat, tingling life's tempo.

I lingered at the cottage because I knew that the occupants were
indeed of the Severn. From their bedroom window they saw it.
From their garden they heard it, whenever the cattle plunged
udder-deep into summer coolness. During a flood they felt it. Very
likely their forebears drank it. Beyond doubt their own grand-
children swam in it. On a Sunday afternoon they themselves
strolled beside it. And although I should come here every day for
the rest of my life, still these cottagers would know the river
more precisely and with a deeper insight, for it was among the

first things they had ever seen, and would, if they had their way, be among the last.

"Lovely morning!"

I looked up, and saw the cottager at his porch, grey-haired and pippin-cheeked.

"Yes," I agreed. "Lovely."

## THE COLOURED COUNTIES:
## UPTON-ON-SEVERN TO
## STOURPORT-ON-SEVERN

COMPARISONS are not necessarily odious. Well-used, they heighten a definition. For example, not a single mile of the Severn could be mistaken for the Thames. The hinterland alone would identify it. And even were the hinterland hidden in mist, still the height of its banks and the colour of their soil would serve as signposts. Nor has the Severn these small surprises which alert the Thames . . . the curves seeming never to reveal a precisely similar bend . . . gardens sloping to the water . . . avenues of trees supplanted by willowy meadows. The Thames, for its part, lacks the Severn's more conspicuous scene-shifting . . . at Aust the abrupt narrowing . . . at Over the change from seafaring to country clothes . . . and now, beyond Upton, the Cotswolds yielding to the Malverns.

Celia Fiennes called these Hills "the English Alps". If it referred to their height, her description was misleading; but if it referred to their shape, her description was justified, for in all England there are no other hills which so resembled mountains. Miss Fiennes, however, was wide of the mark when she sized them as "at least two or three miles up". Their summit, the Worcestershire Beacon, is only 1,400 feet. Even so, the Malverns do carve a dramatic sky-line, seven miles long. Like the Langdales in Westmorland, they stand tiptoe on their own contours, seeming to gain several cubits from the level ground below. Defoe sighted them from the Wiltshire Downs: "They say," he reported, "that they are seen from the top of Salisbury steeple, which is above fifty miles." An Oxford geologist, Dr. D. C. Rex, has suggested that the Malverns' pre-Cambrian rock may have been sandstone or shale a thousand million years ago. Certainly they are relics of an upheaval which still conditions the lives of local people. Cotswold houses, for example, are replaced by half-timbered homes; and the red soil yields fruit, flowers, and vegetables, confirming Jane Austen's Emma when she said: "Many counties, I believe, are called the garden of England . . ." In that garden the Severn seeks seclusion, though for a mile or more it does flow beside a main road, almost within sight of a village called Hanley Castle, nowadays a suburb of Upton.

The castle at Hanley was pulled down by Sir William Compton at about the time when Bishop Bonner was demolishing his own reputation. Edmund Bonner (or Bower) was born at Hanley Castle, whence he went up to Pembroke College, Oxford, through the generosity of the lord of the manor. As chaplain to Wolsey, he visited Rome, hoping to hasten the annulment of the King's marriage. He became Bishop of Hereford in 1538 and of London a year later. Having acknowledged King Henry VIII as Head of the English Church, he refused to enforce the use of the next King's new Prayer Book. After two sojourns in the Fleet prison, Bonner was restored by Mary Tudor. In 1551 he began to persecute the Protestants so brutally that even the French and Venetian ambassadors were shocked. He declined to acknowledge Queen Elizabeth, who sent him again to the Fleet, where he died. His apologists have pleaded that he urged the Protestants to save their skins by denying their faith; which seems a poor defence. The English hated Bonner because his regime was both alien and clerical, of all tyrannies the most odious.

Bonner served awhile as chaplain to Wolsey; and Wolsey had been tutor to Sir Richard Nanfan, Constable of Calais, at his home, Birtsmorton Court, a splendid Severn house, moated, bridged, with a hiding-place in which, they said, Queen Margaret sheltered.

The name Birtsmorton offers a clue to the river's geology and ethnology. Morton means 'marshy place'; Birt means le Bret, the name of a twelfth-century lord of the manor; and le Bret means 'The Breton'. So, one family of Celtic people came to live near another Celtic people, the Welsh.

Birtsmorton Court had been the seat of the Hakluyts, who settled in the Marcher country during the thirteenth century, when they called themselves Haklitch or Haklutel. Among their descendants was Richard Hakluyt, sometime Prebendary of Bristol and Archdeacon of Westminster.

As a boy at Westminster School ("that fruitful nurse", he called it) Richard Hakluyt one day found some maps in the chambers of his cousin, a member of the Middle Temple. These so impressed him that he asked to be instructed. His cousin consented, telling him to take down a Bible, and read the twenty-third and the twenty-fourth verse of Psalm 107: ". . . they which go downe to the sea in ships and occupy the great waters, these see the works of the Lord, and his wonders in the deep."

In 1570 Hakluyt went up to Christchurch, Oxford, to read navigation and geography ("geography," he declared, "is the eye of history"). Later he became chaplain to the English ambassador in Paris; and there he began his lifetime's task of collecting and publishing the narratives of English sea captains. In 1589 he issued the first edition of a book which Froude hailed as "the prose epic of the English nation". Dedicated to Sir Francis Walsingham, and commonly known as Hakluyt's *Voyages*, this vast anthology bears a more impressive title: *The Principall Navigation, Voyages and Discoveries of the English nation made by sea or over land, in the most remote and furthest distant quarters of the earth at any time within the compass of these 1500 yeeres.* Hakluyt's own prose rolled like the sea which it described, as in the first volume of a second edition, dedicated to the Lord High Admiral: ". . . what restless nights, what painfull days, what heat, what cold, I have endured; how many long and chargeable journeys I have travailed; how many famous libraries I have searched into; what varietie of ancient and moderne writers I have perused; what a number of old records, patents, privileges, letters, etc., I have redeemed from obscuritie and perishing." Hakluyt died in 1616, and was buried at Westminster Abbey. Two centuries later he received a monument *aere perennius*, the Hakluyt Society, which was formed in order to print ". . . rare and valuable Voyages, Travels, Naval Expeditions, and other geographical records". By 1968 the Society had published more than 250 volumes.

In Queen Victoria's time Birtsmorton Court was the home of William Huskisson, President of the Board of Trade, the first man to be killed in an English railway accident. He stumbled in the way of Stephenson's *Rocket*, at the opening of the Liverpool to

Manchester line. On 27th September 1830, *The Times* described the disaster: ". . . the wheel went over his left thigh, squeezing it almost to a jelly. . . . Mrs. Huskisson, who, with several other ladies, witnessed the accident, uttered a shriek of agony, which none who heard it will ever forget." The scene of the accident is marked by a memorial stone at Newton-in-Makerfield, Lancashire.

Beyond Hanley Castle the Severn seems so intent upon going its own way that it flows for a dozen miles without entering a village. This is the only sector whose riverside houses can be compared with those along the Thames. First, on the left bank, comes Severn End, ancient seat of the Lechmeres, destroyed by fire and then rebuilt as a replica of the original.

Another large house, only a short distance up-stream, Severn Bank, stands among woods near Severn Stoke. There is a fruity story about a greenhouse at Severn Stoke, which William Cobbett narrated, not in his customary crisp prose, but with a sentence of 125 words:

"It belonged to a parson of the name of St. John, whose parsonage house is very near to it, and who, being sure of having the benefice when the then rector should die, bought a piece of land, and erected his grapery on it, just facing and only about fifty yards from, the windows, out of which the old parson had to look until the day of his death, with a view, doubtless, of piously furnishing his aged brother with a *memento mori* (remember death) quite as significant as a death's head and cross bones and yet done in a manner expressive of that fellow feeling, that delicacy, that absence from self-gratification which are well known to be characteristics almost peculiar to the cloth."

Many people are surprised when they hear of grapes beside the Severn; supposing that such tender fruit demands a frost-free climate. But a vine will withstand twenty degrees of frost; what it cannot endure is a dryly cold spring and a cold autumn. Domesday Book mentions several English vineyards, and the thirteenth-century Bishop of Hereford had a vineyard at his manor of Ledbury. The first shipment of Gascon wine did not reach England until 1213. Nearly a century later the Earl of Cornwall was drinking wine from his vineyards beside the Thames at Isleworth and Wallingford.

*Parish church, Upton-on-Severn*

Another mile up-stream discovers Clevelode (the river by a cliff), a cluster of half-a-dozen cottages, some black-and-white, some of mellow brick, perched on a knoll within a few yards of the water. Nearby are Cliffley Wood and the lane leading to a riverside farmhouse. Here you will meet Izaak Walton's company of anglers, the men who are ". . . lovers of virtue, and dare to trust in His providence, and be quiet, and go a-angling".

Fishing, of course, is a familiar feature of the portrait; but at Clevelode an unfamiliar feature appears—the hop fields. Now ale, as we noticed, supplanted mead as England's national drink; and this it did at about the time when the wool trade had brought Englishmen into close contact with the beer-drinking Low Countries. The pupil eventually became the master, for in 1617 Moryson's *Itinerary* stated: ". . . English beere is famous in Netherlands, made of barley and hops, for England yields plenty of hops." When King Henry III fixed the prices of bread and ale, the latter fetched one penny per sixteen pints. The phrase 'scot-free' recalls the medieval 'bottle parties' to which every reveller brought his own bottle or 'scot'. In 1240 the Bishop of Worcester waved a white ribbon, declaring: "We forbid the clergy to take part in these drinking parties called scot-ales. . . ." During the fourteenth century the ale-taster appeared, charged with the task of grading ales. Severnside folk soon grew accustomed to the taster's sedentary occupation: having spilt some ale on a wooden bench, he sat on it for half-an-hour. If, when he arose, his breeches stuck to the puddle, he down-graded the ale because of its excessive sugar content. Shakespeare's father was ale-taster at Stratford-upon-Avon. Even so, these extensive Severn hop fields did not exist during the middle ages. As late as 1468 the Brewers' Company deplored the new custom of adding hops to ale. Indeed, they wished to outlaw everyone who leavened ale with ". . . any hoppes, herbs, or other like thing but only licquor, malt, and yeste". English hops were not grown in quantity until about the year 1524, when Flemish immigrants introduced them to Kent. Thereafter the English followed suit. Samuel Smiles reckoned that tens of thousands of Victorian working-class families spent half their annual wages on alcohol.

Hops do not take kindly to an English climate, which was one reason why they remained neglected until the Flemings set an

6

*Freshwater sailors, Upton-on-Severn*

example. As the man said in Francis Brett Young's *Fair Forest*: "Hops be faddy mortals . . . you've got to humour them. . . ." Even when hops did become an important crop, the harvest was so uncertain that members of Tattersalls wagered large sums on the annual hop prices. The gamblers certainly took chances. In 1823, for instance, Worcestershire and Herefordshire paid only £4 3s. duty on their hop yield; but two years later they paid £11,911. It was not until 1876 that Pasteur's *Études sur la bière* analysed the role of hops as a preservative and clarifier of sugar solution. Hops nowadays are valued chiefly for their oils and resin; and the Severn hop fields have almost doubled their acreage during the past century.

As John Philips was the bard of cider, so Christopher Smart sang of hops, in what he styled "verse Miltonian":

> When to inhume the plants; to turn the glebe;
> And wed the tendrils to th'aspiring poles:
> Under what sign to pluck the crop, and how
> To cure and in capacious sacks infold,
> I teach in verse Miltonian . . .

Totally abstinent, the Severn now steers north, still avoiding all villages. Clifton, a hamlet of handsome old homes on the right bank, is a full half-mile from the water, though its woods are visible from Great Malvern on the far side.

Great Malvern (from the Welsh *Moel-fryn* or 'bare hill') is an ungainly museum of Victorian and Edwardian houses which sprang up at the behest of Dr. Gullson, whom Charles Reade satirized in *It Is Never Too Late To Mend*. This Gullson was a fiction based upon two facts—Dr. James Gully and Dr. James Wilson. The former was born in Jamaica; the latter came from Liverpool, and was physician to Lord Farnham (the patient soon died from an overdose of colchium). Together these two practitioners transformed a quiet village into a fashionable spa; charging, as some of their modern counterparts still do charge, a great deal of money in return for very little food. Wilson rented 'The Crown Hotel' while Gully took 'Tudor House'. When Mrs. Charles Dickens came to take the cure, her husband dismissed the patients as "Cold-Waterers". In 1843 Tennyson arrived, hoping that a psychic ailment would yield to physical treatment. It did not. The Poet Laureate complained: "Of all the uncomfortable ways of living, sure an hydropathic is the worst; no reading by candlelight, no going near a fire, no coffee, perpetual wet sheet and cold bath and alternation from hot to cold." In 1848 Charles Darwin arrived; and he, too, discovered that physical treatment is not always the best minister for a mind dis-eased.

Despite hydropathic despoliation, Great Malvern contains some beautiful houses, notably on the steep road leading to the Hills. Many footpaths flow from that road; and if you climb the Worcestershire Beacon on a clear day, your binoculars will sight the summits of Exmoor.

There is a priory church at Great Malvern—part of a vanished Benedictine monastery—and in it a stained glass window, showing God measuring the heavens with a pair of compasses. This picture may explain why some inns were called 'The Goat and Compass' . . . God having been corrupted into Goat. At the Dissolution the priory church was bought by the townsfolk for £20.

Great Malvern holds an annual drama festival, a legacy from Sir Barry Jackson of Birmingham.

Finally, there are the headquarters of the Severn River Authority, which was established in 1964 to supervise not only the Severn but also a number of its tributaries, including the Teme, Tern, Roden, Vyrwny. Until 1964 the river had lacked an overall controller, for the Severn Commission, instituted in 1842, was responsible only between Gloucester and Stourport. The present Authority covers an area of 4,410 square miles in sixteen counties from Northamptonshire to Cardiganshire, and from Cheshire to Avonmouth, with responsibility for land drainage, fishery, water resources, river cleansing; but not for navigation between Stourport and Gloucester, which is controlled by the British Waterways Board. The Authority has divided the river into three sectors: Lower Severn, from Avonmouth to Tewkesbury; Mid-Severn, from Tewkesbury to Upper Arley; Upper Severn, from Upper Arley to the source.

Great Malvern was the nursery of William Langland—his friends called him Long Will—whose identity has puzzled many scholars; some saying that he was indeed a man; others, that he was two men (though none, happily, went so far as Samuel

Butler when he announced that Homer was a woman). Most
people now agree that Langland was born *c.* 1332 at Ledbury in
Herefordshire, the birthplace also of John Masefield; that he was
the bastard of Stacy de Rokayle; that he went to school at the
Benedictine monastery in Great Malvern; that he took minor
orders, lived in London, married a wife (named Kitte), by whom
he had a daughter (called Calote); and that he wrote *The Vision
of William Langland concerning Piers Plowman.* Like the Ripple
carvings, Langland's immense poem evokes the essence of medieval England, but with this difference, that it is a commentary as
well as a description; an indictment of the ways in which the
commonfolk were too often maltreated by the Church, the Court,
and Mammon. One might describe Langland as an English
Voltaire, a Malvern Marxist, a clerical Cobbett; but that would be
a poor substitute for the study of what he wrote. *Piers Plowman*
does not portray the Severn—it does not even mention it—but,
like the poet himself, it was nurtured by the Severn scene:

> . . . on a May morning on Malvern hills
> A marvel befell me of fairy, methought.
> I was weary with wandering, and went me to rest
> Under a broad bank by a brook's side . . .

That extract is one of several translations, into modern English,
of Langland's alliterative Middle English:

> . . . on a May mornynge on Maluerne hulles,
> Me byfel a ferly of fairy, me thoughte;
> I was very forwandred and went me to reste
> Vnder a brode banke bi a bornes side . . .

Resting there, the poet slept, and sleeping saw a vision:

> A fair field full of folk found I between,
> Of all manner of men, the rich and the poor.

The vision is a report on the state of the nation; political, economic, spiritual. It is an epic of the soul of a people, sustained
through more than two thousand lines; and it was conceived
within sight of the Severn.

Beyond Great Malvern the river confronts a level reach, still
refusing to enter a village, although it does pass within a mile or

so of Powick Bridge spanning a tributary, the Teme, where
Prince Rupert attacked some rebels. But already the suburbs have
arrived from Worcester.

When Lely came to paint Cromwell's portrait, the dictator said
to him: "Paint me as I am. If you leave out the scars and wrinkles,
I will not pay you a shilling." How does one paint the wrinkles
and scars of modern Worcester? Are they worth painting? I think
not. So, I shall dismiss them, as follows: of all the towns beside the
Severn, Worcester has been the most grievously desecrated. No
matter how you approach—whether from the north, or from the
east, or from the south, or from the west—you are greeted by suburbs, traffic, factories, offices, chimneys. The city's chief glory, its
cathedral, is out-flanked and out-topped by industry. Such old
buildings as do remain are likewise jostled and hemmed-in. The
streets are a maze of one-way congestion. And in the cathedral
close you may need to shout in order to speak. At Llangurig, near
the source of the Severn, I once met two visitors who, they said,
dreaded going home to Worcester, which they had known and
loved for seventy years.

These things being so, even the briefest account of Worcester's
past must seem irrelevant and in the base sense academic. Deafened by traffic, who would know, or guess, or care even to be
told that this pandemonium was once called Wignorna ceastra or
'camp of the Wigoran', a tribe taking their name from the Forest
of Wyre . . . that Worcester first became a city in 880, but was
burned by the Danes, and rebuilt when King Alfred held a Witan
there . . . that in 983 Bishop Oswald raised a new cathedral, and
that in 1041 the Danes destroyed it . . . that the present cathedral
was dedicated by Bishop Sylvester in the presence of King Henry
III . . . that in it King John was buried and, in 1874, exhumed,
retaining some grey hairs and enough burial robes to show that
they tallied with those on his effigy.

If you do explore this bower of Babel, you will find a Deanery
that was once the Bishops' Palace; an eighteenth-century Guildhall and, from the same period, a redbrick Almshouse (deafened
by lorries and cars) endowed by one of the Berkeleys; a Cathedral
School, founded by King Henry VIII (Samuel Butler was an Old
Boy) and a Grammar School (Queen Victoria made it Royal).
Also hidden in the hideousness are (or were, because Worcester

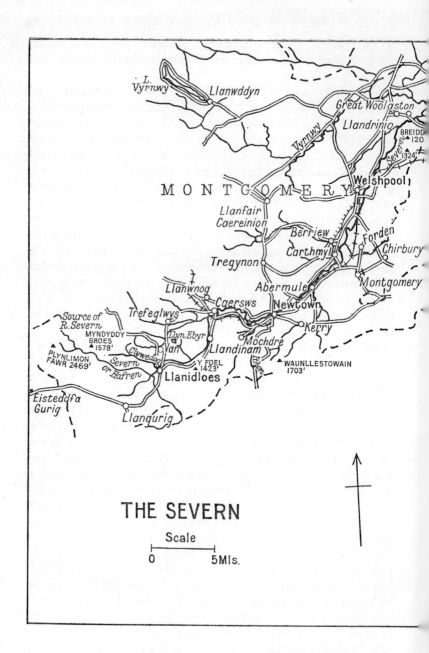

THE SEVERN

Scale

0 —————— 5 Mls.

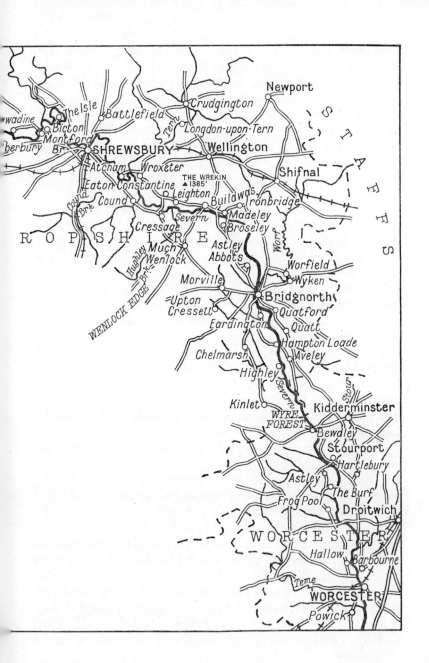

razes itself rapidly) a half-timbered house, near the old corn market, bearing an inscription: "Love God, honour the King." From that house King Charles II led his troops against the rebels, and into it again was snatched by Lord Wilmot, once more to leave (by the back door) while the rebels were entering through the front. There is, too—or was—in New Street a tea shop with a plaque stating that on Wednesday, 11th March 1772: "This building was opened by the Rev. John Wesley, MA, Fellow of Lincoln College, Oxford." The plaque adds: "The first Methodist Chapel in this city."

And yet, as I say, it seems irrelevant to speak of a place that has destroyed itself. Ruskin diagnosed the suicide: "Whenever I travel in England . . . I see that men, wherever they can reach, destroy all beauty. They seem to have no other desire or hope but to have large houses and to be able to move fast."

Worcester, which used to be a country town, now manufactures uncountable quantities of God-knows-what; and in the midst of it I take my stand, against desecretion of the Severn in particular and of this kingdom in general. Disregarding chambers of commerce, associations of artisans, consortia of executives, and all other oddfellows, I say of Worcester what Max Beerbohm said of London: ". . . it has been cosmopolitanized, democratized, commercialized, mechanized, standardized, vulgarized, so extensively that one's pride in showing it to a foreigner is changed to a wholesome humility."

However, Worcester does have one good story to tell, all the better for being true. On 23rd August 1651 King Charles II and a few thousand of his troops, chiefly Scotsmen, limped into the city, having marched thither from Scotland, three hundred miles in three weeks. Eleven days later Cromwell attacked them. The young King led a sortie, but was beaten back. Within a few hours his men were either dead, or captured, or in flight. The King himself wished to ride south before news of the defeat should make it even more difficult for him to reach France. But his advisers disagreed. He must, they said, play for safety. The King acquiesced. With a handful of followers he galloped away, through failing light, into the shadows of the Severn; guided by a Roman Catholic, Charles Giffard, who owned estates in a remote part of the country.

At Stourbridge the fugitives dismounted, and led their horses quietly, hoping not to awake the townsfolk. Soon after daybreak the King was introduced by Giffard to a Roman Catholic family of woodcutters, the Penderels, who gave him some farmworker's clothes. Lord Wilmot then began to crop the royal ringlets, but made such a ragged job that Richard Penderel was invited to do better, with a pair of shears.

The King now entrusted himself solely to Penderel, hoping that the forester's skill would lead him through the encircling rebels. Only once did Penderel's courage fail, and that was when they had to cross a river, for he could not swim. The King lived to dictate an account of that crossing, to Samuel Pepys: "So I told him," said the King, "that the river, being but a little one, I would undertake to help him over. Upon which we went over some closes to the river side, and I, entering the river first to see whether I could myself get over, who knew how to swim, found it was but a little above my middle, and, thereupon, taking Richard Penderel by the hand, I helped him over."

After many adventures and much hardship the King reached Penderel's home, a hunting lodge in the woods of Boscobel. Already the rebels were offering a huge reward to anyone who should betray—and death to all who sheltered—"Charles Stuart, a long dark man, above two yards high". Tradition says that at Boscobel the King hid among the branches of an oak tree while the rebels searched nearby. He did indeed hide in an oak, with Colonel Careless, but not among its branches, for the tree was hollow, so that the two men were able to creep inside; and there the young King fell asleep, with his head on the Colonel's lap. The Colonel, in fact, supported the head for so long that his own arm became numb. And that was how King Charles escaped from Worcester, on his way to exile.

The Severn, by contrast, escapes to freedom. The noise of Worcester falls astern, and soon the high ground of Upper Broadheath appears, the birthplace of Elgar.

Edward William Elgar was born at a cottage, in 1857. His father kept a small music shop in Worcester, and was organist at the Roman Catholic church there. Although the son never did receive a formal musical education, he early mastered the violin. As a youth he played alongside his father at the Three Choirs'

Festival. Later he directed a band at the County Lunatic Asylum. During a scripture lesson, he resolved one day to compose a music honouring the Apostles. "Destiny," said Virgil, "will find a way." For Elgar, as for many artists, the way was long and hard. It led first to London, at a time when English music was held in international disrepute. "Living," as he himself put it, "on two bags of nuts a day," Elgar acquired a few violin pupils; among them Caroline, daughter of Sir Henry Gee Roberts. The couple fell in love and soon afterwards were married; but the bride's parents, shocked by her social and financial insouciance, disowned the couple, and withheld from them the few weekly guineas that could have added so much joy—and who knows how much music —to Elgar's life. Lacking that pittance, his best years were squandered on teaching. For decades the Elgars lived close to poverty; at Great Malvern, at Hereford, at Hampstead (where Elgar named his house 'Severn'). The long and anguished annals of English art contain no love story braver nor more devoted than the Elgars'. One inclines to ask whether Elgar ever could have triumphed without his wife's fortitude and faith. She it was, when the world passed by, who bade him stand fast; she the one for whom he composed the music which announced that the heirs of Byrd and of Purcell were not extinct.

As a child Elgar had confessed to his mother a wish to become so famous that people throughout the world would write to him as 'Edward Elgar, England'. That wish was fulfilled. After years of neglect, he became a member of the Order of Merit, Master of the King's Musick, Baronet, Doctor *honoris causae* of the Universities of Oxford and Cambridge. When Lady Elgar died, the wellspring withered. Only to her, it seems, could he offer his best. To mark his seventy-fifth birthday the B.B.C. invited him to compose a third symphony, but he lived to make no more than some notes for it. He died in 1934, and was buried beside his wife in the churchyard of St. Wulfstan's at Little Malvern near the Severn.

With Ralph Vaughan Williams, Elgar was the only Briton who has composed great symphonies. His devotional music delights even those who reject its creed. The so-called 'patriotic' music proves that he could do well what most of his detractors cannot do at all. After an exile that had lasted for nearly three hundred years,

English music received from him its passport as a citizen of the world. And the passport was sealed by the Severn. Elgar himself said, that if men do haunt their old home, then he will be found on Malvern Hills. To hear his violin concerto, or the fourth movement of the second symphony, is to feel a breeze from those Hills. The music of Sir Edward Elgar was set to words by his contemporary, Robert Bridges:

> ... out of his heart there falleth
> A melody-making river
> Of passion, that runneth ever
> To the ends of the earth and crieth,
> That yearneth and calleth;
> And Love from the heart of man
> To the heart of man replieth ...

And so to the river again, which has flowed some seventy miles from Gloucester, touching only the three towns of Tewkesbury, Upton-on-Severn, Worcester. Even at Hallow, north-west of suburban Worcester, the Severn keeps to itself, and actually inclines away from that village, unlike Queen Elizabeth I, who stayed at Hallow Hall (now demolished) as guest of the Habington family. Her retinue of 1,500 horses must have cropped many a Severnside meadow.

There is a weir hereabouts, and one of the Severn's few islets, called Bevere, to which the men of Worcester retreated when the Danes came by. When William Cobbett came by he noted with approval that many Severnside cottagers earned good pin-money from making gloves; but factories soon appeared, and the craft of glove-making was mechanized, though a few cottagers still accepted work which the factories farmed to them. Now, like the lacemakers of Buckinghamshire, the Worcestershire glovers are gone. You may find an elderly woman practising the skill of her youth, but it will be a self-conscious pastime, never again a service to those for whom the best of everything is good enough.

Above Bevere the Severn makes for Ombersley, but presently sheers away, as though it could not endure the traffic that shakes the foundations of the black-and-white houses which make Ombersley a sight for sore eyes, though never a sound for sensitive ears. Two centuries ago a less erosive traffic plied over these roads,

carrying the Royal Mail. An order of 1727, signed by "S. Wood-
cock, Surveyor, Glocester," issued a warning to the staff of the
Worcester and Hereford Coach: "NB. This Mail must be conveyed at the Rate of Six Miles in The Hour at least, . . . Every
Deputy or Contractor will be responsible (at their Peril) for the
regular Performance of their Riding Duty. And if any Post-Boy
or Rider, carrying this Mail, is found loitering on the Road, he
will be committed to the House of Correction, and confined to
hard Labour for one Month." There was a postscript to that
warning, for the "Post-Boy or Rider" referred to the girls who
sometimes galloped so furiously that they overtook the squire
hurrying home on his Newmarket mare. This feature lingered
long in England. A stage-coach was running between Lynton
and Minehead fifty years ago.

Having avoided Ombersley, the Severn makes for Holt, where
a Norman church stands between the river and the road. Nearby
is Holt Castle, towered and embattled; partly a modern residence,
partly a sixteenth-century mansion, built by Gilbert Bourne, a
contemporary of Edmund Bonner, whom Mary Tudor appointed as Bishop of Bath and Wells a Secretary of State. The
castle was purchased by one of the Bromleys, one of whom, Sir
Thomas, presided at the trial of Mary Queen of Scots. The Queen,
an anointed Sovereign, declined to recognize the Commission's
validity, yet defended herself with eloquence and dignity, putting
Sir Thomas Bromley in his place: "God forgive you lawyers,"
she told him, "for you are so sore fellows. God bless me and my
cause from your laws, for it is a very good matter that they cannot
make seem bad."

Wooded, grass-green, patrolled by swans, Holt Fleet is a beautiful place and true to its name, which means a river beside a wood.
It is also a place to be visited out of season or between hours, for
at most other times it becomes a jamboree of motorists and cara-
vaners. Bless them all. Doubtless they do indeed work hard, and
pay their taxes, and cherish their families, and understand all those
abstruse matters which every parliamentary elector ought to
understand. Bless them again a second time and for a third if you
feel it may do them some good. But never pretend that their
presence enhances the Severn.

At Shrawley the woods come down to the water, and so too

does a tributary, Dick Brook, flowing from Astley, two miles to
the east. Astley's Norman church contains some monuments to
the Actons, of whom the greatest was the historian, John Emrich
Edward Dalberg-Acton, first Baron Acton. Born of a German
mother at Naples in 1834, Lord Acton studied under Wiseman at
Oscott, and became Regius Professor of Modern History at
Cambridge. *Lectures on Modern History* is his best-known book
("All power corrupts, and absolute power corrupts absolutely").
Lord Acton helped to design, but did not live to see the launching
of, *The Cambridge Modern History*. He must have been an impressive lecturer. According to Sir John Pollock, who studied under
him: "There was a magnetic quality in the tones of his voice, and
a light in his eye, that compelled obedience from the mind." Each
of his lectures, we are told, was ". . . a wonderful work of art, such
as in all likeliness will never again be witnessed." Acton was an
ecumenical Roman Catholic at a time when the Papacy imposed a
less flexible attitude. He disliked the dogma of *ex cathedra* infalli-
bility, and wished rather to unite than to divide Christendom. His
essay on Luther is admirably just and not without good humour,
as when it reveals Luther hiding in Wartburg Castle ". . . disguised
as a country gentleman. He wore a moustache, dined joyously,
carried a sword, and shot a buck."

Above Shrawley the river continues to avoid all villages. At
Linccomb there is a long and foaming weir, inland at Hampshill a redbrick inn (the landlords used to be ferrymen), and among
the woods some herons and many birch trees. You seldom see a
barge here, yet the traffic two centuries ago was so heavy that
Andrew Yarranton built several locks on Dick Brook so that
barges might reach a forge which then worked in the forest. The
sandstone remains of those locks are still visible. Inland a little,
left and right, black-and-white houses blend with others of redbrick and thatch, as though to ask a question: why do we admire
old buildings? It cannot be solely for their age, else logic would
conclude that a Queen Anne house is less handsome than a Tudor
mansion, and a Norman castle superior to both. Partly, of course,
we admire a past which our own rose-tinted spectacles have
imagined. Walking beside the Severn at Shrawley, or along the
lanes above it, even an historian may forget to remember what
used to lie behind the façades of these timbered farmsteads . . .

the stench from their privy . . . the life which expected to end before it reached fifty, and was amazed if all its children survived
infancy . . . the illness which nowadays a chemist might cure . . .
the dread of landlords, or a fire, or two bad harvests . . . the heavy
odds against any man rising above his class. These facts grow dim
when we come upon a timbered cottage peaceful as still-life.
Nevertheless, we continue to admire such places, and are left once
again to ask why. The ultimate answer eludes us because there is a
point beyond which no dissector can pursue his self-analysis. He
might as well inquire why pain hurts while pleasure pleases. Even
so, we can cite some justification for our love of old homes. They
were made-to-measure by hand. Strip the average modern house,
and not even its owner could identify it among the crowd of
similar houses. But a Tudor farmer would recognize his own
kitchen simply by glancing at the beams, none of which exactly
resembled any other in the world. "Houses," said Francis Bacon,
"are built to live in, not to look on." That comes strangely from a
man who adorned what we now rate as an era of superb domestic
architecture. In any event Bacon was wrong; even the cave-
dwellers decorated their home. And we envy our ancestors' ability
to make useful things beautifully. Morever these old houses are
numinous. They have observed history. They were built when
Queen Elizabeth rallied her troops against the Armada. They were
enlarged when Cromwell became a military dictator. They were
repaired when Nelson defeated Villeneuve.

Among such buildings—partly older, partly younger—is
Hartlebury Castle, two miles inland, near a point where the river
is joined by a stream from the castle grounds. Built during the
thirteenth century, on land that had been given to the See of
Worcester 1,100 years ago, Hartlebury Castle has for centuries
been the Bishop's Palace. Most of the present sandstone castle was
built by Bishop Hough during the late seventeenth century. One
hundred years later Bishop Hurd bought the libraries of Alexander
Pope and his contemporary, William Warburton, Bishop of
Gloucester, who helped Theobald to edit Shakespeare. Bishop
Hurd then designed a long gallery to contain the libraries. Hartlebury Castle has been adapted to receive the many deputations—
pastoral, administrative, theological—which wait upon a bishop.

Near the castle stands an obsolete feature of the portrait, a watermill. Domesday Book mentions 5,624 watermills in England, but the total number must have been greater than that because Domesday ignored sizeable parts of the kingdom. In 1086, at all events, Worcestershire had sixty-nine watermills, most of them beside the Severn; Gloucestershire had 128; Shropshire had 187. Nor did the mills provide bread alone. In 1168 a watermill was working for the fullers, beating textiles in water, to increase their durability by shrinkage. In the fourteenth century, watermills were crushing woad for the dyeing trade. Others were used to produce oil, tobacco, copper, paper, leather. The steam engine put them out of business, yet they died hard. The miller in Daudet's *Letter From My Mill* spoke—indeed, shouted—for all his kind. This miller, said Daudet, ". . . had known sixty years among the flour and was inordinately proud of his craft. The setting up of steam infuriated him. For a whole week he was to be seen about the village, stirring up the people, and shouting at the top of his voice that the new miller's flour was going to poison all Provence". And not only Provence: in our own time Dr. W. G. Hoskins analysed the average white loaf as ". . . an obscene caricature of bread". However, not every watermill became obsolete. In 1948 a privately-owned watermill generated electricity for Swaledale in Yorkshire; in 1968 a watermill was generating electricity at Cotehale in Cornwall; and in John o' Groats I recently visited a watermill (there was only one other in all Scotland) still grinding 'meal' or oats.

Quays and locks are the places from which to study a river in breadth, but its depth is best plumbed at a watermill, even although the sounding must now be retrospective. John Constable, a miller's son, said that he was never so happy as when "surrounded by weirs, backwaters, nets and willows, with the smell of weeds, flowing water and flour in my nostrils". These Severn watermills were a rural *rendezvous*. A small watermill served its own village and the outlying farms. A large mill served several villages and perhaps a small town. Housewives baked their own bread, and anyone who was able to carry a bag of flour would join the gossips at the mill.

With lawyers and friars, the miller was often an unpopular figure in the medieval economy, for he received payment in kind, keeping a percentage of each customer's flour; and it was he

alone who decided how much flour each customer had brought,
and how much each had taken away. The miller could indeed
afford to be "jolly".

As a child I spent many happy hours beside a watermill beyond
the hamlet that lay beyond the village, along a narrow lane over a
hump-back bridge among trees at the foot of hills. There, had I
then known it, I might have echoed Tennyson's praise:

> I loved the brimming wave that swam
> Thro' quiet meadows round the mill,
> The sleepy pool above the dam,
> The pool beneath it never still,
> The meal-sacks on the whiten'd floor,
> The dark round of the dripping wheel,
> The very air about the door
> Made misty with the floating meal.

Poetry, alas, plays no part in the landscape waiting around the
next bend, at an eighteenth-century town that was designed and
built as an industrial centre, and may therefore be called the first
of Britain's trading estates.

Before we do arrive, it will be helpful to glance backward and
forward through time, because a shifting perspective may enable
the portrait to represent more accurately what it undertook to
portray. And the matter—which is revolution—seems especially
urgent because it moves so swiftly that anyone under thirty years
of age may regard it as part of *l'ancien regime* and co-eval with the
hills. For example, until the beginning of this century, country
life drew its identity from one basic source, which was distance.
That source is failing, and will soon die. From Land's End to John
o' Groats the same cheap music and the same trivial horseplay
pervade any household that cares to invite them. A generation
which flies to Majorca, is no longer excited, as its grandparents
were excited, by the prospect of visiting friends ten miles across
the mountains. Nothing imaginable can revive a past that will die
with its last remembrancer. Nor will anyone wish that the past
could be completely revived. Change is another name for life.
The issue is, not whether, but in what ways, life ought to change.
If, after all, events are governed by certainty, not by probability
—if, in Bergson's words, *tout est donné*—then, given the invention

*Near the Malverns*

of the wheel, a seer might have foretold death on the roads and a
trip to the moon. Whether technological revolution ever can respect the basic conditions for human health and happiness, is a
question that may one day be answered. From sheer stupidity, or
utter fatalism, men may subordinate their own happiness and
health to the basic conditions for technological revolution.
Meanwhile, old cities are desecrated, new factory-towns created,
farmland destroyed. Britain has become its own parasite, self-
consuming in order that it may continue to exist and to consume
more of itself. An early example of this proliferation, posing as
natural regeneration, may be seen at Stourport-on-Severn.

Two centuries ago this town did not exist. In its place stood the
hamlet of Lower Mitton, where the Severn met the Avon, and
was later joined by the Staffordshire and Worcestershire Canal.
Mitton, in short, was doomed; and James Brindley became its
executioner. During the 1790s a group of businessmen commis-
sioned him to build a new town there, with houses, docks, and a
bridge that was swept away and replaced by another (rebuilt in
1870). There is no evidence that Brindley himself designed the
houses, yet the new town may properly be called his own creation.
They named it Stourport, after an alehouse in the old hamlet.
Nowadays, by calling itself Stourport-on-Severn, the town co-opts
both rivers.

Because the architects of 1790 were incapable of designing ugly
houses, it follows that their eighteenth-century town was pleasanter than the twentieth-century additions to it. If you arrive
before traffic-time, or on early-closing day, you may, by half-
shutting one eye, imagine what Brindley's town looked like.
Climbing the main street from an obsolescent harbour, the
eighteenth-century houses are well-built of red brick. Several old-
fashionable establishments continue to make shopping a pleasure.
But the twentieth century has built an unsightly hotel by the
bridge; a post office in bright red; an ezcema of chain stores; a
permanently decrepit fun-fair; and a litter of power-houses,
petrol pumps, factories, coal dumps, and rail-yards sprawling in
sour disorder.

Brindley, in short, built for a future that now contemplates its
past. His dry docks are damp with disuse; the boatbuilders' yard
is a mausoleum of rubble and weeds; the quays and the derricks

7

*Worcester: Berkeley's Almshouse*

grow rusty. Some river-traffic does find its way here, but the only craft I ever saw were pleasure-boats and a barge half-submerged. In 1816, by contrast, traffic was so heavy that the canal locks were kept open from 5 a.m. until 9 p.m.; by 1830 they were open throughout the twenty-four hours; and in 1839 the Stourport bargefolk protested, on religious grounds, against Sunday work. According to a census of 1841 there were in England and Wales 23,226 "boat and barge men" and 132 female accessories. At Stourport, as on many other canals, the companies began by running their own barges, but soon found it more profitable to sell them to individuals, and thereafter to levy tolls. So arose the family barge with its gipsy-like decor. But, as I say, all has changed. And the change is epitomized in the surveys of Worcestershire during the early years of the twentieth century. These contain no reference to the craft of cheese-making; instead, the cry goes up "no milkers can be got". France not only feeds itself but also exports a surplus of food; England cannot produce even one-half of the food which Englishmen require. At Stourport-on-Severn you may see the ghost of a town which was built in order to celebrate the birth of that precarious policy. And I say "ghost" despite Stourport's busyness and off-peak pleasantness, for the town is neither one thing nor the other. It has lost commercial status without regaining rural identity.

# THE INDUSTRIAL MIDLANDS:
## STOURPORT-ON-SEVERN TO BUILDWAS

THE next six miles of river reveal a battle between town and country. Fouled by industrial excreta, and sandwiched between two roads, the Severn might have become a slut. Instead, sheering westward from Stourport, it enters an enchanting reach, rippled by swans; and comes at length under the lee of Stagborough Hill, whence Ribbesford Woods dip down to the water. The village of Ribbesford no longer exists, but its church and the house (with an eighteenth-century wing) abide and are beautiful.

The church has a Norman tympanum, an arcade of oak arches in the south aisle, and a window by Burne-Jones.

The House stands on ground that was held by the Saxon monks of Worcester, and passed in time to the Mortimers, who granted it to the de Ribbesford family. Among later owners were the Herberts, and after them the Ingrams and the Winningtons who begat a twentieth-century Bishop of London. A path leads through Ribbesford Woods, to join a lane near Horsehill Farm. Seen from this high ground, the Severn winks like a blue eye. Here indeed is a land of woods—Areley Wood, Burnt Wood, Rock Coppice—paving a way for the forest that lies ahead.

Facing Ribbesford House, Blackstone Crag seems ill-named because its earth is red. Unfortunately, the road at this point becomes narrow, dangerous, and so close to the river that the banks are fouled by litter and broken bottles. On this reach the summer hordes jostle for a picnic-place. As though trying to shake them off, the Severn swings north-east, bending gracefully into Bewdley, which used to be famous and still is handsome.

The arms of Bewdley show an anchor *non sanz droict* because this inland town, set among woods and hills, was Bristol's clearing-house for the northern half of England. Having received help from

Bewdley men after the battle of Tewkesbury, King Edward IV excused them from paying river dues. These bargemen were both famous and ferocious: famous for their skill at navigating the fords and races between the quay and Blackstone Crag; ferocious in their opposition to change. In 1803 about 150 men were employed to haul barges from Bewdley to Coalbrookdale; a livelihood which Telford described as "the present barbarous and expensive custom of performing this slave-like office by men". Telford reckoned that, whereas one man might haul three tons, a horse could haul thirty-six, at one-third of the cost. During the 1830s a tow-path for horses was laid between Gloucester and Shrewsbury; and against it the Bewdley bargemen rioted. Having accepted horses, they rioted a second time, when tugs took the oats from the horses' mouth.

Leland came to Bewdley soon after the town had rebuilt itself on the crest of a prosperous wave. His description was lyrical: "The town itself is sett on the side of a hill, so comely that a man cannot wish to see a towne better. It riseth from the Severne bank upon the hill by west, so that a man standing transpontem by east may discern almost every house, and att rising of the sunne the whole towne glittereth, being all of new building, as it were of gold." Time has dealt kindly with Leland's vision. As a riverscape, admittedly, it is disappointing because no one has troubled to create a pleasant promenade. Even so, Bewdley—the *beau lieu* or 'beautiful place'—lives up to its name. If you enter from the right-bank, you notice first a miniature black-and-white cottage, and Telford's graceful stone bridge, and beyond it the main street climbing to an eighteenth-century church astride the traffic. On Severnside South a group of weathered houses gaze across the river at Tudor, Caroline, and Georgian houses (Georgian because many of the half-timbered homes were rebuilt during the eighteenth century). Then came the Stourport Canal, leaving Bewdley high and dry. Now only the inns—'The Anchor', 'The Pack-horse'—testify to a lost eminence. In 1967 Bewdley was named as a town which the Civic Amenities Act ought to protect against 'development'. But no formal litany can evoke the essence of this place. You must come here several times at several seasons—before the traffic and after—leaning over the bridge; loitering among the venerable homes in Load Street; hoping that the dilapidated houses near the church will be restored and occupied.

Bewdley is dominated by a great house, 'Tickenhill', built in 1738 to incorporate parts of a palace which King Henry VII made for his heir, Arthur, the only English Prince who was *de jure* and *de facto* of Wales; for this Prince became President of Wales and the Marches, ruling often from Ludlow and sometimes from his new palace at Bewdley. "A fayre mannour," Leland found it, ". . . on the very Knappe of an hill that the Towne standeth on." Royal indeed was 'Tickenhill'. Here by proxy the young Prince Arthur announced his betrothal to Katharine, Princess of Aragon . . . not foreseeing that her marriage to his successor would impel the Reformation. Here lived Princess Mary . . . not foreseeing that Calais would carve her heart. And here King Charles I learned of the disaster at Marston Moor . . . not foreseeing the defection of his General, the Marquis of Newcastle (who, wrote Clarendon, "hoped that his meritorious actions might outweigh his present abandoning the thought of future action; and so, without further consideration . . . transported himself out of the kingdom . . ."). 'Tickenhill' has experienced several changes of fortune. Fifty years ago it became a school. On my last visit it was a private residence.

Bewdley's most famous son was Lord Baldwin, who came of Methodist stock, took his title from the town, and retired within a few miles of it. Born in 1867, Stanley Baldwin was educated at Harrow and Cambridge. He wished to become a country parson, but chose to enter the family manufacturing business. Having succeeded his father as Member for Kidderminster, he served as parliamentary private secretary to Bonar Law at the Treasury. Six years later, in 1923, he became premier, and remained so for most of the next fourteen years of national decadence, against which his private life was more commendable than his public perspicacity. Like most British premiers until recent times, Earl Baldwin of Bewdley was a country landowner. Often he longed to return to a realm of (as he put it) "old castles and black and white buildings". Instead, he shouldered the obligations of privilege.

As the Severn leaves Bewdley, it passes a clutter of shacks and caravans above the bridge; thereafter flowing between a road and a railway, so that anyone coming here for the first time, expects to find more factories, and is therefore pleased when his expectations are not fulfilled. Certainly the Severn has reached the industrial Midlands, but you would not guess so, for at Bewdley it approaches a riverscape which many Midlanders prefer above all others *en route*. First, on the left bank, comes the Forest of Wyre, with a railway running through it, and beside the railway a brook called Dowles, whose name either came from or went to a small and beautiful Tudor manor house overhung by riverside woods. The name Dowles is a foretaste of the Marcher Country, being a corruption of Dalch, which was itself a hybrid, gotten of the British *dubo* or 'black' and of the Welsh *glais* or 'stream'. Like Worcester, the word Wyre is a corruption of *Wigoran*, the name of a local tribe. In the ninth century Wyre Forest covered a vast area of the left bank. Now it is a relatively small region of woodland north and south of Dowles Brook. Yet it remains wild, peaceful, baptized with evocative place names . . . No Man's Land, Uncless, Longdon Orchard, Lord's Yard Coppice. England has nothing else quite like Wyre Forest. Here are miles of scrub oak set among birch saplings speckled with heather and gorse. On a still day in the heart of the Forest never a leaf will flutter nor any footfall stir the silence; though in times past the blackgrouse flourished here, and eagles made an eyrie on the hills. But Wyre Forest is not a tomb, for the ghosts of its former busyness are active. Charcoal is burned; besoms are made from birch twigs; skeps or oval baskets are fashioned from Wyre oak. Some people regret that Mammon has neglected Wyre in favour of quick profits from foreign soft woods. Others rejoice that Wyre goes its own way, unbalanced by any sort of payments.

Shropshire now joins Worcestershire, and both are met by Staffordshire pointing a long finger at the Severn, as though to stake its claim on classic ground. The lie of the land is emphasized by the loops of the Severn, which, in its search for a level passage, flows through two right angles and between two woods— Exymoor on the east, Seckley on the west—and from them emerges at Upper Arley, the loveliest hamlet on the Severn, with a Norman church, a cluster of cottages, a cobbled quay, and a castle built by Lord Valentia on the site of an old mansion and an older fortress. For the rest, the recipe is as usual: if you come here on a summer Saturday, and do manage to weave a way through the

cars, you will bump into more cars and therefore into more
people.

I first came to Arley in October. From Kinlet I came, on high
ground above the left bank. As the lane loped downhill, I saw a
skyline of woods on the far shore, though the Severn itself was
invisible deep below; and when I glanced back, there also were
trees. I passed a good inn (which is to say, an old one); a good (and
therefore ancient) barn; a single railway line whose station slept;
a second good inn; and finally a car park harmoniously empty
except for a bicycle and one gym shoe. Then the lane turned left,
and entered the river. Across the river were three rowing boats,
and a punt half-ashore on the cobbled beach. Beyond the cobbles, a
causeway led to some redbrick houses among gardens glowing
with dahlias and honeysuckle. And over all, I saw a tower above
trees.

I walked to the end of the lane, and there let the Severn slap my
shoes. It was then that I noticed the fisherman, gazing at his rod as
intently as Buddha had contemplated his belly. The man must have
heard me, for he looked up—he was plain and elderly—and gave
a smile of such benevolence that I nodded, not only to him but
also to the shade of Izaak Walton, who said: ". . . a brother of the
Angle . . . is cheerful . . . is worth gold." Then came a youth and
his girl, and sat beside the water, holding hands: and after them
came a swan, glancing neither right nor left, sometimes gliding and
then again sometimes surging forward upon lawful occasions
known only to itself. And that was how I first saw Arley.

When I last saw Arley I was still repeating a phrase which I
could not improve—"typically English"—and as though to con-
firm the phrase, England appeared as a place-name beside Bole
Brook flowing to join the Severn in Shropshire. Yet Shropshire
contains names that are not at all English: Llanymynech, Llanvair,
Bettws-y-crwyn. This, in short, is a border county and the
Marcher country: and through it the Severn flows, among red
and treeless banks that are best seen from high ground to the left,
where Kinlet is worth visiting, even although the old village has
disappeared.

Kinlet Hall was built (1727–29) of red brick with stone dressings,
to a design by a Warwick architect, Francis Smith. In 1968 it was
a preparatory school.

Kinlet church, in the Hall grounds, has part of a Norman tympanum, and a rare feature, a church stable, with a rarer stone mounting block. Among the effigies are some which carve the history of England: Sir Humphry Blount, for instance (*obiit* 1477), who, for his valour in the northern campaigns, was dubbed "The Terror of Scotland" . . . a name, said Camden, "very famous in these parts . . .".

The next place, Highley, sounds as though it were on high ground. In fact, it lies within a few hundred yards of the water meadows, and was anciently Hugga's leah. Hugga would not now recognize his *leah*, for the new settlement is a geological accident, a mining community of brash brick, exacerbated by a suburb of the 1930s and by another of the 1960s. The only sights worth seeing are the Norman church, the base and shaft of a medieval cross, and a timbered Church House overlooking the churchyard.

Above Highley the river enters a reach that to me has always seemed very lonely. However, a dearth of people is balanced by herds of cattle. Writing of Shropshire and Herefordshire as they were during the 1870s, John Masefield recalled their ". . . fine pastures, feeding a kind of cattle that has gone all over the cattle-raising world". They are massive indeed, these Herefordshires, with their thick necks, tawny hair, pale noses. They are a beef breed, reaching maturity soon and cheaply. When I was a farm pupil, long ago, only 2 per cent of a large Herefordshire herd reacted to tuberculosis. The cow is a first-rate milker.

As for the sheep, many of them on this reach are Shropshires, not unlike the Southdowns. I think it is correct to say that they came from crossing Staffordshires with the old native Shropshires. They are prolific, well able to adapt to various soils, which is one reason why so many of them were exported. Even on this reach you will see some of the Clun Forest sheep, descended from the black-faced Longmynd rams. On the hills a dozen miles inland I have noticed a few Welsh Mountain sheep, scarcely changed for centuries. They have yellowish faces and curled horns.

On the left bank a lane passes Chelmarsh church with its red-brick tower (1720) and chantry (1345).

Chelmarsh Hall, formerly a grange or granary of Wigmore Abbey, was granted to the monks by Edmund Mortimer, Earl of March, in 1379. Now it is a Victorian mansion with some late medieval doors and windows, and fragments of a timber roof. Its chief glory is a vision of the Severn far below.

The next hamlet, Eardington, forms part of the parish of Quatford on the opposite shore. The best buildings are a black-and-white Post Office; the redbrick Grange Farm; and a Georgian house, Hay Farm, with one seventeenth-century window.

If you feel in the mood to follow Mor Brook to Upton Cressett, the journey will prove memorable, for this is an endearing place, perched on a hill. Take first the lane to Oldbury (a suburb of Bridgnorth), and then turn left, along a lane to Morville; and after that, take the second lane on the left, and so across the Brook into Upton Cressett, whose name means 'the upper part of the hamlet' which, during the thirteenth century, came by marriage to Thomas Cressett (and *his* name was a nickname, *crais*, the Old French word for 'fat').

The church has a timber-framed porch and some Flemish glass of the Renaissance. A brass (1640) to Richard Cressett, with his wife and five praying children, is signed (a rare event) by its maker "Fr. Grigs" who designed the memorial to Sir Robert Hitcham of Framlingham in Suffolk. The Tudor Hall retains a gabled and turreted gatehouse. For one night Prince Rupert slept there. The Hall is now a farmhouse. At Upton Cressett an Englishman may join with any other villager who believes that his parish is the one which Francis Thompson described:

> And let thy vales make haste to seem more green
> Than any vales are seen
> In less auspicious lands,
> And let thy trees clap all their leafy hands,
> And let thy flowers be gladder far of hue
> Than flowers of other regions may . . .

So far we have followed the left bank above Bewdley. Now is the moment at which to explore the right, starting from Alveley, nearly 400 feet up, in sight of the Clee Hills.

Alveley church has a Norman tower, and an altar frontal (embroidered during the late middle ages) whose faint colourings are still discernible. A brass to John Groves (*obiit* 1616) illustrates a theme familiar in English history. Groves, who came of yeoman stock, lived at Pool Hall, a moated manor with a Georgian frontage. Having prospered as a London merchant, he married a daughter of Lord Jermyn, and in his will bequeathed five pounds to "labouring men of honest conversation". It was this movement from one class to another, and the marriages between classes, which saved England from a French revolution and from the excessive inter-breeding which has brought decadence to some of the continental aristocracies.

The Three Horseshoes Inn is said to have been built in 1406. Nearby, some stone cottages and ancient elms enhance the quietude.

From Alveley a lane leads to Hampton Loade (Old English *lad* or 'watercourse'), keeping within sight of the Severn, and then becoming a track at a cross roads marked by what the Ordnance Map calls a Butter Cross, though it more likely signified a general market. Hampton Loade is a riverside haven of trees and white-washed cottages.

Unlike the left bank, this side of the Severn is harried by a main road. Day and night the traffic rumbles through the Forest of Morfe, which in Leland's time covered both sides of the Severn above Bridgnorth, but was so razed by the ironmasters that now only a few coverts remain, and a handful of evocative place-names . . . Morville (anciently Morfield), Morfevalley, and The Mose (a nucleus of farms off the beaten track, one of them having a shed with red sandstone columns).

Quatt village, facing Chelmarsh across the river, took its name from Quatford, four miles to the north, at a ford where Cwatt's people dwelt. In the year 896 the place had a bridge, called Cwatbrycg. Quatt's redbrick Georgian church contains several Norman features and some memorials to the Wolryche family of Dudmaston Hall, one of whom, Sir Thomas Wolryche died in 1701, aged twenty-nine. His wife, whom he had married when she was seventeen, lived as a widow for sixty-four years, dying when she was ninety-three. Near the church is the eighteenth-century Dower House of Dudmaston Hall.

The Hall itself was enlarged by the Wolryche family in 1730. It stands between the river and the road; near enough to overlook the former, and far enough not to overhear the latter. I first saw the Hall by chance, at the end of a long day's motoring. It was May, I remember, and the light failing. Enervated by miles of traffic, I decided to take the very next turning, left or right, in search of sanity; and it led me to Dudmaston Hall. After a while I guessed that this was private property, so I stopped the car, and continued on foot, assured that no reasonable man objects when his home is admired reasonably. Through the trees I saw lights glowing from the Hall; and below them the starlit Severn. Somewhere a clock struck nine, which set me thinking of Sir Thomas Wolryche's lady all those years ago, for in her time the Curfew was sounded, and indeed for a long while after, far and wide, even until the 1870s, as Masefield remembered: "In many parishes Curfew was rung at eight o'clock in the evenings and still called Curfew, though few knew why." Curfew, of course, is the French for 'extinguish your fire', a warning especially urgent in an era of timber houses. Yet there was no precise rule. Common sense and custom were held to be enough. As late as 1531 the Articles of Faversham decided: "Imprimis, the sexton, or his sufficient deputy, shall lye in the church steeple; and at eight o'clock every night shall ring the curfewe by the space of a quarter of an hour, with such bell as of old time hath been accustomed." England did not have a Curfew Law until 1918, when the Board of Trade restricted the use of gas and electricity.

What changes Lady Wolryche had seen. Born soon after King Charles II came into his own, she died to the sound of steam engines from an industrial revolution only twenty miles away. In Bridgnorth on market day she overheard English dissenters theologizing with Welsh chapel-folk; just such a scene as Gregory of Nyssa had witnessed in Constantinople during the Arian dispute sixteen centuries ago: "Ask a tradesman the price of some new article," he reported, "and he replies with a disquisition on generated and ungenerated being. Ask the price of bread today, and the baker tells you, 'The Son is subordinate to the Father'. Ask your servant if the bath is ready, and he answers, 'The Son arose out of nothing'."

Lady Wolryche must have seen and sometimes hailed the ferryman; today she would call in vain, for almost every Severn ferry has betaken itself to Lethe. The right to ply a ferry is a franchise or royal grant, like the licence to hold a market. Such right confers no ownership of the river bank. A ferryman is simply entitled to exact a reasonable toll for his services. No one may start a new ferry, nor compete with an old one, except by Parliament's authority. Lady Wolryche would marvel at the disappearance of a necessity. Yet the changes which she witnessed were slight compared with those that have transformed England within the lifetime of men who are middleaged today. Such men must feel thankful that many past evils have perished; but when they remember the good things which also have perished—the quietude, the craftsmanship, the countryside's façade of beauty that was more than skin deep—then, like Juliet's Nurse, they must say:

To think that I have lived to see thee die.

Quatford lies a few miles north of Dudmaston Hall, and has a footpath which once joined it with Eardington via a ferry. You can find the path near the church, and follow it inland as far as Forest Oak, a place-name recalling the Forest of Morfe. Quatford nowadays is a suburb of Bridgnorth. Its sandstone castle, overlooking the Severn from Quatford Wood, was designed by a builder, John Smalman, for his own use, in precisely the style that one would expect of such a man at such a time; topheavy with turrets, battlements, machicolations.

The church of St. Mary Magdalene surveys the Severn from a knoll. The Norman chancel and nave were rebuilt in 1714. Nearby stands an ornamental look-out post, another of J. Smalman's follies. Danes Ford speaks for itself.

After Quatford the river sheers westward from the traffic, along an impressive reach crowned by Bridgnorth two miles away. Until the thirteenth century, Bridgnorth was *Brycg* or 'The Bridge'. But when Quatford built its own bridge, the citizens of 'The Bridge' asserted their pre-eminence by defining it as *Brugg' Norht* or 'The North Bridge'.

Unlike Gloucester and Worcester, Bridgnorth has not been ruined. On the contrary, it is the most impressive of all the Severn towns, among the most dramatically-sited in England. In fact, it is two towns—Low Town by the river, High Town on the hill—a dichotomy emphasized by an annual custom, for on Boxing Day a posse of small boys from Low Town march up to High Town, their faces blackened, their jackets turned inside-out and decorated with coloured cloth. Each boy carries a broom-handle. The High

Town boys receive the invaders courteously. The opposing armies then hold a mock combat with their broom-handles; all the while chanting ten verses of traditional song, "This old man played one." Money is collected, and the festivities end at noon. Neither in nor out of books have I been able to discover the origin of this ancient custom.

High and Low, at all events, offer so many good things that portraiture must become impressionism, as follows: the remains of a hilltop castle built by the Saxons, rebuilt by Robert Belesme (1098–1101), and razed by the rebels (1646) . . . the tower of that castle, leaning three times more dizzily than Pisa's . . . a grammar school (1629) which nurtured a small benchful of bishops . . . the Governor's Home (1633), roseate in all weathers . . . the town hall (1648–52), timbered and with two belfries . . . a welcome from The Raven Inn (1646), the timbered 'King's Head', and two Caroline taverns, 'The Castle' and 'The Swan' . . . Bishop Percy's House (1580) on Cartway, the old road between High Town and Low . . . some riverside caves that were human hovels when Queen Victoria came to the throne . . . the churches of St. Leonard (Victorian red sandstone) and of St. Mary Magdalene (designed by Telford) . . . the post office (1700) . . . a half-timbered house near the bridge, inscribed "Except the Lord Build the Owse the labours thereof avail nothing. Erected by R. Fos." (alias Richard Forester, a Severn bargemaster whose wharf still bears his name).

Yet dates and buildings are not enough. Bridgnorth must be explored on foot, preferably at mid-week in April, for then the town is companionably busy, with just the right amount of humanity in a still-life of gables and dormers and timbers; of alleys tumbling into the water, and the highway climbing the hill. At such a time you will see the town living as it always has lived, by mixing industry with agriculture. Five centuries ago Leland said of Bridgnorth: ". . . it standeth by clothing." When clothing collapsed, the town made hats and caps. Today it has factories for carpets, electrical gadgets, engineering. As long ago as 1808 the Minute Book of the Grand Junction Canal noted that the canal engineer had lately ordered from Bridgnorth a four-horsepower steam pump. The Minute Book added that Bridgnorth possessed ". . . a Steam Engine invented by Mr. Trevithick on a very simple construction . . .".

The town's river traffic is a memory only. Gone forever are the coal barges that came daily to Richard Forester's wharf, hauled by men harnessed like horses. And yet, after all, the memory is not so faint, for some of the townsfolk told me that in their childhood the horse-barges still plied with a mixed cargo.

The great man of Bridgnorth was Thomas Percy, who first saw the light in 1729, from that same house which "R. Fos." had inscribed. Although Percy's father was a grocer, the son in later life produced evidence of kinship with the ducal Percies of Northumberland; and produced it so persuasively that James Boswell declared ". . . both as a lawyer accustomed to the consideration of evidence, and as a Genealogist versed in the study of pedigrees, I am fully satisfied." Whether simple or gentle, Thomas Percy went up from Bridgnorth Grammar School to Christchurch, Oxford, and then took holy orders. His preferment was not slow —he became Dean of Carlisle and then Bishop of Dromore in Ireland—neither was his eminence idle. He translated several works, but his fame rests upon one book, *The Reliques of Ancient English Poetry*, which appeared (1765) with a title-page: *Old Heroic Ballads, Songs, and other Pieces of our Earlier Poets (chiefly of the lyric kind). Together with some few of a later date*. These *Reliques* or remains came chiefly from manuscripts which Percy obtained from a Shifnal man, Humphrey Pitt, who had been in the habit of using them as fire-lighters. Percy chose and edited many of the manuscript ballads, including 'Sir Patrick Spens' and 'Lillibulero'. His preface was resounding: ". . . the antiquaries who have revised the works of our ancient writers have been for the most part men void of taste and genius, and therefore have always fastidiously rejected the old poetical Romances, because founded on fictitious or popular subjects, while they have been careful to grub up every petty fragment of the most dull and insipid rhymist." The poems, too, were resounding; for example, the opening lines of 'Edward, Edward', which Percy got from Sir David Dalrymple:

> Why dois your brand sae drap wi' bluid,
> Edward, Edward?

These un-Augustan ballads augured well. In 1815 Wordsworth affirmed: "I do not think there is an able writer in verse of the present day who would not be proud to acknowledge his obligations to the Reliques." Wiser than many of our own writers in verse, the ballad-makers knew that men have an ineradicable fondness for what Sir Philip Sidney called "A tale which holdeth children from play, and old men from the chimney corner".

Bridgnorth offers a second literary pilgrimage, to Aldenham Park, the home of Lord Acton, whom we met down-river at Astley. The Park lies in the parish of Morville, near Mor Brook, a tributary of the Severn, about three miles north-west of Bridgnorth. A public footpath leads from the inn through the Park. The house was rebuilt by Sir Edward Acton in 1691. The historian's grandfather, Sir John Acton, was a man of initiative. Born at Besançon in 1736, he joined the Tuscan navy, from which he was promoted—or, more precisely, from which he promoted himself —to the rank of Neapolitan premier, treasurer, and commander-in-chief. Sir John's grandson owed his peerage partly to his friendship with Gladstone. His library was bought, and presented to Cambridge University, by Lord Morley and Mr. Andrew Carnegie.

Now the Severn heads due north, and is joined by another tributary, the Worfe (Old English *worig* or 'winding'), flowing down from Worfield, seat of the Bromleys. Worfield church has monuments to Sir George Bromley (*obiit* 1588) and to another landed family, the Davenports, who, like the Winningtons and the Ingrams, intermarried. Sir Thomas Bromley, Bacon's successor as Lord High Chancellor, signed the death warrant of Mary Queen of Scots, and delivered a famous judgment on the law of real property, known to jurists as Shelley's Case.

On the left bank Astley Abbots was the *east-leah* or 'eastern water-meadow' belonging to Shrewsbury Abbey. Pleasantly secluded, it has a Norman church dedicated to St. Calixtus; two sixteenth-century houses; and a Jacobean mansion, Stanley Hall.

Beyond Astley Abbots the river flows alongside the wooded slopes of Apley Park, a Regency mansion peering down from a knoll. This is indeed an oasis among industry. The riverside squalor above the Park can be gauged by an account of it as it was half a century ago: "Unlovely villages cling to the steep hillsides, banks of slag and refuse present deplorable eyesores, and tall chimneys here and there spring up from the level river, or shoot skyward from the summits." Yet these blots on the landscape do more than hurt the eye; they pilfer the national pocket. Consider the waste land on these industrial dumps, the derelict acres, the tons of potential hay that are never harvested. The Commons Standing Committee on the Countryside Bill reported that in 1968 the derelict land in England and Wales was increasing by some 4,000 acres every year. The total area of dereliction was not far short of 150,000 acres, of which 55,000 acres were so ravaged that it would not be economic to reclaim them. It seems strange that a kingdom unable to feed itself should yearly destroy thousands of acres of farmland.

The Severn now enters a part of "England's green and pleasant land" which proves, not that industry is inherently evil, nor even that it is inevitably ugly, but that its creators are either too gross or too greedy to curb the excesses of their own handiwork.

First among the debris is Coalport, created by John Rose, an eighteenth-century porcelain manufacturer, who started a business which flourished here until 1926. Rose did not choose to live among his squalid creation. Instead, he bought Hay Hill Farm, a Queen Anne house, which in those years was rural. The iron bridge at Coalport was built in 1818.

Broseley comes next, the ancient capital of Coalbrookdale, now famed for its tiles, though for many years a centre of the clay pipe industry. In *Notes and Queries* for 6th September 1913, a correspondent recalled "The old pipe-rack with the long row of church-wardens and Broseleys—at one time an indispensable fitting in most bar parlours . . .". This industry was at least as old as 1619, when the Company of Pipe Makers received its charter from James I despite his pamphlet against smoking, *A Counterblaste To Tobacco*, in which the royal Scot described tobacco as " . . . vile . . . stinking and unsavoury . . .". There is a house here, 'The Lawns' (1727), which became the home of an ironmaster, John Wilkinson, who installed at his Broseley forge (1776) a steam engine for blowing the bellows. Eleven years later he designed, built, and launched on this reach *The Trial*, the first barge ever to be made of iron. Many experts assumed that the thing would sink. It did not. "It answers all my expectations," Wilkinson wrote, "and has convinced the unbelievers, who were 999 in a thousand." John Wilkinson in his will asked to be buried in an iron coffin; hoping no doubt he and his metal would merge in a mutual immortality.

*The Compleat Angler: near Hanley Castle*
*Getting acquainted: above Arley*
*The way to the river: near Bridgnorth*

After Broseley the river passes Coalbrookdale. The name is misleading, for it suggests 'brook in the dale of coalfields'. In fact, the name was originally Caldebrok or 'cold brook valley'. What pitfalls await the amateur English place-namer. I remember being bewildered by Pity Me in County Durham, until I discovered that the name was a corruption of *petit mer* or the small lake nearby. And who would guess that Haltemprice in Yorkshire is a corruption of the *haut emprise* or high endeavour of the monks who in 1322 founded a monastery there? Anyway, in this 'cold brook valley', in 1708, Abraham Darby founded the Coalbrookdale Company, which soon devoured every tree for miles around. The Company was thriving in 1968. Near one of its early Victorian warehouses you can see part of Darby's first furnace.

Coalbrookdale is a hybrid of housing estates, factories, slag heaps. It contains a redbrick Methodist chapel (1886) and a church (1850–4) that was paid for by Abraham Darby. From time immemorial the local people had brewed their own beer, and in 1833 a Report of the Select Committee on Agriculture showed that most of the cottages still retained a brewhouse; but none of the occupiers knew how to brew beer. In 1804 every household baked its own bread; eleven years later most of the bread came from shops.

Abraham Darby's church contains a bronze memorial to Matthew Webb, son of a doctor, who was born in 1848, at what was then the neighbouring village of Dawley. Almost as soon as he had learned to walk, Webb was taught to swim in the Severn, from which he soon afterwards snatched one of his brothers. Later, as a Mate in the Merchant Service, he dived overboard to rescue a rating in heavy seas. For this he received the Royal Humane Society's medal. At the age of twenty-seven he achieved his first command—a small sailing ship, registered at Liverpool—and thereafter styled himself Captain Webb. Having created a record by swimming the twenty miles from Blackwall Point to Gravesend, in less than four hours, Webb became the first man to swim the English Channel (it took him all day and most of the night). After that he lapsed into lunacy. For a trivial wager, and despite the pleas of all who were competent to advise him, he swam the rapids below Niagara Falls, watched by a large crowd. After a few minutes he drowned. His body was found several days later, seven miles down-stream.

8

*Yachtsmen at Holt*

Ironbridge takes its name from the bridge which Abraham Darby designed and cast at his Coalbrookdale forge in 1778. In its day it was a brave new wonder of the world; by 1968, as an Ancient Monument, it had become unsafe for traffic. The railway bridge arrived in 1859, and was called Albert Edward. John Wesley came here, to admire the new bridge, to preach at Broseley, and to visit an old friend, John Fletcher or Flechère, vicar of Madeley, who dedicated his life to the proposition that man shall not live by iron alone, not even though it were cast by Abraham Darby of Broseley.

Jean Guillame de la Flechère, son of a Bernese nobleman, studied theology for seven years at Geneva, but then reversed the example of Loyola by serving as a mercenary in Holland and Spain. During a visit to England he became tutor with a family in Shropshire. John Fletcher, as he now called himself, was so impressed by the good works of Methodism among these Severn slag heaps that he took holy orders. Declining a comfortable living at Dunham, because he regarded the stipend as too great, he spent the rest of his days at Madeley, among a flock that was as black as the coal which fed it. They boycotted Fletcher's church, and tried to intimidate him by violence, forgetful that he had been an Army officer. Fletcher counter-attacked by striding from house to house at dawn, armed with a bell, rousing the sleepers to remember their Maker. He taught children at the village school, and gave them a Sunday School as well. His pastoral work followed the precepts of Methodism, which at that time was an Anglican renaissance. In all this the vicar of Madeley was sustained by his wife, Mary Bosanquet, herself a Methodist and close friend of Wesley. Ultimately they triumphed, though not until Fletcher had collapsed under the strain. Happily, a rich friend took him to Italy, from whence he returned restored. Fletcher's church was replaced (1796) by Thomas Telford's Italianate temple, now containing the original Jacobean altar, Fletcher's sword, a fragment of his wife's wedding gown, and a pestle and mortar with which she prepared medicines for the poor. When Fletcher died, Wesley preached the funeral sermon. He had never met, he said, a man so holy as John Fletcher.

Madeley Court, formerly a grange of the Priors of Wenlock, was bought (1533) by Sir Rupert Brooke, Speaker of the House of

Commons. It is a curious building, much marred. In 1968 the Gatehouse and its two polygonal towers were cottages. Abraham Darby occupied the Court from 1709 until his death. But not everyone admired these industrial revolutionaries and their financial friends. On 4th July 1830, Coleridge remarked to James Gilman: "The stock-jobbing and moneyed interest is so strong in this country, that is has more than once prevailed in our foreign councils over national honour and national justice." Coleridge added that, in order to survive, many of the squires had soiled their own hands: "The country gentlemen are not slow to join this influence. Canning felt this very keenly, and said he was unable to contend against the city trained bands."

If, from all this squalor, the traveller lifts up his eyes, he will receive much help from the hills that now appear; notably the Longmynd (Welsh *mynyndd* or 'hill') whose tumuli are not improved by the caravans and other bric-à-brac left there by a gliding club. A drovers' track, the Port Way, wanders over the Longmynd. Pole Bank, the highest point, is 1,695 feet. From it, on a clear day, you can see deep into England and Wales. Carding Mill Valley becomes a car queue in fine weather, but at Minton Bath solitude prevails throughout most of the year. Before embarking for France in 1914, the Westmorland and Cumberland Yeomanry encamped on the Longmynd. One night a thunder storm swept the hills, and the terrified cavalry horses broke loose and ran with the stallions on the heights, adding a new strain to the Marcher stock.

But now the Severn approaches yet another classic ground, the *gebyldu* or 'building' on *waesse* or 'damp soil' at Buildwas. How pithily our fathers named their places, for at Buildwas there is indeed damp soil, and beyond it a building, the remains of an abbey. Industry tried hard to ruin Buildwas. It has dumped a vast power house by the abbey. It has thrust a railway between the abbey and the river. It has even destroyed some of its own handiwork, Telford's iron bridge (1795-6). Yet the beauty of Buildwas prevails.

Buildwas Abbey was founded by Roger de Clinton, Bishop of Coventry and Lichfield, for the monks of the Order of Savigny in France, soon to become Cistercians. These monks were an important feature of England in general and of the Severn in particular.

The foundations of the Cistercian Order were laid when a Benedictine, Robert of Thierry, led a small party of brothers from
Molesme, in search of deeper solitude. Having travelled sixty
miles through the mountains and forests of the Côtes d'Or, they
came at last to a remote valley, named Cîteaux (Latin *Cistercium*),
and there, helped by some servants of the Duke of Burgundy,
they felled trees, diverted streams, and on St. Benedict's Day, 21st
March 1098, solemnly and joyfully dedicated the timber abbey
which they had built. These Benedictines had no wish to re-
nounce their old Order; but, as the years passed, they found themselves creating a new one: first under an Englishman, their third
Prior, John Harding; then under St. Bernard. Because they wove
their habit from undyed fleece, they were known as White
Monks; and by giving to manual labour those hours which St.
Benedict had appointed for study, they became the chief farmers
in Christendom and the finest shepherds in the world.

Gradually the most desolate regions of England were lit by
these beacons of learning and labour; many of them beside a river
that would provide fish and remove sewage. Indeed, the first
English Cistercian foundation (1128) was on the River Wey at
Waverley in Surrey. Another, Tintern, stood beside the Wye, on
the fringe of the Forest of Dean. A third overlooked the Lowther
west of Shap in Westmorland. Together with other Orders, these
monasteries formed a chain of hospices, without which, travel in
medieval England would have been almost impossible, except to
the King and a handful of his richest subjects. In 1431, for example,
the Countess of Warwick, having returned from the coronation
of King Henry VI in Paris, set out from London to Warwick
Castle with fifty-eight retainers. Travelling 194 miles at an average speed of twenty miles a day, the party relied largely on the
hospitality of monks. They stayed first at Syon Abbey by the
Thames, and again by the Thames at Bisham Abbey and at a
nunnery whose Prioress was a kinswoman of the Countess. At
Reading, still on the Thames, they were received by monks, and
yet again by monks at Abingdon. From Abingdon they travelled
to another abbey, this time at Tewkesbury; and from Tewkesbury
they followed the Severn to Worcester Priory.

As for Buildwas Abbey, it is the noblest ruin beside the Severn;
and because it transcends its ruin, it is not wholly ruinous. Seen

from a distance, or through mist, the walls appear intact; their tower half-finished rather than half-fallen. Fourteen nave bays support the massive walls on pillars fourteen feet thick. The west and the east windows are unbroken; the latter having three narrow lights, eighteen feet high. Parts of the thirteenth-century Abbot's House were incorporated with a private residence. The ground-plan and certain features at Buildwas are typically Cistercian; notably a vaulted presbytery and the lay brothers' quarters west of the cloister.

No one knows when Buildwas Abbey was built, though some put the date at about 1150. I have seen the abbey only once, because the Severn between Broseley and Buildwas deters me with its industrial hinterland. Nevertheless, that single visit remains vivid. I arrived to a scene which Sidney Keyes had set:

> Spring night, plovers calling
> Over the fallow, and the dew falling.

A sunset showed the abbey as Leland saw the town of Bewdley, so that it shone, as though the walls were new; and while I wandered among them, I understood more vividly than ever before the famous passage in Gibbon's *Autobiography*: "It was at Rome . . . as I sat musing amidst the ruins of the Capitol, while the barefoot friars were singing vespers in the Temple of Jupiter, that the idea of writing the decline and fall of the city first started to my mind."

Yet the ruins of Buildwas did not set me thinking about decline; rather, they reminded me of a rise from simple beginnings. Every church beside the Severn, as elsewhere throughout England, is an extension of the earliest Saxon churches whose purpose was to provide shelter for a priest and his congregation celebrating Mass before an altar. These churches contained a chancel and a nave. The former, facing east, holds the altar and the choir. The latter contains the congregation. Later churches increased the size of their nave by adding aisles and by raising the walls of the nave, piercing them with clerestory windows. A great family would build their private chapel, and other chapels were added for public worship. The hammerbeam roof was devised in order to reduce pressure on the walls.

Towers were added, not only to contain bells but also to guide travellers and to serve as look-out posts during troubled times. To some towers a spire was added. A few churches had no tower, but housed their bell in a bell-cote, as at Kelmscot on the Thames near Lechlade. Because medieval baptismal services began in the churchyard, a porch was added as shelter against rough weather. In time the porch became almost a market place. The summit of this evolution may be seen at Buildwas and other great churches of Europe.

From Buildwas I walked a short distance to the river, beneath wooded hills and beside red banks; and there I made certain small discoveries, resembling those of an earlier pilgrim, Rev. Francis Kilvert of Clyro, who walked through Herefordshire and Shropshire in 1876, and wrote in his journal: "... came slipping, sliding, scrambling down the precipitous path of deep red mud . . . in a field adorned with a noble pear tree of majestic height and growth in full bloom . . . I found cowslips and the first bluebells".

Yet truth will out; and out of the twilight came the smoke from a new temple, Buildwas power-house, smudging its *Tekel* on the sky.

## LIGHT AND SHADE: AN INTERLUDE

I‍T HAD been just such a day as Edward Thomas savoured when he confessed:

> To say 'God bless it' was all that I could do.

Near Tewkesbury it began, where the Severn and the Avon salute each other in passing; and from Tewkesbury I wandered among unknown lanes toward Ledbury, past fields of hip-high corn, beside black-and-white farmsteads, down vistas of cottages pulling the thatch over their eaves as though against the sunlight. And from Ledbury—since Time seemed eternal—I returned to the Severn, tracking one of the tributaries which, by heading always westward, made the day seem like Traherne's corn that should abide "from everlasting to everlasting". The pleasant illusion persisted until I noticed how steep the shadows slanted, stroking the grass with ebony fingers. So I turned back, and found the car where I had left it, six miles away; and by then the sun really had set, taking the shadows with it, though little of the warmth and none of the hay-scent that had travelled with me since early morning. Having nothing specific to do, I drove slowly on, following any lane or signpost that beckoned more invitingly than the rest.

The moon was up now, and Sirius pre-eminent. A tractor trundled past, its headlamps twinkling like something new in astronomy; and I followed it into a village where two tributaries of the Severn met. There I halted, in a stillness which echoed some words that had been spoken on the road to Emmaeus: "Abide with us: for it is toward evening, and the day is far spent."

There was a small hotel in the village, with a garden sloping to one of the tributaries. I walked across the street, and became the hotel's only resident that night, though two Welshmen were dining well in homely state.

After coffee, I went into the bar, among the Borderfolk whose forefathers had always mistrusted and often fought one another. Now, the races mingled easily; talking of sheep, fishing, the weather; much as the Romans had talked while they built their camp on a hill nearby.

Then the bar closed. An English "Good night" answered the Welsh "So long". Within five minutes the world, or at any rate this corner of it, was as the world ought always to become at bedtime, which is to say reposeful. And the repose grew so profound that my footsteps down the street sounded alien and untimely. This was W. H. Auden's hour:

> . . . late in the evening,
> The lovers had gone,
> The clocks had ceased their chiming,
> And the deep river ran on.

Presently I left the village, following a lane past some scattered cottages and one farm whose black-and-whiteness heightened the moonlight that enhanced it. To my left the hills of England rose like a rampart against stars; on the right, Wales was mountainous; and all around, woodland and wheatland and sheepland and orchard, for miles and miles and miles. Honeysuckle trailed across the lane, not tangibly but in swathes too subtle to be grasped. From time to time some ghosts loomed, or might have been ghosts, except that they stood thirty feet tall and several yards long; these were the white farmsteads, luminous by moonlight. Deep country talks in its sleep, but at this place on this night not even the sound of its breathing reached me. It was as though the silence of Clun were abroad, making these hills

> . . . the quietest places
> Under the sun.

Hills lead their own nightlife, not at all like a town's. If you wish to meet badgers, or to consort with owls, you must do so by appointment. And as for the essence of a river—its water—that never looks so well as when it bears the moon and stars.

On how many such nights, I wondered, had the Welsh crept

down to avenge an old wrong, or the English gone up to redress
a new one? Here, surely, the tales of *The Mabinogion* might come
true, as in Rhonabwy's dream: "He could see two troops of men
slowly approaching the ford across the Severn; and a brilliant
white troop, and a mantle of white brocaded silk about each man
of them; and the fringes of each one pure black, and the knee-
caps and the tops of the horses' legs black, and the horses pale
white all over save for that; and their standards pure white, and
the top of each of them pure black." But no such vision appeared
when I returned to the river, for nothing impossible can happen in
an era which believes that only the conceivable occurs. Yet there
were other sights to be seen . . . stars on the water, unruffled until
a breeze shivered the images which Debussy re-composed into a
waterscape. Had rivers been birds, I thought, one might ring
those ripples, and thereafter await news of them as they were
sighted at Arley, or in the grime of Gloucester, or undergoing a
sea-change westward of Portishead.

It was nearly midnight now, so I returned to the hotel, through
swishing meadows, munching cattle, starlight, stillness, seclusion.
And suddenly, as I passed over the bridge, a lark began to sing,
more blithely than the nightingale and less to be expected, for
although larks do chant Evensong, they are *par excellence* the
makers of Matins. Perhaps I was never so surprised in all my life.
Yet there it hovered, invisible through starlight, as though it had
heard and were come to fulfil J. M. Synge's birthday wish:

> Lark of April, June and May,
> Sing loudly this my lady-day.

The bird was still singing when I went indoors.

Like Pepys as he too knocked at the door of an inn late at night,
I found ". . . the master of the house a sober, understanding man,
and I had good discourse with him about this country's matters, as
wool, and corne, and other things".

There is a sense in which you may learn more about a river
from its tributaries than from the river itself. It is like consulting
the parents in order to understand a child. Tonight I was in a
countryside utterly English—'mere English', as Shakespeare
would have said—yet poised upon the brink of Wales, and by
that fact alone made vividly aware of its Englishry. In Cornwall

or Rutland—even among the Westmorland mountains, so close to Scotland—you seldom overhear the words 'England' or 'English'. But in the Marcher Country of the Severn you do hear them, quite often; no longer uttered as insults nor war cries, yet still with the realism that is common among people whose windows overlook another nation and a different language.

Before turning-in, I observed my custom of saying goodnight to the world. Sometimes—during a gale or in fog—this benediction is brief and may seem simply a habit; but tonight it resembled a child's reluctance to put away its toys and go to sleep. I was fascinated by an apparent paradox, that having reached a place far from home, I found there the thing which I had left at home . . . quietness. Mary Webb summed it up: "When you lean from your window into the silence of a country night you are not aware of it at first. It is like an invisible, enclosing bowl, and you become aware of its depth only when a fox's bark rings in it, like a sharp silver thing. . . . "

The lark had long ago piped-down; but when I opened the bedroom window, I could hear the tributary hurrying to join the Severn with a song, as though it, too, would

Sing loudly this my lady-day.

This was not my own lady-day, but it did become and has ever after remained a rubric of remembrance, from dawn till dusk enriched by those events which compile what we mis-call a day when nothing happened.

## MARCHER COUNTRY:
## BUILDWAS TO SHREWSBURY

EVER since Tewkesbury the course of the Severn has led steadily
north despite many deviations, but at Buildwas it has already
begun the westerly wandering that will sweep through Shrewsbury and thence south into Montgomeryshire. This change of
direction is due neither to chance nor to any inherent wayward-
ness of water; it is caused by rocks. In simple terms, the course of a
river can be divided into three parts. The first of these is the upper
or mountainous part, where the river flows steeply through a
narrow channel, and can therefore brush aside quite large boulders. The second is the middle part, where mountains have become
hills, and the river loses its youthful vigour. The third is the lower
part, where the river meanders through level countryside, carrying and often discarding the silt and sand which it acquired during
the middle part. At Buildwas the Severn is still in its second or
middle course. It cannot erode the Wrekin, nor the Stipperstones
(1,731 feet), nor Wenlock Edge (with an average height of 750 feet).
Under the lee of those hills, having cast industry astern, the river
becomes pastoral. Its companions are cattle, sheep, orchards, corn;
the spectators are villages adding an iota-subscript to English
history.

First, on the right bank, Leighton (Old English *leac-tun* or
'settlement where leeks are grown'), an endearing village with a
redbrick Hall (1778) overlooking the Severn from grounds containing a church (1714) with medieval masonry. The churchyard
is cluttered with ironmasters' iron-railed graves. The eighteenth
century was indeed a second Iron Age; John Wilkinson, for
example, bespoke his own iron coffin, and designed an iron pulpit
for the Staffordshire church of Bradley. More impressive is a
thirteenth-century brass to a member of the Leighton family,

which was removed hither from Buildwas Abbey at the Dissolution. The Leightons rose to power when John Leighton went over
to Henry Tudor at Bosworth. Leighton's son was knighted by
King Henry VIII, and the grandson married a cousin of Queen
Elizabeth. Tom Jones, on the other hand, was lucky to be recorded
at all, for his gravestone says: "Underneath Lies interred the Body
of Revd. Thomas Jones, late Curate of this Parish. His wealthy
Relatives refusing Expense of a small Monument in Memorial of
his Services The Principal Parishioners of LEIGHTON erected
this Stone Buried 6th June, 1789." The Hall stables, on the far side
of the church, have a clock tower or lantern. Leighton is a place of
yew trees. I never saw so many, so well-tended, in one village.

It is always interesting to compare notes *en route*. They show
where we agree and when we disagree about a vista, a factory, a
birthplace; and any list of eminent Severn birthplaces must in-
clude Leighton, first home of Mary Webb. Of all the artists of the
Severn, it was she who portrayed its people and places most
lovingly, most vividly, most minutely.

Mary Webb was born on 25th March 1881. Her father was a
Welsh schoolmaster; her mother, an Edinburgh member of Sir
Walter Scott's clan. Like Wordsworth and Emily Brontë, Mary
Webb lived almost the whole of her life in one English county.
Part of her childhood was spent north of the Severn, at Stanton-
upon-Hine-Heath. As a young woman she lived awhile in Meole
Brace, which was then a village, and is now a suburb of Shrews-
bury. In 1912 she married a Cambridge graduate, Henry Bertam
Ian Webb, who wrote under the pen-name John Clayton. To him
she dedicated *Precious Bane, Gone To Earth, The Golden Arrow.*
For their honeymoon she chose Church Stretton under The
Longmynd in Shropshire. Even when she joined her husband at
school in Weston-super-Mare, still she saw the Severn Sea and
beyond it the Welsh hills. Returning to Shropshire, they lived at
Pontesbury, in a house named Roseville, where she wrote *The
Golden Arrow.* Later they built a home on Lyth Hill overlooking
Shrewsbury ("my own town", she called it), and at Shrewsbury
market they sold their garden produce. Like Thomas Hardy, to
whose "illustrious name" she dedicated *Seven For A Secret,* Mary
Webb re-baptized her places: Shrewsbury became Silverton, and
Church Stretton was Shepwardine. During the 1914 War she

wrote a number of poems and country essays which—published in 1928 as *Poems And The Spring Of Joy*—contain some of the best nature mysticism in modern English literature. Walter de la Mare once said to me: "She was as observant as Richard Jefferies, and better disciplined." Her novels fell upon stony ground. *Precious Bane*, in fact, received the *Femina Vie Heureuse* prize, which is reserved for work that the public has misguidedly rejected. Though she hid her disappointment, it crept between the lines of *Precious Bane*, where a character cries: "I was like one standing at the lane end with a nosegay to offer to the world as it rode by. But the world rode me down . . . it rode me down."

When Mary Webb was dead, a man whom she had never met made a speech, at a Royal Literary Fund dinner, praising her work. That man, himself a Severnsider, was Stanley Baldwin, the Prime Minister. As a result of his speech Mary Webb became famous overnight. *Precious Bane* was re-issued once a month for a year. In his preface to the 1928 edition of that book, Baldwin wrote: "The stupid urban view of the countryside as dull receives a fresh and crushing answer in the books of Mary Webb." The art and the ethos of Mary Webb's novels are at present out of fashion. In any event her genius was mystic rather than analytic. As Earl Baldwin noted, her strength "lies in the fusion of the elements of nature and man, as observed in this remote countryside . . .". Mary Webb herself declared: "Shropshire is a country where the dignity and beauty of ancient things lingers long, and I have been fortunate . . . in being born and brought up in its magical atmosphere." That atmosphere makes all her writing luminous.

But Mary Webb was more than a landscape painter, more than a portraitist. She probed to the core, and was conscious of the stars. How much nonsense about 'realism' and 'objectivity' is swept away by a sentence from one of her characters: "You canna write a word, even, but you show yourself—in the word you choose, and the shape of letters, and whether you write tall or short, plain or flourished. It's a game of I spy, and there's nowhere to hide." Not Job himself more vividly evoked human suffering: "The deep lament," she called it, "old as the moan of forests and falling water, that goes up through the centuries to the aloof and silent sky, and remains, as ever, unassuaged."

At the end of her short life she suffered a severe collapse, which

in retrospect heightens the description of Abel in *Gone To Earth*:
". . . he had dark places in his soul, and that is the very core of art
and its substance." She died at St. Leonards, Sussex, in 1927, and
was buried at Shrewsbury; remembered, if at all, as the author of
some unsuccessful novels. Freud long ago revealed that we are
always more complex than we suppose, and sometimes wiser
than we know. Thus, in a poem about Shrewsbury, written from
the depths of apparent failure, Mary Webb foretold her own
fame:

> And I shall dwell where once unknown
> I passed, and all shall be my own,
> Because I built of joy and tears
> A city that defied the years.

At Cressage, on the opposite bank, the Severn makes an easterly
turn, and then bears westward past the Wrekin. Cressage Bridge
has a wide elliptical arch and two semi-circular ones. On it a
plaque recalls that the bridge replaced a timber trestle bridge
of five spans (1800), adding: "The oak frame of this inscription
plate was made from a portion of the old structure." It is pleasant
to find a county council caring for such things."

Cressage church is Victorian, but the Old Vicarage, overlooking the river, is hale and half-timbered.

Domesday Book calls the village Cristesache or 'Christ's oak'.
For centuries the place was said to have been the site of St.
Augustine's meeting with the Celtic bishops. We have already
noticed two other claimants; a fourth was Abberley near Worcester.

I came to Cressage on a summer morning. For a full hour I lay
in the sun, on a narrow spit of land, almost under the bridge; and
having closed my eyes, I heard only the water, and some sheep,
and so many birds that I gave up trying to sift their songs.
Wordsworth had done the same thing many times by northern
rivers: "He thought," says Dorothy in her *Journal*, "that it would
be as sweet thus so to lie in the grave, to hear the *peaceful* sounds of
the earth, and just to know that our dear friends were near."
When at last I opened my eyes, I saw the Wrekin, framed by the
arch of the bridge, beckoning like a celestial destination.

Above Cressage the Severn is joined by Cound Brook—much

chub and many trout, they told me—flowing through Cound
village, a quiet place with a timbered post office.

The thirteenth-century church contains memorials to the
Pelhams and Cressetts: notably Dr. Edward Cressett, Bishop of
Llandaff, for whom the stately redbrick Cound Hall was built
by John Prince of Shrewsbury in 1704.

It is worthwhile to follow Cound Brook inland to Condover
by way of Berrington, which has a gabled and timbered Manor
House (1658) and a red sandstone church containing the oaken
effigy of a cross-legged knight, known locally as Old Scriven.
When Old Scriven was young he courted a lady at Easton
Mascott (a corruption of Marescot, after William Marescot, who
held the manor in 1242). Young Scriven, at all events, one day
found a lion between himself and his lady. So, drawing a sword,
he bisected the beast, though not until he had been clawed in the
face. Sure enough, Old Scriven's effigy rests its feet upon a lion,
and bears a scar on its face. It seems unlikely that young Scriven
really did slay a lion, but a wild boar might have caused the inci-
dent. In these matters wisdom distributes its unbelief equally
between the credulous and the incredulous.

Condover church, of pink sandstone, is partly Norman, with
several Tudor monuments (for example, to Thomas Scriven and
his wife) and a Victorian monument to Sir Thomas Cholmondeley
as depicted by G. F. Watts.

Condover Hall was built (c. 1598) for Thomas Owen, sometime Justice of Common Pleas, by Walter Hancock, a Shropshire
man whose letter of commendation came from Sir Francis
Newport: "I pray you let mee commende a Mason of approved
skyll and honestye, one Walter Hancock... you cannot match the
man in these parts (with any of that occupaycon) nyther in scyence
and judgement of workmanship, nor in playnes and honestye to
deal with all . . ." Shaped like the fashionable E of its period,
Condover Hall ranks with the great Tudor houses of Shropshire.

But there is another reason why I have taken you further than
usual from the Severn, and that is Dick Tarlton, Queen Elizabeth's
favourite jester. Tarlton, a swineherd, attracted the Earl of
Leicester with his nimble wit. The Earl took him to Court, and
the Court took him to heart. There were moments when only
Dick Tarlton could dispel the Queen's cares. "When Queen

Elizabeth was . . . out of good humour," wrote Fuller, "he could undumpish her at his pleasure. Her highest favourites would in some cases go to Tarlton, before they would go to the Queen; and he was their usher, to prepare their advantageous access to her . . . he cured her melancholy, better than all her physicians." Tarlton joined the Queen's Twelve Players; and in 1611 a book called *Tarlton's Jeasts* was published. Tarlton himself was too old to have played for Shakespeare, but Shakespeare may have met him, and some scholars believe that he was ". . . poor Yorick . . . I knew him . . . a fellow of infinite jest, of most excellent fancy". The stage door-keeper in Jonson's *St. Bartholomew's Fair* says: "I kept the stage in Master Tarlton's time, I thank my stars." Tarlton had a tavern in Paternoster Row, and afterwards another in Gracechurch Street. He died in 1588, and was buried at St. Leonards, Shoreditch. Some thirty years later a wit composed his epitaph:

> Here within this sullen earth
> Lies Dick Tarleton, full of mirth . . .

Across the river, Eaton Constantine took its name from Thomas de Costentin, lord of the manor in 1242, who came from Costentin in Normandy. The Victorian church holds no attractions, but Richard Baxter's home is so easy on the eye that, whenever I do pass this way, I lean over its five-barred gate, staring at the tiled, gabled, dormered motley of black-and-white, topped by the Wrekin and a television aerial. Baxter was not born here—he first saw the light from his mother's home at Rowton, a few miles away —but he did spend his childhood in this house. His education he got at Wroxeter and Ludlow, where he read in the castle library. When he was eighteen, he tried his fortune in London, but disliked what he found there, and returned home. Having been ordained by Bishop Thornborough of Worcester, in 1638, he was appointed headmaster of Dudley Grammar School, then curate at Bridgnorth, and after that an assistant preacher at Kidderminster, where his statue is in the Bull Ring, and his pulpit in the Unitarian chapel.

Although Baxter served with the rebels, he regarded the King's execution as murder. At the Restoration he became chaplain to Charles II, and twice declined a bishopric. In 1662 he defied the

*The Wrekin: winter floods*

Act of Uniformity, and was tried by Judge Jeffreys, who bawled: "Richard Baxter, thou art an old knave." Fined and for two years imprisoned, Baxter died in 1691. The best-known of his writings, an autobiography, *Reliquiae Baxterianae*, became Coleridge's textbook of English church history. "It is," he declared, "an inestimable work." Dr. Johnson so admired Baxter's books that he urged Boswell: "Read any of them; they are all good." The autobiography is a social and religious history of England under the Stuarts, with particular reference to the laxity of some parish priests. "At Eaton Constantine," Baxter remembered, "there was a reader eighty years of age, Sir William Rogers, who never preached yet he had two livings, twenty miles apart from each other. His sight failing, he repeated the prayers without book, but to read the lessons he employed a common labourer one year, a tailor another; and at last his own son, the best stage-player and gamester in all the country, got orders and supplied one of his places. Within a few miles around were nearly a dozen ministers of the same description, poor, ignorant readers, and most of them dissolute livers." At other times Baxter turned his criticism inwards: "I was once wont to meditate on my own heart, and to dwell at home and look higher ... yet I see more need of a higher work, and that I should look often upon Christ, and God, and heaven ..." Good Richard Baxter was neither the first nor the last politician who discovered that there are times when the surest way of getting knocked down is to squat in the middle of the road.

One would suppose that the Severn at this point had supplied enough good tales; but not so, for at the next village, Eyton-on-Severn, we find another notable, Edward Herbert, first Baron Cherbury, of the illustrious family that we shall meet up-river at Montgomery. Born in 1583, on an estate which his mother inherited, Edward Herbert went up to University College, Oxford, when he was only fifteen; having already taken a wife, Mary Herbert, daughter of his kinsman, Sir William Herbert of St. Julians in Monmouthshire. The young Benedick may have been the only Oxford undergraduate whose mother and whose wife went into residence with him. His *Autobiography*, published by Horace Walpole in 1764, is disarmingly naïve: "It is well known to those that wait on me in my chamber, that the shirts, waistcoats

9

*Daffodil-time near Leighton*

and other garments I wear next my body are sweet beyond what can easily be believed, or hath been observed in any else . . . All which I do in a familiar way mention to my posterity, though otherwise they may be thought scarce worth the writing."

King James I knighted Herbert, and King Charles I ennobled him. Having served for two years in the army of the Prince of Orange, he returned to England, mixing much with the wits— Jonson, Donne, Carew, Selden—but then took the air again, this time as English ambassador at Paris, whence he was recalled after a quarrel. His *Life and Reign of King Henry VIII* expresses an anglicized Welshman's approval of the Tudor union between England and Wales: "The king, now considering that it was but reasonable to unite this part of the kingdom to the rest . . . caus'd an act to be past for executing justice in Wales, in the manner as in England." Horace Walpole edited the *History* and the *Auto-biography*, with a dedication to Lord Herbert's descendant, the Earl of Powis: "Hitherto," Walpole wrote, "Lord Herbert has been little-known but as an author. I much mistake, if hereafter he is not considered as one of the most extraordinary characters which this country has produced." Walpole over-estimated a man whom posterity regards as a racey individual and author of some lively books of history and comparative religion.

Lord Herbert took his title from a village up-river, scarcely a mile from the Welsh border; but the Severn at Eyton is already so deeply in the Marcher Country that the Marches themselves must be examined as an important feature of the portrait. These Marches included the whole of the present counties of Denbigh, Radnor, Brecon, Monmouth, Montgomery; with large areas of Shropshire and Herefordshire; three manors in Gloucestershire, one in Worcestershire, and some outposts in Merionethshire, Cardiganshire, Carmarthenshire. The word 'march' came from the Germanic *mark*, which was used to describe, first, the waste-land separating one village from another, and, second, the boundary line between them. The Welsh Marches began to be created when William of Normandy, unable to conquer Wales, set certain of his subjects to contain it for him. The process went somewhat as follows: armed with the royal assent and his own retainers, a Norman would seize some suitable area from the Welsh. One Norman got his swag by captivating rather than capturing; he married a Welsh heiress. Though they remained tenants-in-chief of the King, these early Marcher Lords became absolute rulers, with power of life and death. The King, however, controlled them by sending trustworthy men to three key points: Roger of Montgomery, a former Regent of Normandy, at Shrewsbury Castle; William Fitzosbern, a veteran soldier, at Hereford Castle; and at Chester Castle, Hugh de Avranches, the King's nephew. To these castles he added a fourth, at Montgomery, as an outpost of Shrewsbury. Finally, Chester became a royal palatinate; the King's writ ran throughout large areas of Shropshire and Herefordshire; and Pembroke and Glamorgan became quasi-counties.

Matters went more smoothly than might have been supposed, chiefly because the Normans had something of Rome's genius for colonization. Thus, each Marcher Lord employed Englishmen (or at any rate Normans) to deal with English affairs; and Welshmen to handle Wales. English law ran for Englishmen; the Welsh were subject to their own laws. When both nations were involved in litigation, a body of Anglo-Welsh law was devised. Known as the Custom of the Lordship, this compromise was, as a rule, based on the Custom of Breteuil in Normandy.

In 1478 Edward IV established the President and Council of Wales and the Welsh Marches, which sat usually at Ludlow Castle, but occasionally also at Bewdley, Shrewsbury, Worcester, Hereford, Tewkesbury, Hartlebury, Bridgnorth, Oswestry, and as far south as Gloucester. Officially a Court of Appeal for the whole of the Marches, it was charged to restrain the Lords' independence. Henry VII, himself a Welshman, used the Council as a type of provincial Star Chamber. Under Henry VIII Wales became "incorporated, united and annexed to and with the Realm of England". A decree went forth that "no person or persons that use the Welsh speech or language shall have . . . any office . . . within the realm of England, Wales, or other the King's Dominion . . . unless he or they use and exercise the King's speech or language." Now it may seem strange that Henry VIII should have waited until the twenty-seventh year of his reign before completing a union which Edward I had made imminent when he defeated Llywelyn ap Gruffydd, the last of the great Welsh leaders. In fact, the union with Wales was conceived and, in its earlier stages, executed by Thomas Cromwell, ever zealous to strengthen the prerogative by tautening its administration. The union occurred peaceably. Lord Herbert of Cherbury, in his *Life and Reign of King Henry VIII*, quoted a petition from Wales: "We . . . inhabiting that portion of the island which our invaders first called Wales, most humbly prostrate at your highness's feet, do crave to be receiv'd and adopted into the same laws and privileges which your other subjects enjoy. . . ." Although this petition may have been instigated by Thomas Cromwell via his friend, Sir Edward Herbert, the historian's great-grandfather, it heralded the taming of the potentates "and reduc'd the lordship marchers to shire-ground". The union was confirmed by three Statutes between 1536 and 1542. The second of the three, commonly known as the Act of Union, was entitled "An Act for the laws and justice to be ministered in Wales in like form as it is in this realm". Wales however, received its own assizes, the Courts of the King's Great Sessions, excluding Monmouthshire (whence that county's spurious Englishry). The Council was retained as an administrator and a judiciary for personal pleas. It survived until 1689, when the government of the Principality was divided between the Lords Lieutenants of North Wales and South Wales. With the abolition of the Great Sessions in 1830, Thomas Cromwell's policy was at last realized, and the administrative and political systems of Wales became identical with England's. After twenty-seven years as President of the Council, Sir Henry Herbert paid each nation a compliment when he declared: "A better people to govern than the Welsh, Europe holds not." Nor does every Welshman look back in anger. The borough of Laugharne, for example, cherishes the charter which in 1307 it received from Sir Guy de Brian, Lord Marcher. The town's constitution was the same under Queen Elizabeth II as it had been under King Edward II; and at the annual Portreeve's dinner the corporation still drinks, if not to the health of Sir Guy's body, then at any rate to the repose of his soul. Even today the old regime still lingers in Pembrokeshire, where the mayor of Newport is *ex officio* Lord Marcher of the Barony of Kemaes, which Henry VIII excluded from the general abolition.

And from that feature the Severn salutes another, the Wrekin, which now dominates the scene. This hill has borne several names. In the year 975 it was called Wrocene; in 1278 La Wrekene; in

1248 La Wrokene. All those names are British versions of Wroxeter or 'The Roman fort of Viroconion'. But the Wrekin is older than Rome. Urging through the grass, fragments of Pre-Cambrian rock can be seen, the oldest things in Britain. Two centuries before Christ a tribe built a fortress here; its trench and the ramparts can still be traced. This tribe may have been the Cornovii, the earliest citizens of Viroconion or Uricon. Every Englishman ought to climb the Wrekin. The view from the summit will take his breath away, and so will the winter wind, as A. E. Housman discovered:

> On Wenlock Edge the wood's in trouble;
> His forest fleece the Wrekin heaves;
> The gale, it plies the saplings double,
> And thick on Severn snow the leaves.

The Wrekin seems a timely place from which to look down upon Housman and his poems, *A Shropshire Lad*: noting first that Housman was not a Shropshire lad. He himself admitted: "I was born in Worcestershire, not in Shropshire, where I never spent much time . . . my topographical details . . . are sometimes quite wrong."

Albert Edward Housman was born in 1859, at the Worcestershire village of Fockbury, where his birthplace, Valley House, has been re-named 'Housman'. He was by nature a townsman; first in London, as a clerk of the Patent Office (he had taken a disastrous degree at Oxford), then at Cambridge as the foremost Latinist of the twentieth century. Much of *A Shropshire Lad* was written in a London suburb, at 17 North Hill, Highgate. Why, then, did Housman name his book *A Shropshire Lad*? His own answer was: "I had a sentimental feeling for Shropshire because its hills were our western horizon."

Like several other English classics, the book appeared at the author's expense, having been rejected by Macmillan. Housman's profit on the first edition was £2 5s. 3d. Although the poems are sprinkled with Shropshire place-names, they nowhere suggest that the poet loved the tang of a byre or the company of cottagers. Sir John Squire hit the mark when he complained: "Landscape poets are very often townsmen, with an eye for colour and shape and feeling, but not necessarily a knowledge of the characters or even names of any but the commonest and most conspicuous country things." Housman's well-wrought poems have a narrow range. In 1936 both the manner and the matter of his poems were exactly as they had been in 1896. Like the man himself, they are fixated. Puzzled by Thomas Hardy's pessimism, Edmund Gosse asked: "What has Fate done to Mr. Hardy?" This generation is better equipped than his to perceive what Fate had done to A. E. Housman, for his poems, and much else that is known about him, reveal that he was predominantly homosexual. *A Shropshire Lad* arraigns "whatever brute or blackguard made the world." . . . and in particular the tormented world of A. E. Housman. It cries out against a lifetime of suppression. Said Emerson: "Upon the degree of our despair we build our characters." The character of Housman may be assessed by comparing him with Beethoven, who suffered an affliction even more terrible because it menaced the very music by which alone he might remain sane and alive. Yet Beethoven achieved a serenity not elsewhere to be found in art. Housman's greatest achievement was as a Latin philologist, but his popular fame will rest upon a few lyrics:

> Loveliest of trees, the cherry now
> Is hung with bloom along the bough,
> And stands about the woodland ride
> Wearing white for Eastertide.

Wroxeter, a small place, north of the Wrekin, is linked to the Severn by a green tract of Watling Street. Part of the nave of Wroxeter's Saxon church was built of Roman stone. Ahead the Kerry Hills rise up, grazed by 15,000 sheep. The riverside meadows draw a good depth of soil from the Old Red Sandstone. I have seen a second crop of hay taken here before the Aberdeenshire farmers had carried their first. At Wroxeter you may wander among these fruits of the earth without at first understanding that you are stepping on the stones of Uricon, in its heyday the fourth city of Britain. Parts of that city have been uncovered and are open to inspection . . . a lump of the basilica, twenty feet high, seventy feet long . . . the hot baths that were part of a Roman legionary's equipment . . . a row of broken pillars leading to the forum.

Uricon was built *c.* A.D. 60. Thirty years later the Romans en-

larged the city, but thereafter the work flagged, perhaps because
of military operations against the Welsh. Then came the Emperor
Hadrian from Rome, champing like a Churchill through the
province of Britannia Secunda; and forthwith the masons and the
carpenters and the smiths laid out a new city, dominating the
Severn for many miles and through many years; imposing justice,
efficiency, hygiene. But already Mammon and Demos were
sapping Rome's patrician *gravitas*. The Empire fell victim to its own
internationalism. Besieged and impoverished, Rome recalled her
troops, leaving the savages to their own British devices. Bede
described the general desolation: "When the Romans departed
. . . the British abandoned their cities . . . and fled in disorder.
They were driven from their homes [by Picts and Scots], and
sought to avoid starvation by robbery and violence . . . their
internal anarchy adding to the miseries inflicted on them by
others." The Dark Ages had dawned. Uricon was rubble:

> The pillars stand, with alien grace,
> In churches of a younger race;
> The chiselled column, black and rough,
> Becomes a roadside cattle-trough.

That was how Mary Webb saw the ghost of Uricon's departed
glory.

Older than Rome, the river Tern now joins the Severn, flowing
from a countryside that has a private railway, and used to own
several. One of them, the Bishop's Castle Line, faced bankruptcy
within a year of its opening (1865). Bailiffs tore up part of the
track, and erected a fence across the line. Undeterred, the Company spanned the breach with a service of waggons. The loco-
motive which surmounted—or at any rate broke through—these
obstacles was aptly named *Perseverance*. The last working loco-
motive, *Carlisle*, went to the scrap heap when the line was closed
during the 1930s. Some of the rails were used to support the frames
in which H.M.S. *Prince of Wales* was built.

The Shropshire and Montgomeryshire Line was more successful. In 1930 it ran Thursday excursions from Shrewsbury to
Llanymynech, at eightpence return. The tickets bore a caption:
"Support the local line. Travel in Safety across the country,
away from the crowded roads, over Home-made Steel instead of

Imported Rubber." A postcript added: "Enterprise of Colonel Stephens." This Colonel—son of the *Athenaeum*'s art critic—was the line's managing director and chief engineer. He studied in France and Germany before serving an apprenticeship at the Neasden sheds of the Metropolitan Railway Company. He later built 340 miles of branch lines in East Kent, Somerset, and on this reach of the river.

Now the Severn enters Atcham, which has two handsome bridges; Severn Bridge (1769–71) built by a Shrewsbury man, John Gwynn, founder-member of the Royal Academy, and designer of Oxford's Magdalen Bridge; and Tern Bridge (1774), built by Robert Mylne. From this bridge you gaze across water to Attingham Hall owned by the County Council. It was built (1783–5) for Noel Hill, first Lord Berwick, by George Steuart, who, by incorporating parts of an earlier house, Tern Hall, created the most majestic eighteenth-century home in Shropshire; eleven bays wide, two-and-a-half storeys high, with a portico of four Ionic columns. In 1807 John Nash made some changes and additions. This was the house in which Fletcher of Madeley served as tutor to the sons of Thomas Hill.

Atcham village lies to the west of Tern Bridge. In Domesday Book it was Atingeham, 'the home of Eat's people'. The red sandstone church, built partly of rubble from Uricon, is the only British church dedicated to St. Eata, whose protegé was St. Cuthbert. According to Bede: "Cuthbert first entered the monastery of Melrose on the banks of the river Tweed, then ruled by Abbot Eata, one of the gentlest and simplest of men, who later became Bishop of Lindisfarne."

Atcham's most famous native was Odericus Vitalis, nicknamed 'The Clerk' because of his erudition. Born in 1075, he was baptized in Atcham church by his godfather, Oderic. At the age of five he went to be schooled at the church of St. Peter in Shrewsbury; thereafter living a long life in the Norman monastery of Ouche. Two years before he died, he completed his *Historia Ecclesiastica*, on which he had been working for eighteen years.

Among several interesting memorials in the church are two that were removed from Bracton church in 1811. One is to Miles ap Harry (that is, Parry); the other is to Blanche Parry of Newcourt in Herefordshire, for many years chief gentlewoman of the

Privy Chamber to Queen Elizabeth I. When Mistress Parry died, blind, at the age of eighty-three, the Queen was deeply grieved by the loss of a loyal and loving friend. Blanche Parry's memorial is lengthily resounding:

I Parrychays' dorghter Blanche of Newe Covrte borne
That treynd was in pryncys' covrts . . .

Another line recalls that, like the Queen, she died a spinster:

A maede in courts and never no man's wyffe . . .

The first time I saw Atcham was in November, when the local Hunt came by, moving warily, for the Severn was in spate, and had lately swept away the master of the Albrighton pack, drowning him in the fierce currents. If you have read that instructive fantasy, *Utopia*, you may remember that the wellborn citizens of Sir Thomas More's ideal State were not hunting folk: "The Utopians consider hunting below their dignity of free men, and leave it entirely to butchers, who are baseborn. In their opinion, hunting is the vilest department of butchery compared with which, all the others are quite useful and honourable." On this reach of the Severn they order things differently. Quite respectable people follow the David Davies Pack, the Plas Machynlleth, the Tanatside, the United. Other respectable people hunt the otter, or shoot mallard, snipe, teal, partridge, pheasant. And fishermen are esteemed.

Atcham's two bridges, with the roads and the railway, maintain a tradition which began when the Romans built roads across Wales, and linked them with lesser highways. The Severn itself was crossed by Via Julia Maritima, running from Bath to St. David's; by Via Julia Montana, an upper route, joining the river near Gloucester; and by Via Devana, which followed the Severn at Caersws. When Rome withdrew from Britain, the roads, like Uricon, decayed. In vain the medieval church offered indulgences to any who would help to mend the rutted tracks. At the Reformation many parishes were required to provide labour and materials for highways between market towns, but not until the Industrial Revolution did English roads regain something of their Roman efficiency.

Two centuries ago the Atcham bridges were used by Welsh

drovers leading their herds and flocks across the border into Shrewsbury and thence through the Midlands to London. George Borrow painted a harsh portrait of a drover. Even Twm o' Nant spoke unkindly of the dead:

> His world is now a narrow bed—
> So, let him cheat the dead instead.

But farmers would never had employed consistently dishonest men. Most of the Welsh drovers were trustworthy. Some acted as Government agents on minor duties; others became rent collectors *en route*; a few founded their own banks . . . the Black Ox Bank (Banc yr Eidiou Dbu) at Llandovery, and the Black Sheep Bank at Aberystwyth. Drover Benjamin Evans became a Congregational minister; Drover Edward Morus was a Caroline poet; and when Rhys Jones solicited subscribers to his anthology of Welsh poetry, *Gorchestion Beirdd Cymru*, the appeal was answered by Drovers Thomas, Jones, Parry, Roberts (and by Dr. Samuel Johnson from London). It was such men whom Defoe had in mind when he said of Shrewsbury: ". . . they all speak English in the town, but on market-day you would think you were in Wales."

And what does one say of Shrewsbury itself, now in view above Atcham? Old people can remember Shrewsbury when it was the most beautiful town on the Severn. Today its skyline is scarred by offices, factories, chimneys. The streets are tortured by traffic. The beauty is hemmed-in and harried. You may reply that the town has been adorned with parks and gardens, that many of the timbered houses are cared for. But who cares for a timbered house that has been filleted into a television shop, or wedged between chain stores?

"The Towne of Shrewsbury," said Leland, "standeth on a Rocky Hill of Stone." Out of that stone, and from the timber surrounding it, our fathers made a town of such splendour that men still admire whatever of it has not been razed or ruined by their contemporaries. There are remains of the castle which Roger de Montgomery built a thousand years ago . . . the Benedictine Abbey of Holy Cross, another of de Montgomery's creations, in which he died, three days after he had entered it as a monk . . . churches, too, for Roman Catholics, Methodists, English Presby-

terians, Welsh Presbyterians, Unitarians, Christian Scientists . . . a
library and museum that were Shrewsbury School three centuries
ago . . . Old Market House (1596) which Defoe described as ". . . a
kind of hall for the manufactures which are sold here weekly in
very great quantities." . . . English Bridge (1768–74), Welsh
Bridge (1791–5), Kingsland Bridge (1883), Porthill Bridge (1922),
Castle Bridge (1949) . . . and everywhere a Babel of traffic.

Early in the morning, or under a midnight moon, you may, by
closing one eye against modernity, catch a glimpse of what old
Shrewsbury looked like . . . Butcher Row, for example, and its
Tudor houses overhanging the cobbled curve of Fish Street topped
by a tower . . . the half-timbered house in Dogpole . . . the black-
and-white Council House Gateway . . . the Severn itself, looping
northward among trees, with Shrewsbury School peering down
upon it, redbrick on greensward. Not all was well, within that
beauty. There is horror between Defoe's lines: ". . . here broke
out that first unaccountable plague, call'd the sweating sickness,
which at first baffled all the sons of art, and spread itself through
the whole kingdom of England. This happen'd in the year
1551." Nevertheless, if you come here at sunrise, and choose a
vista that has escaped modernity, you will share Wordsworth's
reverie:

> This City now doth, like a garment, wear
> The beauty of the morning. . . .

Shrewsbury, of course, is not a city, though King Charles II did
offer to create a diocese there; but "proud Salopians" declined,
preferring to remain as they were. Defoe chided Camden on this
point: "Mr. Cambden calls it a city: 'Tis at this day, he says, a
fine city well-inhabited: But we do not now call it a city,
yet 'tis equal to many good cities in England, and superior to
some."

Since 50,000 people inhabit Shrewsbury, one assumes that they
manufacture vast quantities of God-knows-what. Let us hope that
a comparable number of customers will continue to pay the pipe-
line, because if they do not, the factories and housing estates must
go the way of Uricon, and Shrewsbury will again become a
country town of medieval, Tudor and Georgian houses, but with
this difference—that the occupants will earn their bread by sitting

at home, doing unskilled piecework for the American rag-doll industry.

As at Gloucester and Worcester, so now in Shrewsbury—some respite from the din may be had by contemplating the portrait as it used to be; starting at Shrewsbury School, which King Edward VI founded in 1552. Staff problems seem to have occurred, for the first masters were required to swear that they would neither steal nor in any other way defraud their employers. Eight hundred pupils were admitted during the first six years, of whom 300 paid nothing. In 1882 the school moved to its present site, overlooking the Severn, in what had been Captain Coram's Shrewsbury Foundling Hospital (1765). Today the school ranks next after Eton College as a nursery of oarsmen. It won the Ladies Plate at Henley Royal Regatta as long ago as 1924. Nearly one hundred Old Salopians have rowed in the Boat Race. Shrewsbury's greatest pupils were Sidney and Darwin.

Philip Sidney entered the School in 1563, a few days before his tenth birthday and at the same time as his future biographer, Fulke Greville, Lord Brooke. From Shrewsbury he went up to Christ Church, Oxford, and then for a while to Cambridge. His father being Lord Deputy of Ireland, the son obtained from Queen Elizabeth her licence ". . . to go out of England into parts beyond the seas, with three servants and four horses etc., to remain the space of two years . . . for his attaining the knowledge of foreign languages". In fact, he accompanied the Earl of Lincoln on a diplomatic mission to France. Then and during later travels he acquired a culture so wide that it earned him the nickname "a general Maecenas of learning". Sidney became a Tudor version of Chaucer's perfect and gentle knight; scholar, courtier, soldier, poet. His best sonnets stand close upon Shakespeare's:

> Leave me, O Love, which reachest but to dust;
> And then, in mind, aspire to higher things;
> Grow rich in that which never taketh rust;
> Whatever fades, but fading pleasure brings.

Sidney's *Arcadia*, which he wrote for his sister, Lady Pembroke, is a romantic idyll, perennially fresh. By temperament and breeding an amateur, Sidney in his will required his writings to be burned when he died. Fortunately his sister and his friends pre-

served and published them. When Dr. Johnson was compiling
his dictionary, he consulted little that had been written after the
early seventeenth century: "I have," he said, "fixed Sidney's work
for the boundary, beyond which I make few excursions."

Having failed to enlist with Drake, Sir Philip Sidney became
Governor of Flushing. Later, while commanding the English
cavalry, he was wounded at Zutphen. Though he was not killed
on that battlefield (he died at Arnhem twenty-six days later), the
manner of his death has passed into history, for when they brought
him a cup of water, to ease his agony, he passed it to a soldier,
saying, "Thy need is greater than mine."

Charles Darwin evolved differently. He was born in Shrewsbury, at a house called 'The Mount', where his father practised as
the town's leading physician. He entered Shrewsbury School in
1818, when the boys were rioting against bad food. The head-
master, Dr. Butler, handled the revolt with a firmness which
pleased the Master of St. John's College, Cambridge, who observed: "Children nowadays very early imbibe most pernicious
notions, if not from their parents and relations, at least from the
spirit of the times." But bad food was not the only bane. The lad
who was soon to eat hard tack and swing a hammock in H.M.S.
*Beagle*, complained to his father that the school beds were "damp
as muck".

Darwin had nothing good to say of a classical education. In *An
Autobiography*, written many years afterwards, he declared: "The
school as a means of education to me was simply a blank." Such
blankness is never unilateral. Moreover Darwin failed even at a
scientific education, retiring *re infecta* after two years as a medical
student at Edinburgh. He was a famous instance of neurotic
genius. His own son admitted: ". . . for nearly forty years he
never knew one day of the health of ordinary men . . . his life was
one long struggle against weariness. . . ." This lethargy led him to
postpone publication of his *Origins* for so long that another Englishman, Alfred Russell Wallace, beat him to it. In the end, Darwin's
theory appeared jointly with Wallace's; the two papers being read
to the Linnean Society on 1st July 1858, entitled "On the Ten-
dency of Species to form Varieties; and on the Perpetuation of
Varieties and Species by Natural Means and Selection." That was a
mouthful indeed, which England and America swallowed whole;

but several French scientists, having chewed it over, spat some of it out. That men evolved from non-men is what the Irishman called probably certain; but that a creature, having lived its life under water, should suddenly decide to implant in itself the ability to grow wings, seems less than an inspired guess; many wise men look beyond Darwin, to a *Deus ex anima*. Karl Marx regarded the *Origins* as '. . . a basis in natural science for the class struggle in history". He offered to dedicate to Darwin the English translation of *Das Kapital*, but Darwin declined, saying that it would pain his family were he to identify himself with such an atheistical book. Nevertheless, he told Marx, ". . . we both earnestly desire . . . to add to the happiness of mankind". That, of course, was before Lenin and Stalin had contributed their own comradely joy.

Despite his scientific achievement, Darwin was a pathetic figure and the logical conclusion to a method which either ignores or denigrates whatever will not submit to scientific measurement: "Up to the age of thirty," he confessed, "poetry of many kinds . . . gave me great delight. . . . But now for many years I cannot endure to read a line of poetry. . . . I have also almost lost any taste for pictures or music. . . . My mind seems to have become a kind of machine for grinding general laws out of a large collection of facts. . . ."

To those two great men a third must be added, even although he was in no sense an Old Salopian. Now Dr. Johnson was a famous talker, and in our own time Mr. Gillie Potter has been known to descant upon medieval canon law, Edwardian music halls, heraldry, the Royal Artillery, nineteenth-century sporting writers, the technical problems of steam locomotion, China during the Boxer rebellion and the best way to get from Hereford to Huntingdon. Yet neither Mr. Potter nor Dr. Johnson ever, so far as I know, excelled the performance of Samuel Taylor Coleridge when he was appointed as successor to Hazlitt's father, the Unitarian minister at Wem. Hazlitt described Shrewsbury's first encounter with ". . . a redfaced man in a short black jacket . . . which scarcely seemed to have been made for him". Having alighted from the London coach, this total stranger began talking ". . . at a great rate. . . . He did not cease while he stayed: nor has he since, that I know of." Metaphysics, theology, optics, politics, ethics, poetry, painting: so melic was the monologue, its

wings so wide and soaring, that, even although they compre-
hended only a few stray notes, the townsfolk of Shrewsbury
agreed, said Hazlitt, ". . . to have heard no such mystical sounds
since

> High-born Hoel's harp or soft Llewellyn's lays."

But their amazement was brief. Within a few days of his arrival,
Coleridge received (from one of the Wedgwoods) the offer of a
pension if he would quit Shrewsbury, and give himself wholly to
poetry and metaphysics. So, said Hazlitt, instead of remaining
". . . the pastor of a dissenting congregation at Shrewsbury, he was
henceforth to inhabit the Hill of Parnassus". Alas, Hazlitt himself
had already detected the symptoms of a famous failure. "His
nose . . . the index of the will, was small, feeble, a nothing—like
what he has done." Coleridge did things that were neither feeble
nor small, but Hazlitt hit the mark. While he was still at Shrewsbury, Coleridge aspired ". . . to write a Sonnet to the Road between Wem and Shrewsbury, and immortalize every step of it
. . .". But instead of succeeding, he failed even to try, protesting
that he lacked ". . . the quaint Muse of Sir Philip Sidney".

A feminine view of old Shrewsbury comes from Celia Fiennes,
who notices first the three schools; each of which is ". . . free for
children not only of the town but for all over England . . .". After
that, she notices an elegant forerunner of the present Girls' High
School: ". . . a very good schoole for young Gentlewomen for
learning work and behaviour and musick". Next, she observes
that the houses are large, old, convenient, stately. Her conclusion
is pithy: ". . . it's a pleasant town to live in. . . ." And polished as
well, for it has fine public gardens: " . . . every Wednesday most
of the town and Ladyes and Gentlemen walk there as in St.
James's Parke and there are abundance of people of quality lives
in Shrewsbury. . . ." Celia Fiennes lived too soon to have read the
extract from Thomas Fuller's collection of proverbs: "He that
takes a wife at Shrewsbury must carry her to Staffordshire, else
she'll drive him to Cumberland." It seems unlikely, however, that
the ladies of Shrewsbury were more feminine than any others.
During the 1960s the damsels of the town celebrated May Day by
dancing around a perambulator wheel decorated with tricolour
streamers.

Shrewsbury's *noblesse* was manifest in its ancient earldom and the Talbots who held it; of whom the sturdiest must surely have been John Talbot. On 21st October 1451, being then eighty years of age, this veteran led an army that drove the French from Gascony. The natives, thankful to live under English rule, received the Earl of Shrewsbury with enthusiasn. "King Talbot", they called him, *Le Roi Talbot*.

Shrewsbury's *politesse* was thriving in 1706 when Farquhar put the town on the map with his play *The Recruiting Officer*, which he dedicated, in the words of an old Shropshire toast, to "all friends round the Wrekin". There are two curious facts concerning this play: together with Shakespeare's *Twelfth Night* and Jonson's *Epicoene*, it mentions the famous Great Bed of Ware; and it was chosen by David Garrick when, as a schoolboy, he first became an actor-manager by producing *The Recruiting Officer* as a school play wherein he took the minor role of Sergeant Kite (in later years he played Captain Plume and Brazen, and the clownish Costain Pearmain). Garrick may have been attracted by something other than the play's dramatic merits, for he was born at The Angel Inn, Shrewsbury, where his father commanded Tyrrell's Dragoons.

Farquhar himself was born at Londonderry in 1677. Educated at Trinity College, Dublin, he had wished to enter the Church, but transferred his ambitions from the pulpit to the proscenium. Though he did play Othello, he never could vanquish stage-fright, and when he had almost killed a fellow actor during a duel scene, he took the advice of his friend, Robert Wilks, resolving rather to write than to recite. *The Recruiting Officer* was based on his own experiences as a subaltern serving at Shrewsbury.

Like one or two other members of the theatrical world, Farquhar fell upon hard times. In other words, he overspent. The Duke of Ormonde (the "General" of the play's dedication) advised him to pay his debts by selling his commission, and promised to reward him with a Captaincy. Farquhar followed this advice, but the Duke failed to honour his promise. In the midst of his troubles Farquhar married a woman who had posed as an heiress, though in truth she was a pauper. It is to Farquhar's credit that he fulfilled a bad bargain faithfully and without rancour. But poverty and despair overwhelmed him. He was discovered in a

*Welshpool: Grace Evans' Cottage*

garret in St. Martin's Lane, by his friend, Bob Wilks, who lent him twenty guineas, and urged him to write. Within six weeks Farquhar completed his masterpiece, *The Beaux' Stratagem*. But, wrote Wilks, suffering had broken his health: ". . . before he finished the second act, he perceived the approaches of death." Happily, the dying man lived long enough to learn that his last play was a triumph. Bequeathing two daughters, Farquhar left a manly tribute to his friend Wilks: "Dear Bob, I have not anything to leave thee to perpetuate my memory, but two helpless girls; look upon them sometimes, and think on him who was to the last moment of his life thine, G. Farquhar."

The Senior Service, too, has a Shrewsbury man, Vice-Admiral John Benbow, who was born here in 1650. His famous exploit begins on 19th August 1702, when he intercepts a French squadron off Santa Marta. At once he makes a signal, "Engage the Enemy." Four of the seven English Captains disobey that signal (a thing, one assumes, without a parallel in the history of the Royal Navy). With less than half his force, Benbow leads the attack, hoping, as he afterwards said, that his "own People for shame would not faile to follow a good Example". The chase continues throughout the night, but dawn shows that only Benbow's *Bredah* and the *Falmouth* are within range of the enemy. The rest of the English vessels lag "3, 4, 5 miles astern". Soon the *Falmouth* falls away, and for two more days *Bredah* fights her own running battle, once or twice supported by *Falmouth* bearing within range. On the sixth day a chain-shot shatters one of Benbow's legs. Refusing to go below, he orders the ship's carpenter to rig-up a cradle on the quarter-deck; and there he lies, directing a battle so impossible that the French escape, and Benbow has to put-about for Jamaica, where two of his seven Captains are court-martialled and shot. On 4th November the Vice-Admiral dies of his wounds, deserving more than he received from English poetry:

> Brave Benbow lost his legs,
> Yet on his stumps he begs,
> "Fight on, my English lads, 'tis our lot, 'tis our lot."

Finally, there was Robert Lawrence, the man who put Shrewsbury on the map, and thereafter kept it well-posted. As owner of The Lion Hotel at Shrewsbury, Lawrence used his influence to

10

*At Berriew*

have the Holyhead Mail diverted from the Chester to Shrewsbury route. A memorial in St. Juliana's Church acknowledges
that to him the Salopians owed ". . . the first Mail Coach to this
town". In 1797 the Shrewsbury Mail left London at 8 p.m.,
reached High Wycombe four hours later, entered Shipston-on-
Stour at 7.22 in the morning, stopped an hour for lunch at
Birmingham, and was in Shrewsbury at 7.45 p.m., after a journey
of twenty-four hours. The guard of the Shrewsbury coach was a
famous figure. In *The Torrington Diaries* we have a description of
him by the Honble. John Byng, who was staying at The Lion Hotel:
"The guard of the coach is one of the grandest and most swagger-
ing fellows I ever beheld, dressed in ruffles and nankeen breeches,
and white stockings; and is here named the Prince of Wales." The
Shrewsbury coach was probably the most impressive vehicle, and
her guard the most dashing figure, ever seen by the cottagers
along the Severn, for the guard of a mail coach wore a scarlet coat
of military cut, with the emblems of his royal duties. Moreover
the coat was made to measure (in 1796 the Post Office wrote to a
posting-house on the Shrewsbury route, saying: ". . . if you will
send the measure we will have the uniforms sent for him"). One
man volunteered to serve as guard without pay, simply in order
to wear a royal uniform. Another was allowed to keep his uniform
when he retired, as a mark of long service. Every guard carried a
tool kit for repairs. Among its contents were two trace chains,
two hammers, two gimlets, a saw, hatchet, spade, nails, screws,
cord. All other traffic yielded precedence to the Royal Mail. On
one occasion the guard ordered his coachman to drive through a
party of Household Cavalry that had refused to give way.

But that was long ago. Shrewsbury today is clogged with cars
and lorries; and having left them behind, the Severn becomes
more than ever remote, though always the Severn, not simply a
river. If, for instance, you ask a Fawley cottager or a Kelmscot
farmer the way to the Thames, they will say, "First left and then
over the river." But whenever I have sought a lane between
Tewkesbury and Shrewsbury, I have been told, "First left and
then over the Severn". I cannot account for this, nor do I cite my
random experience as evidence of a general law; but there it is.

Finally, a problem of pronounciation; is the name Shrosebury,
or Shroosebury? Again I cannot claim to have Galluped along this

reach, but I have asked many people how they pronounce the name; and about three-quarters of them said 'Shrosebury'. In the year 901 the town's name echoed a Latin past, Civitas Scrobbensis: in 1086 it was Sciropesberie: in 1094 it was Salopesberia. The root of the matter is 'Scrobb's burgh'. But who, or what, was Scrobb? You will find some sort of an answer among a few stones on a heathy hill above the hamlet of Richard's Castle, which is partly in Shropshire, partly in Herefordshire. Those stones are the remains of the castle that was built *c.* 1050 by Richard, son of Scrob, allegedly a pre-Conquest Norman. Now Scrob, not being a Norman word, may have been the Saxon's nickname for their new lord, *skrubb*, a Norwegian word, meaning 'gruff fellow'. Or is Scrobb a variant of *scrob*, a Germanic word, meaning 'brushwood'? Certainly there is brushwood at Richard's Castle, and at Shrewsbury a thousand years ago there must have been a great deal more. So, Shrewsbury may mean either the town among brushwood or the town in the territory of a gruff Norman.

There are no gruff Normans hereabouts now, and not much brushwood. The Severn wanders through a pastoral plain, with the English Wrekin astern, and the Welsh Breidden ahead. This is the core of the Marcher country, poised between England and Wales. It is the land that John Masefield foresaw when he came on deck, and scanned the Atlantic, homeward-bound:

> There, somewhere, nor-nor-east from me,
> Was Shropshire, where I longed to be,
> Ercall and Mynd,
> Severn and Wrekin, you and me.

## CROSSING THE BORDER: AN INTERLUDE

ENGLISHMEN need not cross the sea in order to go abroad. A Fenlander may feel himself more at home in Holland than among the Westmorland mountains; and for every hundred thousand Londoners who smatter their way through France, not one can say to a Welshman: "*Ple may I pletty gore yne?*" To regard Wales as though it were an outpost of the Greater London Council is like visiting Rome with the sole purpose of admiring its cinemas. History, language, religion; they are the keys to a proper understanding of the Welsh people; and if a stranger declines to carry those keys with him, he may indeed cross the Severn into Wales, but he never will span the gulf between himself and the natives.

At certain points along their border the Welsh display a sign bearing the word 'Cymry', which many foreigners misconstrue as Wales. In fact, Wales is a corruption of Wealas, the Saxon name for all foreigners. The Britons, however, described themselves as *cymry* or 'fellow countrymen'. Who were these *cymry*? Sir John Rhys, the Victorian scholar, believed that the Celts, having reached Europe from the East during the Iron Age, divided their race into three parts—Gaulish, Cymric, Goildelic. Recent scholarship takes a different view. In 1967, for example, Dr. Anne Ross maintained that, although the Gauls did call themselves *Celtae*, there never had been a Celtic race. At most the word 'Celtic' may be used to denote certain linguistic and ethnological attributes of a people who appeared in Europe, north of the Alps, about the year 1300 B.C.

The first Celtic immigration may have reached north-east Scotland during the sixth century B.C. England experienced two incursions, about 500 B.C. and again about 250 B.C. To their Roman conquerors these Celts or Britons seemed an artistic albeit aggressive people. Their clothes were gay and exquisitely woven;

their weapons wrought with a finesse exceeding anything that
came out of Rome. Place-names prove that the Anglo-Saxons
never exterminated the Celts, but either married with them or
drove them into the south-west, or across the Irish Channel, or
into Wales. Neither the Romans nor the Saxons were able to
conquer these early Welshfolk; and when King Edward I did
subdue them, it was partly because they had already tamed themselves by civil war under jealous princelings.

During the later middle ages many of the Welsh nobility and
gentry either went to England or aped its fashions, uttering Glyn
Dwr's boast, but without his patriotism:

> I can speak English, Lord, as well as you;
> For I was train'd up in the English Court . . .

It was fashionable to anglicize one's surname; the Sitsyllts, for
instance, became Cecils; Writhe became Wriothesley; Keys
became Caius (founder of a Cambridge College); and Bugge
blossomed into Willoughby. The lesser Welsh gentry were so
poor that Cromwell's Major-General, who had been sent to
govern Wales, rated most of them as worth less than £100 yearly.

Henry VII is commonly regarded as the first Welsh King of
England, but Fluellen had already reminded King Henry V " . . .
the Welshmen did goot service in a garden where leeks did grow,
wearing leeks in their Monmouth caps; which your majesty
knows, to this hour is an honourable padge of the service; and I
do pelieve your majesty takes no scorn to wear the leek upon
St. Tavy's day." To this the King of England replied:

> I wear it for a memorable honour;
> For I am Welsh, you know, good countryman.

The King was topographically correct, for he had been born in
Monmouthshire.

When Henry Tudor became Henry VII his fellow-Welshmen
flocked to London, as the Scots were to follow James First and
Sixth. Among the most prominent beneficiaries were the Herberts,
a family of Raglan yeomen, whose senior branch were created
Earls of Pembroke and Knights of the Garter; reaching their
zenith when Katherine Herbert became Henry VIII's sixth
Queen. We have already noticed the Lords Marchers and the

union of England and Wales. For nearly a century Wales enjoyed royal favour. Queen Elizabeth's favourite guards were Welsh; and she chose two successive Welshmen as Deans of Westminster. King James I appointed a Welshman to improve London's water supply.

The Prince of Wales had not always been the King of England's eldest son. It was Edward I who bestowed that title on an Englishman. In 1404 a Welsh synod at Machynlleth retaliated by proclaiming Owain Glyn Dwr as Prince of Wales *dei gratia*. Meantime, although many of their nobility and gentry had Englished themselves, the Welsh people maintained their identity by asserting their religion and language.

Wales until the Reformation was staunchly Roman, not least because of its Cistercian monks, who excelled as sheep farmers and as custodians of Welsh culture. Long after the death of Henry VIII, a Bishop of St. David's was celebrating Mass in the Romish manner. Even in 1710 a Rural Dean discovered that many Welshfolk said prayers for the dead. But dissent was already abroad, though several of its pioneers lived and died as Anglicans, like Rev. Thomas Worth, for nearly forty years rector of Llanfaches. Dissatisfied with the Establishment, Worth built a Welsh dissenting chapel in 1639. For this he was defrocked, yet his allegiance lay so deeply with the Church of England that he asked to be buried in the chancel of Llanfaches church. Worth himself told his Bishop: "There are thousands of immortal souls around me thronging to perdition, and should I not use all means likely to succeed to save them?" In the event, what had begun as a religious revival, ended as a political and national protest. Cottagers attended chapel in order to snub the squire and to annoy the English. After a slow start, Welsh dissent gathered speed during the eighteenth century. When Queen Victoria was born, the majority of Welshmen went to church; when she died, the majority went to chapel. The Baptists had been among the first on the scene, with a chapel near Swansea in 1649. The Methodist Association did not arrive until 1742, and made little impact until the following century.

Welsh dissent is basically Calvinism, that dourest of all the perversions of the teachings of Jesus. The theocracy which Calvin imposed on Geneva made Roman Catholicism appear liberal. His ministers held the power of life and death, and they exercised it against hundreds of men, women and children; basing their creed on St. Augustine's doctrine of predestination whereby some people are foredoomed to Hell, others to Heaven. There is an irony in the Welsh acceptance of Augustine's neurosis, for its chief medieval adversary was a Welshman named Morgan (the Welsh for 'seaman') who, while studying in Rome, was dubbed Pelagius (the Greek for 'seaman'). Unlike Augustine, Pelagius believed that men do possess some control over their destiny. The gift of sight, he argued, comes from God alone, ". . . yet it is in our power that we may make good or bad use of our eyes." Calvinism, on the other hand, bred the terror and unctuousness which Caradoc Evans portrayed in his stories of twentieth-century Wales. Many Welshmen are still compelled to answer "Yes" when faced with Shakespeare's question: "Dost thou think, because thou art virtuous, that there shall be no more cakes and ale?" H. T. Buckle diagnosed the complaint, in his account of early Scottish Calvinism: "The clergy deprived the people of their holidays, their amusements, their shows, their games, their sports; they repressed every appearance of joy, they forbade all movement, they stopped all festivities, they choked up every avenue by which pleasure could enter."

In 1920 the former Bishop of St. Asaph was enthroned as first Archbishop of the Church of Wales. By 1968 that Church had regained a little of the ground which its predecessor had lost to dissent. Nevertheless, religion on the Welsh river means chapel, and chapel means Calvinism, neat or diluted. The choirs of Bethel and Zion do indeed enjoy themselves as they rejoice: "Christ the Lord is risen today. . . . " But they are never so happy as when they mourn: "Oft from the flames of Hell a sinful heart. . . . "

As a national emblem, however, the Welsh religion is less potent than the Welsh language. That language has changed with the years, but not greatly since the eighteenth century. It pays its way without borrowing from a base currency. There are no Welsh words for 'okey-doke' nor 'hospitalization'.

Three centuries ago a former Bishop of St. David's, William Laud, Primate of All England, decreed that only Welsh-speaking priests could be consecrated as bishops in Wales. Dr. Johnson, that most Anglo of Saxons, dipped his pen in Welsh ink when he

wrote: "Their language is attacked on every side. Schools are
erected in which English alone is taught, and there are lately some
who thought it reasonable to refuse them a version of the Holy
Scriptures that they might have no monument in their native
tongue." By and large, England has not supported Dr. Johnson.
Matthew Arnold proclaimed himself a Philistine by confessing:
"I quite share the opinion of my brother Saxons as to the practical
inconvenience of perpetuating the speaking of Welsh . . . The
Welsh language has ceased to be an instrument of living culture."
Nor was Arnold's Philistinism confined to Victorian England.
Many of the Welsh gentry had long ago spurned their vernacular,
though Dr. Robert Griffiths, a Tudor scholar, was not among
them. In the preface of his *Welsh Grammar* he declared: ". . . you
will find some that no sooner see the river Severn, or the clock-
towers of Shrewsbury, and hear the Saxon say in his tongue,
'good morrow' begin to forget their Welsh and speak it with a
foreign accent. Their Welsh is Englishfied, and their English, God
knows, is Welshy." John Ruskin defied the Victorian Mam-
monites: "God forbid," he said, "that the Welsh language should
ever die. It is the language of music." That was in 1889, when
more than half of Wales spoke Welsh, and thousands knew no
other language. The number of Welsh-speakers has dwindled
steeply since then, but remains larger than most Britons suppose.
In 1968 hundreds of thousands of Welshfolk spoke Welsh. A few
old people spoke no English at all, other than the blasphemies
bequeathed to them by tourists. As Caliban boasted:

> You taught me language, and my profit on't
> Is, I know how to curse.

Many people will ask why the Welsh language deserves more
than a valedictory paragraph; but to ask that question is to reveal
oneself incapable of understanding even the simplest answer to it.
However, I offer two replies: first, when a language dies, the
nation which spoke it is already dead; second, Welsh medieval
poetry was as great as the French, and greater than the English. I
am not competent to assess ap Gwilym, but everyone who can,
knows that his best lyrics are great. Wiser than England, the Welsh
poets still observe those rules of prosody which liberate by
challenging the power of language:

*Os oes yna ddynion,*
*All blethu englynion,*
*O showch i'n atebion—nos heno.*

Meanwhile a monoglot traveller may feel that it will be time to read Welsh poetry when he has learned to translate the Welsh place-names confronting him across the Severn. I therefore offer a miniature glossary, which may impose on the map of Wales a meaning where formerly none was perceptible. Thus, *aber* means the mouth of a river; *ap* means the son of; *bach* means small: *bryn*, a wood; *cwym*, a valley; *dinas*, a fortress; *dwr*, water; *llan*, church; *llys*, a palace; *maes*, a field; *myndd*, a mountain; *nant*, a stream; *pant*, a combe or hollow; *pen*, the head of a river or of a valley; *pont*, a bridge; *pwyll*, a pool; *rhyd*, a ford; *sarn*, a causeway; *tal*, an end or cul-de-sac; *tref*, a tarn; *ty*, a house; *y* or *yu*, the; *ystrade*, a vale. Welsh, by the way, retains traces of its continental past; the French and Welsh words for window, bridge, and church are almost identical.

To translate is not necessarily to utter; so, I offer some advice. *Ch* may be pronounced as in loch (which never was lock). Although *ll* sounds safest as *l*, the adventurous may try it (via loch) as *chlan* (but not clan). *Rh*, I have discovered, must be rendered as *r*, lest the Sais find himself spitting in the face of Cymry. Emphasis is usually on the penultimate syllable of each word. Welsh has no *j, k, q, v, x,* or *z* (a deficiency which it makes good with a spate of *l, y, w*).

A word of dismissal may be accorded to the extreme Welsh Nationalists, who wish to see their fellow-countrymen swell the number of delegates at the Disunited Nations. The words and deeds of such persons are symptoms of hatred, not of love. They seem not to know that they long ago lost their battle to Mammon, one of whose prophets, Nathan Rothschild, said: "Give me control of the currency, and I do not care a damn who rules the country." Whether they like it or not, the Welsh are linked inextricably with the rest of the kingdom. Their task is to maintain their language, their faith, and their farms. All other symbols of Cymry are trivial.

Why, one may ask, is a sense of belonging so strong on the Welsh Severn, so weak on the English? The cause is partly physical.

Wales is smaller than England, and therefore more easily apprehended. At a time when any Welshman could make himself understood anywhere in Wales, the Cornish spoke their own language, and so did the Northumbrians and the East Anglians. This Babel was a legacy from Rome, Germany, Scandinavia, Normandy. It emphasized that the English came of a stock more mixed than the Celts. Between north Welsh and south there is indeed an ancient division, but there never was anything resembling the tones which every English county still utters. A modern Welshman does not find that his county blurs his country; but in 1940 the Yorkshire regiments might have served even more gallantly had the war officially been described as Yorkshire versus the Rest. In Westmorland, where I spend much time, a Cumbrian farmer said to me: "There's nobbut two English counties. And the second is Westmorland." In short, English nationalism always has been tinged with regionalism; but in Wales an alien presence long ago subordinated local to national allegiance. This, of course, is not the whole answer. To account for the Welsh proper pride, and for the improper English lack of it, one must assume in the Welsh a stubborn self-respect which the average urban Englishman neither possesses nor wishes to regain.

What, finally, are the Welsh people like? The correct answer to that question is: the Welsh people are like every other people insofar as all flocks, being grey, contain many white sheep and not a few black ones. This commonplace seems so profound that the English cannot easily fathom it. Celia Fiennes dismissed Cymry with one sentence: ". . . they speake Welsh, the inhabitants go barefoote and bare leg'd a nasty sort of people." Landor fanfared his own aggressive nature when he shouted: "I shall never cease to wish that Julius Caesar had utterly exterminated the whole race." Even Beatrix Potter complained: "They net the river, steal the scanty game, and commit petty thefts." What nation does not?

I have spent much time among the Welsh mountains. The scenery there is incomparably finer, the inhabitants more courteous, more imaginative, healthier, hardier, and happier than in Liverpool or London. It may be argued that the Welsh are not wholly objective in their estimate of the English. The recipe for mutual understanding was prescribed by Hilaire Belloc:

> Of Courtesy, it is much less
> Then Courage of Heart or Holiness,
> Yet in my Walks it seems to me
> That the Grace of God is courtesy.

In his own Walks across the border, a visitor will do well to agree with Sir William Watson's portrait of the Welsh:

> A people caring for old dreams and deeds,
> Heroic story, and far-descended song . . .
> An ancient folk, speaking their ancient speech,
> And cherishing in their bosoms all their past . . .

Let the last word come from the land that we are about to explore. In the year 1163 an old Welshman said to King Henry II: "I am persuaded that no other race than this, and no other tongue than this of Wales, happen what may, shall answer in the great day of judgement for this little corner of the earth."

# II

# THE WELSH RIVER:
## SHREWSBURY TO NEWTOWN

THE Welsh border, of course, is marked on the map, but the Severn seems in no hurry to reach it. Looping many loops, it eludes roads, villages, paths; and when at last you do find it, you are surprised because it is almost as wide as it was at Arley, though in places stonier.

I came here once in November, when gales had toppled a tree into the river, forming a dam that collected fleece, leaves, twigs, weeds, straw; and the sound of the water through that dam resembled a human laughing, sobbing, quarreling, cooing.

And what of the voice of humans? It has changed indeed since the old men of Awre uttered a West Country lilt. Here the North and the Midlands have an outpost. 'You must' becomes 'You mun'. The brow of a hill is 'top o' the bank'.

This region used to be called the Isle of Rossal because the Severn encircled it. The great family here were styled Sandfords of the Isles. Their house, near Bicton, had been built for a London merchant, Mayor of Shrewsbury in 1682; and within a dozen years he had to pay a window tax. You will notice the effects of this tax throughout the Severn. The first rating was two shillings a year on all houses with more than six windows and £5 rental (in those years a tidy sum). Dairy windows were exempt if they were marked, which is why some parsonage outbuildings still bear the word 'dairy' above the door. But not every blocked window was a protest against the tax; in 1743 the rector of Gorham in Nottinghamshire blocked several of his windows—he had 120—because they were draughty.

The hamlet of Battlefield on this reach took its name from a famous encounter between King Henry IV and the Marcher Barons under Percy. Shakespeare set the scene with three lines:

> How bloodily the sun begins to peer
> Above yon busky hill. The day looks pale
> At his distemperature.

So said the King. His chief adversary, Percy, was chivalrous enough to wish that he might settle the matter in single combat with the Prince of Wales.

> O, would the quarrel lay upon our heads:
> And that no man might draw short breath today
> But I and Harry Monmouth.

A certain fat knight would have agreed, for when the battle did begin he saved his skin by losing his honour: "Can honour set to a leg? no: or an arm? no: or take away the grief of a wound? no: . . . Therefore I'll have none of it." So said Falstaff.

When the King spoke of "yon busky hill" he may have been staring at the Breidden Hills, which here succeed the Longmynd. This range of three peaks reaches its zenith at Moel-y-Golfa (1,324 feet), Breidden Hill itself has an obelisk (1781) commemorating the services of Admiral Sir George Rodney, whose victory at Dominica in 1782 resounded less favourably then than it did thereafter. The French Admiral de Grasse was court-martialled for lack of initiative; and Rodney displeased his second-in-command, who complained to a brother-officer: "After the glorious business of yesterday, I was most exceedingly disappointed and mortified by the commander-in-chief . . . for not making a signal for a general chase the moment he hauled down that for the line of battle . . .".

Unlike Vice-Admiral Benbow of Shrewsbury, Rodney had no connections with the Severn. One therefore asks why it was that the gentry of Shropshire and Montgomeryshire subscribed to elevate the memory of a stranger in their midst. Perhaps their gratitude was not wholly altruistic, for these woodlands sent much oak to the naval shipyards. Even in 1815 the local gentry and their ladies were still holding annual picnics beside Rodney's monument, from which, on a clear day, they saw Cader Idris and the Wrekin.

This peaceable hillscape has a second martial memory, of Thomas Churchyard, a Severn farmer's son, both soldier and poet. Born in 1520, Churchyard served in Scotland, Ireland, and the Netherlands. He was captured, but escaped to England. His poems I have never read, though good judges rate them smooth, after the manner of Sir Thomas Wyatt. I did once peruse his *General Rehearsall of Warres* (*Churchyard's Choise*), a lively account of some famous English sailors and soldiers. When he was seventy Churchyard received a small pension from the Queen. He died fourteen years later, having been described by Edmund Spenser as "old Palaemon", a veteran nonentity,

> That sung so long untill quite hoarse he grew.

One other literary feature deserves a tribute, and he was Francis Brett Young, whom G. M. Trevelyan praised for "his love of the English countryside and its folk". Young enshrined that love in many novels about the Marches northward from Worcester to the Wrekin and the Forest of Clun. Fame fades, and one lyric may outlive a hundred novels; yet Francis Brett Young's portrait of the Severn countryside half a century ago deserves its place in the gallery . . . "an exceptional and honourable place", said the *Times Literary Supplement* when reviewing the Severn edition of the novels. Joan Hassall's wood engravings (1937) for his *Portrait Of A Village* evoke a landscape with no housing estates, no factories, no aircraft, no chain stores, and hardly any cars. Dr. Young's *Portrait* shows these villages as they were in those years: ". . . the depth of the soil is so great, its nature so fruitful, and the Atlantic air that ebbs and flows over the Severn basin is so bland, that these villages, set within orchards and gardens, still wear a woodland air. Their gentle shapes and hues do no violence to the surrounding greenness, adopting, indeed, in their dapplings of rusty lichen and clambering ivy and mossy thatch, a sort of protective colouring that makes them appear as a natural part of it."

Beyond Montford Bridge lies Shrawardine with a mere and many kinds of birds. Henry I built a castle at Shrawardine, which the Welsh razed. A successor was built by the FitzAlans, who called it Castle Isobel, that being a favourite name among their womenfolk. During the sixteenth century the castle was bought by the Sir Thomas Bromley whom we met down-river; and in the seventeenth century it was held by Sir William Vaughan for the King against the rebels. The better to withstand assault by clearing the ground, Sir William demolished the vicarage and part of the church; but on the sixth day of the siege the castle was destroyed—some say by treachery, others by accidental fire—and parts of the ruins went down-river to build Shrewsbury's Welsh Bridge and Frankwell Quay.

There is another castle hereabouts, two miles south-west of Ford, a hamlet astride a stream that joins the Severn. The original castle was destroyed by Llywelyn in 1482. Three hundred years later a redbrick house was erected on the site; and in 1828 George Wyatt finished transforming the Queen Anne house into a Regency castle.

At the next village, Alberbury, there really is a medieval castle, or at any rate its tower, covered with ivy. This was one of a chain of border fortresses. Its nearest neighbour, at Wattlesborough, was long ago destroyed, except for the medieval keep, fifty feet high, tacked to a Georgian farmhouse. Alberbury church almost touches the remains of the castle walls. About a mile away another farmhouse contains parts of an Augustinian priory (c. 1225) that was excavated in 1925. Here indeed Worcester and Coalbrookdale seem faint, and Newport invisibly forgotten, for this is deep farmland, and the Severn a solitary river winding among many hills. Only the cattle, and sometimes a fisherman, are aware of its existence.

Two features show how nearly the Severn has approached Wales. The first is a place-name, Llanymynech, which is in England, overlooking a Welsh tributary, the Vrynwy. Here the hills were mined by Romans seeking zinc, copper, lead and lime for their new town of Uricon. The second feature is a plaque in Loton Park recording a visit (1809) by the Prince of Wales, who walked one mile thence into his principality, and returned with a twig of Welsh oak.

And now, within a few hundred yards of the border, the Severn flows near the home of its raciest character, Old Parr, who was born at Glyn, a hamlet of Great Wollaston. The church (1778) contains a long memorial to Parr, stating that he was: ". . . born at Glyn in the year of Our Lord 1483. He lived in the reigns of ten kings and queens of England: Edward 4, Edward 5, Richard 3, Henry 7 and 8, Edward 6, Queen Mary, Queen Elizabeth, James I, Charles I; Died the 13th, and was buried in Westminster Abbey

... aged 152 years and 9 months." *De mortuis nisi bonum*; but the good implies the truth; and the truth is, nobody knows at what age old Parr did die, because nobody knows when he was born. The date given on his memorial cannot be verified. Parr, it is said, assured King Charles I that he went into service when he was seventeen, and returned home at the age of thirty-five, to inherit his father's small-holding. Some accounts say that he married his first wife when he was eighty; others, when he was a hundred. Most agree that he did penance in Alberbury church for begetting a bastard by Catherine Milton. At the age of 122, they say, Parr took a second wife. Thirty years later the Earl of Arundel shipped him to London as a gimmick. When pressed by the King to recall the most memorable moment of his life, Parr cited its latest amorous adventure; whereupon the King cried, "Can you remember only your vices?" They say that when Parr died, William Harvey dissected the body, pronouncing its organs vigorous and healthy, but attributing death to the London air and diet. John Taylor, the Gloucester jingler, made a different diagnosis, describing Parr as nearly blind, almost toothless, and very frail; though of good appetite, a sound sleeper and merry withal:

> He would speak heartily, laugh and be merry,
> Drink ale, and now and then a cup of sherry.

Parr certainly lived long enough to justify Taylor's description of him as "The Old, Old, Very Old Man". But one must say of parts of his biography what Hume remarked of Berkeley's philosophy, that it admits of no refutation, and carries no conviction.

Parr being by all accounts unseemly, is not the man to bid us *bon voyage* as we leave England. It is more fitting that we seek help, or at any rate a mood, from the hills that rise on all sides, so tenaciously that we wonder where and how the Severn shall lead a way through them.

These last few yards of England are something more than a border country. They are the border itself. At one moment the Severn is in England; at the next, it flows through Wales. Yet nothing, it seems, has changed. The first house across the frontier looks much like the last behind it: small signs, you feel, to mark

so great a gulf. Even so, the Welshman who takes one pace forward into England, and the Englishman who steps into Wales, enter a land that is different despite the identities.

This difference appears at the first village across the border, which is Llandrinio, set among flat fields beside the Severn, with a bell-turreted Norman church dedicated to three saints: Trinio, Peter, Paul.

Llandrinio Bridge, only twelve feet wide, is one of the pleasantest on the Severn. Built in 1775, it has three semi-circular sandstone arches and cutwaters. The house beside the bridge used to be a tavern. This hamlet once held a weekly market and two yearly fairs that were redletter days for the English who sailed up-river from Shrewsbury, and for the Welsh who flocked from their own place-names . . . Rhydescryn, Maesydd, Cae-Uein, Maerdy, Tir-y-Mynnch, Farchoel. These and many other tongue-twisters line the north bank of the Severn as it indulges a looping of loops knottier even than those at the Isle of Rossal; and one of those loops reaches Pool Quay, which has two churches. The visible church—isolated and modern—has some timber vaulting inside, and an ugly timber belfry outside. The invisible church is the Cistercian Abbey of Ystrad Marchell or Strata Marcella. Owen Cyfeiliog founded it eight hundred years ago. Now it lies under the grass.

At this point the Severn is joined by the Trewern, a name announcing the affinities between Cornwall and Cymry. Both regions used the same word for a hill or *bryn*, for a headland or *pen*, for a harbour or *porth*, for a village or *trew*. A fortress is *car* in Cornish, and *caer* in Welsh. The Cornish for enclosed land is *lan*; the Welsh for it is *llan*. Saint Llantilo in Wales became Saint Teilo in Cornwall.

Here, too, the Severn passes a dyke that was built by Offa, King of Mercia, during the eighth century; certainly to define, possibly to defend, his kingdom. The dyke ran from the Severn at Tiddenham to the Dee near Prestatyn. Much of it has disappeared, but near Wrexham it is twenty yards wide and about seven feet above the ditch that follows it. The Trewern itself, however, is only one of many tributaries on this reach. The largest, the Vrynwy, flows down from Lake Vrynwy, which is nearly five miles long by half a mile wide, and was created

11

*Montgomery: Broad Street*

(1880–90), by the flooding of fields and houses as a reservoir to supply Liverpool via seventy-five miles of aqueduct. In 1959 a drought revealed the houses that had been submerged seventy years previously.

Meanwhile the Severn almost touches the canal, does touch the Shrewsbury road, and is never above a few hundred yards from the railway. Sometimes you might imagine yourself back at Arley's steep banks. At other times the banks disappear while the river runs between pebbly beaches within sight of Welshpool.

Welshpool, said Lloyd George, is the gateway to paradise. Defoe, a journalist, was less lyrical and more precise: "A thoroughly Welsh Town," he called it, "and the inhabitants . . . speak the ancient British language." During the past ten years I have walked through Welshpool at least twenty times, but not once did I hear "the ancient British language". Such is the measure of Welshpool's fall from grace. Yet this assize town is a pleasant place. It has held a weekly market for seven centuries. The borough was created in 1282 by Gruffydd ap Gwenwynwyn, Prince of Powys, who refused to submit a dispute to Welsh law, claiming that he was a Marcher and therefore entitled to be judged as an English baron by common law. Light industries and a milk depot have out-stripped Rev. Richard Warner who, when he came here by barge in 1797, admired the town's ". . . storehouse of the flannels manufactured in the upper counties, which are brought down here, and disposed of to the wholesale dealers who frequent the place".

Welshpool church, on a knoll above the traffic, was built in 542, rebuilt in 1275, and in 1866 rendered largely unrecognizable. There is a Stuart Royal Arms above the west arch.

The former Cross Keys Inn has a message studded in nails on the door, inviting God to damn "old Oliver, 1661". This invitation may have been inscribed by a veteran of the skirmish that occurred here between royalists and rebels in 1644.

At the end of High Street is a house which Gilbert and Ann Jones built in 1692. They claimed that an ancestor, Richard, who lived during the reign of Edward VI, was the first Welsh Jones. In recent times the Welsh Church Fund joined with local subscribers and the Arts Council of Great Britain to renovate and re-stock the town's museum. In 1968 several handsome old houses in Raven Street and High Street were falling down. The most endearing building in Welshpool is a black-and-white cottage by the church. Known now as Grace Evans's Cottage, it was the home of a maidservant of Lady Nithsdale, daughter of the Earl of Powis. Mistress and maid took part in a dramatic plot which begins in 1715 when William Maxwell, fifth Earl of Nithsdale, joins the Galloway Jacobites supporting the Stuart Pretender. A few weeks later the Jacobites surrender after a skirmish at Preston. In February of the following year Lord Nithsdale and several other Scottish peers are found guilty of treason against George I. While her husband awaits death in the Tower, Lady Nithsdale prescribes a desperate remedy. Accompanied by Grace Evans, she goes to London; and there, mixing courage with cunning, the two women smuggle the condemned peer out of the Tower and into Italy, whence he joins the Stuart Court at St. Germains. Lady Nithsdale's account of her exploit was published in *The Transactions of the Society of Antiquaries of Scotland*.

Welshpool's most impressive building is Powis Castle, on a hill beyond the town, in a wooded park containing the tallest tree in Wales, a Douglas fir, 181 feet high. This Marcher fortress recalls George Dyer's couplet:

> Old castles on the cliffs arise,
> Proudly towering in the skies.

To the Welsh it is Castell Coch, the Red (or Sandstone) Castle, seat of the Princes of Powys, who chose to live near their English allies rather than among their Welsh enemies. When the Powis family failed in its male line, the castle passed by marriage to the Charltons of Shropshire, who raised the oldest parts of the present building. The castle was bought by Sir Edward Herbert in 1587, and captured by the rebels in 1644. At the Restoration it was itself restored, and in 1722 it reverted to the Jacobite Earls of Powis (no connection with the Princes of Powys). Capability Brown was then employed to design terraces and gardens *à la mode*. In 1784 a Powis heiress married the son of Lord Clive, one of the greatest of Old Merchant Taylors; whereupon the Clives called themselves Herbert, and soon afterwards received a third re-creation of the earldom. In 1968 the fifth Earl of that creation resided at the castle by courtesy of himself and the National Trust. So, Powis Castle has been a private residence for 700 years.

And now the Severn shakes itself free of road and rail, for three miles flowing alone until, at the weir near Glen Hafren, both rail and road converge and for more than a mile cling to the left bank. The river then sheers away again, and at Trehelig-gro doubles back on itself, but recovers and drops due south and then bears east as though to enter Berriew, a village on the River Rhiw, which here joins the Severn.

Berriew, a junction for six pleasant country roads, is part of a large estate, Vaynor Park, which belonged to the Devereux, Earls of Hereford. About a century ago the houses were well-restored. Their Jacobean-style chimneys—indigenous and perhaps unique—are designed on what is known locally as the Vaynor pattern. The timbered vicarage (1616) outshines its rebuilt church (1876); but nearby, at Pentre Llivior, the Wesleyans have a decent redbrick chapel (1798). There are many fish in this tributary; with the birds and the trees and the insects they assert that people are not the only villagers.

Scarcely a mile away, the Severn wanders eastward to the fringe of Forden, where Aylesford Brook chimes in. Gunley Hall, formerly the seat of the Pryces, retains part of a Tudor house. The church (1868) is less endearing than a memorial in the churchyard:

> Beneath this tree lies singers three
> One tenor and two basses
> Now they are gone, its ten to one
> If three such takes their places.

After some indecision, the Severn bypasses Forden, and for a while eludes the sound of traffic. Passing an ugly iron bridge, it enters a favourite reach of mine, where a broad meadow slopes to the left bank, and then passes a farmhouse among trees, heading due north, past Rhydwhyman ford, the scene of many Marcher meetings, not all of them friendly. This part of the river is haunted by a ghost commonly regarded as English; but, say the Welsh, King Arthur's homeland was Wales. Most Britons dismiss the Arthurian legend as a fairy tale, though to the medieval French it seemed so important that they called it The Matter of Britain, *Matière de Bretagne*. The story is worth telling.

Once upon a time there lived a man of whom we know little except that he called himself Geoffrey of Monmouth because his Breton ancestors had settled in that county during the eleventh century. In 1152 Geoffrey was consecrated Bishop of St. Asaph, a diocese which he did not feel himself obliged to visit. Sixteen years previously, as a secular canon at Oxford, he had written *Historia Regum Britanniae*, a history of British Kings, which, he claimed, was a translation, into Latin, of "a certain very old book in the British tongue". This book had been recommended to him (so he said) by a friend named Walter. Part at least was true, for the evidence proves that Walter, an Oxford archdeacon, had indeed been Geoffrey's friend. But of the "certain very old book" no trace was ever found nor now seems likely to be. In other words, Geoffrey attributed one fiction to another, being delighted (as Boswell remarked of Johnson) "with the fertility of his own imagination". About one-fifth of Geoffrey's *Historia* is a preposterous account of battles, in which Arthur ejects the pagan English, subdues the Picts of Scotland, the Scots of Ireland, and the peoples of Scandinavia. But all this is only a limbering-up. France becomes his next victim. He defeats the French King in single combat, and accepts the surrender of the entire French nation. The conquering hero then returns to Caerleon, his Court in Wales. There he receives from the Emperor Lucius a command either to surrender or to resist. He resists. The Emperor is defeated, and after him the Kings of Babylon, Egypt, Parthia, Greece, and one or two other nations whose names for the moment escape me. But while Arthur is crossing the Alps, in search of new victims, he learns that his throne has been usurped by his nephew Medrawd. Once more he returns to Wales, but this time not victorious, for although he kills Medrawd, he is himself wounded, both mortally and immortally, and borne away into Avalon, *in insulia Aualloniae*, there to be healed. A medieval translator of the *Historia* into Welsh, added a line of his own, pointing out Geoffrey's ambiguous use of the phrase 'mortally wounded'.

Ambiguous or not, the *Historia* became an international best seller. In 1155 it was popularized as a poem of 15,000 lines, *Roman de Brut*, written in Norman-French by a Jersey scribe named Wace. Half a century later it was put into Middle English as a poem of 32,000 lines. Finally, it inspired not only the French

Vulgate Cycle of Romance but also the English Arthurians from
Malory to Masefield.

England, naturally, followed the example of Joseph of Exeter,
who chose the west of England as the home of the man whom he
called "The Flower of Kings", *Flos Regum Arturus*. Wales,
naturally, followed the example of Geoffrey of Monmouth, who
co-opted Camelot into Cymry. Wales claims also to possess the
Holy Grail or chalice of the Last Supper; maintaining that it was
brought into England by Joseph of Arimathea, and thereafter
found its way to a Welsh monastery. When the monastery was
dissolved, the last seven of its monks were given shelter by the
Powells of Nanteos, one of the oldest estates in Cardiganshire;
and the monks showed their gratitude by bequeathing their Grail,
which is still preserved at Nanteos.

So much for legend: what of the facts? Most Arthurian scholars
agree that, toward the end of the fifth century, or perhaps at the
beginning of the sixth, a military leader may have existed and very
likely did exist somewhere in Britain. There are no contemporary
references to him, but in *Historia Britonnum*, a ninth-century work,
Nennius cited several traditions concerning a hero who had led
the Britons to victory over the Anglo-Saxons at the Badonic
Hill. It was of this battle that Masefield declared:

> All Britons know the stories that are told
> Of Arthur's battle . . .

It seems improbable that these stories arose and flourished without some foundation in fact. Only the most sceptical historian
denies that Hereward the Wake and Robin Hood sprang from a
living prototype. The Germanic peoples, admittedly, believed
that a national hero would return from the dead in order to
revive the living; yet the hero himself had once been very much
alive, in the person of Frederick Barbarossa, Holy Roman
Emperor, who repelled the Muslims, and imposed some order
upon his peoples.

Though many suppose that he never lived, King Arthur is not
yet dead. For the learned an international Arthurian Society
flourishes; for the others, Hollywood propounds its own expensive historiography. And in Wales they claim him as their own,
with Bwrdd Arthur or King Arthur's Table at Anglesey; his resting

place at Craig-y-Dinas in Glamorganshire; St. Dryfig, Archbishop of Caerleon, who was said to have crowned Arthur despite
the absence of archbishoprics in the early Welsh church; a multi-
tude of sites and associations in the Rhydaman area of West
Wales; and on the Welsh Severn a ford frequented by his knights.

According to Sir Thomas Malory, King Arthur's last words
were: "I will into the vale of Avilion, to heal me of my grievous
wound. And if thou hear of me never more, pray for my soul." Is
it entirely fanciful to steer a middle course between bodily resur-
rection and a point of no return? Alfred the Great rallied a reeling
kingdom; so in their time and after their fashion did Queen
Elizabeth and Winston Churchill. Perhaps that is what Tennyson's
Arthur meant when from his funeral barge he cried:

> The old order changeth, yielding place to new,
> And God fulfills himself in many ways.

There is no doubt at all about the existence of the Herberts,
who lived at a Welsh castle on this reach, and took one of their
titles from an English village nearby. The Herberts first entered
history in 1426, when William ap Thomas, fifth son of Thomas
ap Gwilym ap Jenkin, was knighted by Henry VI, having
Englished his name into Herbert. As we have noticed, one branch
of the Herberts supplied Katherine as the sixth Queen to Henry
VIII. Created Earls of Pembroke and Knights of the Garter, they
won renown as the Herberts of Willton in Wiltshire, for several
decades a power behind several thrones. A more lasting renown
was achieved by the two Herbert brothers who remained on this
reach of the Severn. The elder, Edward Herbert, we have met
already at Eyton-on-Severn, where he was born. He took his
title from an English village, Chirbury (spelling it as Cherbury),
overlooking Montgomery across the Severn. This Circberie or
'fort with a church' has a beautiful village school (1675), white-
washed and timbered.

The church contains a memorial to Thomas Bray, who was
baptized here. He graduated at All Soul's College, Oxford, in
1678; and twelve years later became rector of Sheldon in Warwickshire. At the request of the Bishop of London he went as
commissary to Maryland, in America, to supervise the recruit-
ment of clergy. Finding that most of his recruits were too poor to

buy books, Bray set about acquiring libraries for them. In 1706 he returned to England, as vicar of an Aldgate parish. Before he died, in 1730, he had helped to create thirty-six libraries in England, and eighty in America. But his greatest foundation was the Society for the Propagation of Christian Knowledge.

From Chirbury you can see Montgomery clearly, and walk there easily. Having arrived, you will agree that 'charming' is the best description of a village which, being a capital, must be called a town. The population is about nine hundred. Montgomery proves that age *qua* age is not the only reason why old houses are delightful, for few of its own, if any at all, are older than the eighteenth century. This is a Georgian town, the only one in Wales, dominated by the remains of its castle (not to be mistaken for the remains of a castle which Roger de Montgomery built at Hendomen, a mile north). Although Montgomery is smaller than many villages, it wears the look of a country town; and this urbanity, I believe, is due largely to the red bricks, for bricks are manufactured, unlike stone (which is quarried) or timber (which is hewn). Bricks never grew on trees nor in the soil. A brick house, therefore, lacks the earthy appearance of Shropshire magpie or of Cotswold stone. Yet Montgomery is intrinsically rural, set on rising ground at the foot of a hill, from which the landscape unrolls like a green carpet patterned by lanes. It is a netherland, neither typically English nor utterly Welsh, though everywhere fruitful and gracious. One medieval bard found it the fairest place on earth:

> Though a man live until Doomsday,
> He shall never behold a land fairer than this.

Henry III built Montgomery Castle, on a lump of igneous rock, from which you can see Cader Idris many miles to the north-west, and Offa's Dyke, scarcely a mile to the east, marking the Anglo-Welsh boundary, with its ditch in Wales. Owain Glyn Dwr sacked Montgomery, but not even he could capture the castle. It became the Mortimers' stronghold, commanding the road, the river, the ford. In 1607 James I took it from one Herbert, Sir Edward, and gave it to another, whom he had created Earl of Montgomery. Six years later the Earl returned it to Sir Edward in exchange for £500. In 1644 it was surrendered by Lord Herbert of Cherbury to the enemies of the King who had ennobled him. Within a few years the King's heir was restored, and the subject's castle demolished. Yet imagination revives the ruins; a horseman is seen, riding for his life and Montgomery's; left and right shouting to the reapers in the corn: "The English are coming!" or "Glyn Dwr is at Rhydwhyman!" Then indeed Sir Walter Scott's vision appears:

> The battled towers, the donjon keep,
> The loophole gates where captives weep,
> The flanking walls that round it sweep
> In yellow lustre shone.

The centre of Montgomery—which is also most of Montgomery—is a cobbled square, called Broad Street. From one end it looks across the Severn into England; at the other end a redbrick Guildhall (1790) almost touches the foot of the castle hill—Donne's hill, it might be called, because he wrote a poem about it, *The Primrose, Being At Montgomery Castle, Upon The Hill, On Which It Is Situate*:

> Upon this Primrose hill,
> Where, if Heav'n would distil
> A shower of rain, each several drop might go
> To his own primrose, and grow Manna so . . .

Around this three-sided square, and along the two streets leading into it, the Georgian houses and shops are agreeable at all seasons. Montgomery does not require you to serve yourself in a chain store exactly resembling its mass-begotten twins. The staff wait upon you, and show their pleasure in doing so. The counters and their commodities are conducive. I have come here in summer, when the houses shimmered like red roses on a breeze; I have come here in winter, when the stones of the castle were whitewashed snow-posts on a road through the skies; and always the place has looked at its best.

Montgomery's citizens are glad that theirs is still a country town unburdened by the hordes who administer a county (that onus now rests upon Welshpool, the administrative centre). In 1927 Montgomery celebrated its tercentenary as a royal borough, whereon the only blemish is a tin-roofed garage.

Montgomery church was relatively unspoiled by a restoration in 1875. Its graveyard contains the Robber's Tomb, recalling the grassless grave of the girl who was murdered down-river at Nass. The Robber's story goes as follows: in 1821 John Newton Davies, about to be hanged for theft, asserted his innocence by prophesying that no grass would grow on his grave and that a bush of white roses would arise to justify him. In 1968 I saw a rosebush beside his grassless grave.

The church has a hammer-beam roof, a double chancel screen, decorated rood loft, and the canopied tomb of the parents of the man whom I rate the most eminent of all the Herberts; George, fifth son of Sir Richard and Lady Herbert. His elder brother, Lord Herbert, described their father as: ". . . very handsome, and well-composed in his limbs, and of a great courage." The mother, Magdalen Herbert, received a double tribute from John Donne, for he preached her funeral sermon, and composed a more lasting memorial, *The Autumnal*, with a famous introit:

> No Spring, nor Summer Beauty hath such grace,
> As I have seen in one Autumnal face.

George Herbert was born in 1593, either at the castle, which was then the residence of his grandfather, or at the adjacent Black Hall. From Westminster School he went up to Trinity College, Cambridge, where he became Fellow, Praelector in Rhetoric, Public Orator. In London he charmed the Court, and might have captured it, for James I, susceptible to masculine beauty, granted him a pension so that he could indulge "his gentile humor for cloaths". But the London episode was brief. The courtier who had boasted

> I know the ways of Pleasure, the sweet strains,
> The lullings and the relishes of it . . .

resolved, as he put it, "both to marry and to enter into the Sacred Orders of Priesthood". This he did. His wife was a Wiltshire girl, Jane, daughter of Sir John Danvers. His Wiltshire parish was Fugglestone St. Peter with Bemerton St. Peter, a place so poor that, when King Charles was asked to make the presentation, he replied: "Most willingly to Mr. Herbert, if it be worth his acceptance." Herbert had obtained the living through his kinsman, the

Earl of Pembroke, who chose Bemerton in order that its new
vicar might reside at Wilton as domestic chaplain. The vicar,
however, did not concur. Although he had delayed before pro-
ceeding from deacon to priest, and still wore layman's clothes
and a gentleman's sword, Herbert at Bemerton set aside the old
Adam. Having rebuilt the parsonage because one-third of it had
fallen down, he composed a verse that may be seen engraven on
the mantel of the hall:

> If thou chance for to find
> A new house to thy mind
> And built without thy cost;
> Be good to the poor,
> As God gives thee store,
> And then my labour's not lost.

The vicar and his wife were the ideal of their kind. Izaak
Walton said of the marriage: "There was never any opposition
betwixt them, unless it were a contest which should most incline
to a compliance with the other's desires." Herbert practised the
preaching of his book, *A Priest In The Temple*, which describes
the good shepherd whose "parish is all his joy and thought".
Herbert's sermons were suited to his flock, taking their imagery
from "a plough, a hatchet, a bushell, boyes piping and dancing".
   From his poetry a deeper note is heard, echoing a struggle
toward the light and away from a "gentile humor for cloaths".

> Only a sweet and virtuous soul,
> Like seasoned timber never gives:
> But though the whole world turn to coal,
> Then clearly lives.

Herbert was not a prolific poet, but he did seek craftsmanship
assiduously. Of 169 poems in *The Temple*, 116 have patterns that
are not repeated. All were published posthumously.
   Herbert died when he was thirty-nine years old, serving where
he had chosen to serve, far from college or Court. On the last
Sunday of his life, despite intense pain, he rose from his bed,
called for a musical instrument, and accompanied himself while
he sang one of his poems praising God. "And thus," said Izaak
Walton, "he continued meditating, and praying, and rejoicing
till the day of his death."

Whether I flie with angels, fall with dust,
Thy hands made both, and I am there:
Thy power and love, my love and trust
Make one place ev'ry where.

He was buried in Bemerton church, and is remembered by a small tablet bearing his initials.

Could he return, George Herbert would blink at Montgomery. The church he would recognize, and the Severn, and the hills above it; but the pattern of the fields would perplex him, the ruined castle would amaze him, and the houses seem utterly strange. The third chapter of Macaulay's *History* was more or less correct: "Could the England of 1685 be, by some magical process, set before our eyes, we should not know one landscape in a hundred, or one building in ten thousand." Nevertheless, I say of this little town what Herbert himself may have overheard on market day: *Duw rhoddo i'ch lawenydd*: may it live in peace.

Above Montgomery the Severn is again troubled by traffic, but contrives to make an impressive entry into Abermule, flanked by the Kerry Hills. On this reach the natives swim and sometimes paddle a canoe near a bridge with an inscription: "This second iron bridge constructed in the County of Montgomery was erected in the year 1852."

Here the River Mule flows from the Kerry Hills, joined by Becham Brook coming down from the north. Here, too, are the remains of a castle that was built a thousand years ago by Bleddyn ap Cynfan, Prince of Powys; rebuilt by Dafydd ap Llywelyn in 1262; captured a few years later by Roger Mortimer. In Leland's day the castle walls were thirty feet high, on a rocky precipice. This castle was named Dolforwyn or the Meadow of Maidens because, so they say, one of its garrison, being jealous of a beautiful girl, drowned her in the river below the ramparts.

And yet, after all, this is less a riverscape than a realm of mountains and remote villages. The unofficial capital is Kerry, which from 1903 until 1924 had its own narrow gauge railway climbing the Mule valley. The church—Norman and Early English, heavily restored—has a monument of 1788 litanizing the munificence of a naval purser (reminding one of Kirkby Stephen in Westmorland, where the market shelter was built by a naval purser at about the same time).

This remote village was the scene of a famous quarrel between the Bishop of St. Asaph and Gerald de Barri *alias* Gerald of Wales *alias* Giraldus Cambrensis, who was born *c.* 1146 at the castle of Manorbier. "I am sprung," Giraldus declared, "from the princes of Wales and from the barons of the Marchers." He was indeed; his father being a Norman lord; his maternal grandmother, the fair and famous Nest, daughter of Rhys ap Tewdr, the last independent ruler of south Wales. Educated first by a chaplain of his uncle, the Bishop of St. David's, and afterwards on the Severn at St. Peter's Abbey at Gloucester, Giraldus studied in Paris, and thereafter served as Archdeacon of Brecon. He wished to become Bishop of St. David's, a shrine then so remote that one pilgrimage to it was reckoned as pious as two to Jerusalem. The diocese of St. David several times fell vacant during his life, and he declined three other Welsh bishoprics, and four in Ireland, hoping that he might at last receive it; but the prize eluded him, partly because of his eagerness to create a Welsh Church that should be independent of Canterbury. Giraldus was the friend of another Welsh Marcher, Walter Map, to whom he once sent the gift of a walking stick and some Latin elegiacs. More veracious than Geoffrey of Monmouth, Giraldus wrote much history and topography, including an account of a journey of eight days in north Wales, and of four weeks in the south (this latter when he accompanied Archbishop Baldwin, during Lent 1188, to preach the Third Crusade). The journeys yielded some interesting news items. Thus, we are told that Henry II could read but not speak English; and that Caerleon had the remains of its Roman city: ". . . hot baths, relics of temples, and theatres, all enclosed within fine walls . . .". A later travelogue, *Descriptio Kambriae* or *Description of Wales*, claims that the Welsh language is purer in the north than in the south. In Wales, says Giraldus, both sexes cut their hair level with their eyes and ears; they brush their teeth with a woollen cloth on a green hazel twig; they hold poets in high esteem; above all, they so value a pure pedigree and noble descent that even the humblest peasant has his family tree by heart, back to the sixth and seventh generations "and even beyond that".

Disappointment did not sour Giraldus. On the contrary, the Kerry quarrel proved his zeal for the see which had rejected him.

The quarrel itself was both unseemly and exciting, for Kerry church was about to be dedicated, and the Bishop of St. Asaph had decided to co-opt it into his own diocese by presiding at the dedication; but Giraldus, hearing of the plot, hurried to confound the hatcher. After much dispute the two clerics—simultaneously, it appears—excommunicated each other; after which, Giraldus demanded to see the Bishop's charter of possession, well knowing that the Bishop did not possess one. In the end, Asaph withdrew, leaving the field and the church to David's zealous advocate.

The Severn meanwhile passes another Glen Hafren, following the Shropshire Union Canal within a short distance of Llanllwchaiarn, which has a Georgian church (1815) whose nave and chancel were not improved by Victorian improvers.

Approaching Newtown, the river adopts several disguises; sometimes flowing between high banks; sometimes meandering among bankless shoals. Gazing ahead, you see only the hills; some of them treeless and grazed, others dark with conifers. And again you ask how the river shall pierce them, for they bar the way by encircling the sky.

Newtown's Welsh name was Llanfair yn Nghedewain, which became Tre Newydd or New Town in order to distinguish it from the ancient settlement of Caersws, six miles up-river. Although Newtown received a charter from the Mortimers in 1280, it is basically a creation of the eighteenth century, not so compactly beautiful as Montgomery, and less consistently Georgian, yet with an impressive High Street and several black-and-white houses. North of the bridge, woods and fields approach within a few yards of the town; southward a weir sings in all weathers. Most of the wool factories have been converted into shops, but there are still some eighteenth-century cottages where flannel garments were handwoven. The Wool Exchange became a Public Hall and the Court of Assizes and Quarter Sessions. The great house here was Newtown Hall, where King Charles I was received by Sir John Pryce after the battle of Naseby. In the Hall grounds you can see traces of the Mortimer's castle. The Hall itself is now a town hall and council offices.

There are two churches here. One of them, the parish church, is an acceptable essay in Victorian Gothic. The other retains only its thirteenth-century tower and walls (the rood screen and font are at the parish church). In the older of the two churchyards Robert Owen was buried; but the house in which he was born has been demolished by the Midland Bank. The present Bank contains an Owen Museum.

Robert Owen was born on 14th May 1771, the son of a New-town saddler. Having worked for a grocer and a haberdasher, he became manager of a Manchester cotton mill. Thereafter, as what we now call a business tycoon, he launched the famous New Lanark Mills in Scotland. Ignoring the fact that the mills existed in order to make profit, Owen called them "institutions for the formation of character", which is rather like describing the Royal Academy as a place where picture-frames are hung. Between 1812 and 1824 Owen's private enterprise was visited by tens of thousands of people from many parts of the world, all admiring—and rightly admiring—the autocratic paternalism with which the work-people were treated. Owen later became an industrialist in America.

This warm-hearted man meant well and did good at a time when help was needed desperately by the poor. He treated his own workpeople well, and was honest enough to admit that a full belly worked better than an empty one. He supported Francis Place and Richard Carlile when they propagated a species of contraception, coyly calling it "Neo-Malthusianism". But he controlled his factories with strict discipline, and did not consult the employees on matters of high policy.

Robert Owen is commonly accepted as a pillar of the Socialist Establishment and as the founder of the Co-operative Movement. The truth is somewhat otherwise, for he neither approved Socialism nor founded the Co-op. The Co-operative Movement was founded on 24th October 1844, when twenty-eight weavers in Manchester registered a private trading company, The Roch-dale Equitable Pioneers, in order to raise "a sufficient amount of capital" in order to amass an even more sufficient amount of capital.

Owen's son, Robert Dale Owen, contributed to *The Atlantic Monthly* a series of articles describing the first twenty-seven years of his life. These articles were then published as a book, *Threading my way: twenty seven years of autobiography*, in which the son revealed his boyhood ambition to combat the father's irreligion:

"I had a vague idea that God had chosen me to be the instrument of my father's salvation, so that he might not be sent to hell when he died." But it was the father who confounded the son. "There are," he said, "probably twelve hundred millions of people in the world. So out of every twelve persons only one is a Protestant. Are you quite sure that the one is right and the eleven wrong?" The child had no answer to this show-of-hands. Might was right, according to the best democratic principles: "And so ended the notable scheme of mine for my father's conversion."

A more typically Welsh family were the Pryces, the squires of Newtown, who died out toward the end of the eighteenth century. Ask any native above seventy years old, and he will tell you the story of Squire Pryce who, by way of a house-warming for his third wife, confronted her with the embalmed corpses of her two predecessors. But it was the last Squire, Sir John Pryce, who supplies Newtown with its raciest lore. In his declining and debt-ridden years the old man was visited by a couple of well-dressed guests from the principal inn. Having entered Newtown Hall, the guests revealed themselves as bailiffs, and—more to the point—proceeded to conduct themselves as such; taking with them a quantity of the Baronet's goods and chattels *in lieu* of payment. The furious debtor then turned on the woman who owned the inn, as though it were her fault that he had run into debt and been shriven by two spruce strangers. By telling malicious lies, the old man contrived to get the woman's licence withdrawn. However—and it throws some light on the flexibility of Welsh society—the innkeeper was herself the aunt of a local squire, well-able to counter-attack. In the end, Sir John Pryce was sued for slander. Having broken bail, he fled to London, was apprehended, sent to the King's Bench prison, died an undischarged bankrupt, and was buried at Newtown.

The Pryces of Newtown are extinct: its shepherds, happily, are not. Still in the late twentieth century you will see among these hills the son of the father whom Maurice Hewlett noticed on the Wiltshire Downs:

> Under the sun on the gray hill,
> At breakfast campt behind the hedge,
> There ate he, there eats he still
> Bacon and bread on the knife's edge.

*The Severn near Montgomery*

Most of these men have some Welsh; a few affect not to have anything else, unless for foreign business. They are chapel-goers, when they do go; and so wisely conservative that only racial bias can explain their habit of opposing the one political party which might help them to preserve what is worth keeping. In a life spent wandering widely through rural Britain, I have never met an English farmhand who read Milton for pleasure, and Herrick as light relief. But on the Welsh river I have heard ap Gwilym's poem to the lark, uttered in Welsh while the speaker coaxed his ewes toward the dip. Can you direct me to any English farmhand who, while he slices mangolds, will entertain a foreign visitor by saying:

> Sound of vernal showers
> On the twinkling grass,
> Rain-awakened flowers,
> All that ever was
> Joyous and clear and fresh, thy music doth surpass.

Again let us understand each other. I am not saying that all England is lost, and every Welshman an angel. I am certainly not suggesting that men shall live by poetry alone. I am simply writing what I have written.

Poetry, politics, economics: all vital things: and in the last resort every one of them seems less important than the relation between a river and the people who live beside it. The deepest intimacy with rivers is the workaday monopoly of shepherds, farmers, anglers, gamekeepers and other members of a breed whom Richard La Gallienne described as 'out-of-doors men'. Even so, an ordinary countryman lives on good terms with his stream. It so happens that much of my own time is divided between Exmoor (where a stream flows within a foot of my window) and Westmorland (where my daily walk follows a river). I can therefore report from experience how companionable a river is, how changeless, how changed from hour to hour.

I have walked along this reach of the Severn on a wintry day so still that you could hear a single reed plashed by one eddy. The trees were bare as besoms, and no bird seemed ever to have sung. And I have walked here in May, when so many birds did sing, and so many lambs bleated, that the weir went silently unheard.

12

*Llanidloes: the Market Hall*

Yet this was the same Severn; and all who knew it had the meadow where they basked in summer, and hoped to bask again. They had the bridge that was sometimes starry and sometimes sunny, yet ever the same structure. They had the lane that once led to the end of their world, or so they supposed. And they had the woods wherein after all the world did not end.

You may liken a river to a shrine, which men approach for many reasons: for comfort, for courage, for absolution, for thanksgiving. Or you may liken it to a friend who listens, but never reproves, and will advise only insofar as he predicts the destination of a specific course.

The Severn's course at Newtown leads among hills, higher than any astern.

# THE HEART OF CYMRY:
# NEWTOWN TO LLANIDLOES

Is THERE a way through those hills? We know that there is. The river proves as much. Yet the question recurs, even among those who know the landscape closely, because the heights so interlock that their spurs peer round every corner, as though confirming Traherne's awareness that "something infinite behind everything appeared". This labyrinth steers the river; first to the east and then, after a few hundred yards, to the south; and then again east, and then again south, along a course zanier than any since first at Over Bridge the estuary changed into country clothes. Indeed, before it reaches Caersws, the river runs back toward Newtown.

After three miles the Mochdre Brook chimes in, hurrying from its source near Waunlluestowain, remote among hills.

Unlike the source of its brook, Mochdre village is scarcely two miles from the Severn, sheltered by summits of 1,400 feet. The church, badly restored in 1867, has a fifteenth-century roof and carved bosses. Beyond Mochdre you can walk all morning without passing a village.

The opposite bank of the river is equally steep and secluded. In fact, there is no place of any size, except Tregynon, which happens to be small. Here also the church was marred by Victorian restorers, yet retained its timber roof and a wooden plaque to the Blayneys of Gregynog Hall, high among woods two miles away. During the 1920s the Hall was the headquarters of an annual festival of poetry and music, sponsored by the Misses Davies. Between 1923 and 1940 the Gregynog Press published a number of handsome books.

From Tregynon and Mochdre the Severn receives Llyfnant Brook and a stream from Fawchen Pool. These tributaries arrive in time to witness the river's zaniest meandering. This looping of

loops looks vivid enough on a map; and from the hills it appears
even more vivid; but you must walk beside the river in order fully
to perceive the zigging of its zags. At one point, having followed
the river southward for ten minutes, I found myself several yards
north of the place from which I had started.

Very different, this, from the steep banks of Shrawley and the
woodlands of Wyre. Here the Severn is shallow, treeless, pebble-
strewn, sandwiched between two roads. The road on the right
bank is pleasantly rural, but the left bank is loud with summer
traffic, which makes a poor introit to yet another classic ground,
Caersws . . . not the village, which is a debris of dull houses, but
the site of a Roman camp and the line of a Roman road.

The camp was probably built to defend the lead mines at Van
near Llanidloes. Now, all that remains of it is a rectangular mound
on the edge of the village. The first excavation was conducted
during the 1880s by Rev. David Davies. In 1909 a more thorough
search revealed traces of a granary, praetorium, kitchens; with
many coins, ornaments and pottery of the first century A.D.

With the aid of a map and the local people, you may follow
part of the imperial road from Caersws. One section, about two
miles long, leads north-east, following traces of an *agger* and some
metalling below the grass. The second section leads north-west to
Pontolgoch, more or less on the line of the present road to Clatter.
Now there is on the Isle of Wight a village named Clatterford,
the ford where travellers clatter over stones (Old English *clat-
rung*). One wonders whether this Welsh Clatter was so-called
because, centuries after the Legions had departed, the ruins of their
roads were still the best highways in Britain. Anyway, after about
four miles, at a place near Trawsgoed, you may see traces of an
*agger* six yards wide, near a brook.

Caersws had written its own Ichabod when Leland saw it 400
years ago: ". . . at poor Caersws hath been a market and borough
privileged." Privileged indeed, for Caersws had been the seat of
the Lords of Arwystli, administering the Severn scene for many
miles around.

At Caersws the river is joined by Afon Garno and four streams
which become one at Gwynfynydd, having flowed from high
ground above Llanwnog, a beautiful hamlet, where John Hughes
was buried. This man Hughes is worth noticing because he was not

only a poet but also a station-master. Copywriters labelled him "The Burns of Wales", but a more precise comparison would have been with Alfred Williams, a labourer in the railway sheds at Swindon, who wrote poetry and prose about the English countryside.

Sometimes known by his bardic name of Ceiriog, John Hughes was born in 1832, son of a Denbighshire sheep farmer. Much of his best work was done while he worked as a goods clerk at Manchester's London Road Station. In 1865 he returned to the land of his fathers, serving as station-master at Llanidloes, Towyn, and Caersws. To the world, if it knows him at all, Hughes is the author of 'Men of Harlech' and 'God Save the Prince of Wales'. To the Welsh he is a major lyricist of the nineteenth century. Like the poets of the Tudor Court, he wrote often for music. In 1863 he published 100 songs, adapting many of them to old Welsh tunes. Sometimes the tune inspired the lyric, as when he wrote the words for Dafydd y Garreg Wen's *Rising of the Lark*. John Ceiriog Hughes died at Caersws; and is commemorated by a village library and institute at Dolywen in the Ceiriog Valley of his native Denbighshire.

More than any other in the world, this Welsh river honours its poets while they live, and is sometimes able to ensure that their death was not by starvation. Giraldus stated that in Wales a poet not only sings for his supper but also receives it above the salt. To be a Bard is to receive an accolade which money cannot buy nor influence borrow. It is a passport valid throughout Wales; received with as much reverence as now the English accord to goalkeepers and aerobats. George Borrow did well when he knelt by the grave of ap Gwilym; Wales did better when, in 1866, Welsh members of Oxford University founded the Dafydd ap Gwilym Society, which still conducts itself in Welsh.

Bards are as old as Welsh poetry, but the *Gorsedd Beirdd Ynys Prydan* or session of the Bards of the Isles of Britain is relatively new. The Bards have three orders: the Ovates (wearing green robes, to signify a growing novitiate), the Bards (wearing blue robes, to signify a summerlike serenity) and the Druids (wearing white robes, to signify allegiance to truth). Druids control entry into their own order, awarding it solely for outstanding achievement in the arts or in scholarship. Theirs is an ancient heritage, for it was at Christmas 1176 that King Henry II convened the first recorded eisteddfod to which competitors came from all parts of Wales. The bardic crown for music was won by a southerner from the land of Morgan; the crown for poetry went to a northerner from Gwynedd.

The Cornish and Breton *Gorseddau* are by-products of the Welsh Session. At meetings of that Session a Breton representative joins the half-sword of Brittany with the half-sword of Wales; the complete sword was presented by Brittany in 1899, as a symbol of unity between the two Celtic peoples.

Ireland, Scotland, and the Isle of Man have no *Gorseddau*, but they do send representatives to the Welsh ceremonies.

So does Wales honour its artists with a proper pageantry; not burdening them with obsessive experiment nor with lifeless formalism, but adapting new attitudes to traditional manners, and those manners to new attitudes. Since I have no more Welsh than would enable me to pass the time of day, I cannot comment on Welsh prosody, except to remark that its patterns are often intricately beautiful. The Welsh poets anticipated Ruskin's remarks on the relation between art and experiment: "Originality in poetry," he said, "does not depend on invention of new measures . . . A man who has the gift, will take up any style that is going, the style of his day, and will work in that, and be great in that, and make everything that he does in it look as fresh as if every thought of it had just come down from heaven."

From Llanwnog four small tributaries become two just above Gwynfndd, and one just below it, at a point midway along the footpath from Llanwnog to Caersws. Having received them, the Severn leads due south, away from its zany sector, following a more or less even course, this time beyond the sound of traffic.

On the right bank, Llanidnam Hall was bought from the first Lord Herbert of Cherbury by a Carmarthenshire family, the Reades, one of whom remembered himself with an inscription above the door: "I.R. 1700". Later generations, known as Crewe-Reade, resided at the Hall until the close of the nineteenth century.

On the left bank, the village of Llanidnam lies two miles above Llanidnam Hall, at a point where the main road rejoins the river. Near a small bridge stands a statue of David Davies, a local lad who made so good that he became the first of all Welsh millionaires. Born in a cottage on the far side of the Severn, Davies had a flair for finance and engineering. He helped to build the Barry Docks, he sat as a Conservative M.P., he sponsored the Ocean Collieries. Part of his fortune went to buy an impressive estate within a short distance of his humble birthplace; another part helped to found Aberystwyth's University College. His grandson became the first Baron Davies, Lord Lieutenant of Montgomeryshire, and brother of the Misses Davies of Gregynog Hall.

A pleasant lane ventures north, hugging the river for awhile, and then turning left, climbing a country that justified the men who named it Paradwys Cymru, the Paradise of Wales. Among these hills the world seems so quiet that you can hear every aspect of the silence . . . birds, brooks, breeze, sheep, foxes, horses, and a tractor bumping the dusty lane. They farm here, and that is all, being enough.

Several footpaths lead toward Llyn Ebyr, a lake three-parts surrounded by woods, from which the Wigdwr Brook joins the Severn near Hengynwydd. On the opposite bank some brooks arrive from Pegwyn-bach, a summit only eighty feet short of being a mountain.

North of Llyn Ebyr a lane crosses two rivers, Afon Ceirist and Afon Trannion, and then reaches Trefeglwys, which is indeed *tref eglwys* or 'hamlet with a church'. The great house here (now faced with brick) was Queen Elizabeth's gift to her favourite, the handsome Robert Dudley, Earl of Leicester, Chancellor of the University of Oxford, who used part of the Trefeglwys estate to breed horses for the royal stud. The Queen loved Dudley, and would have married him had it been possible and politic. Six days before he died, he wrote to the Queen, enquiring after her health, which he called "the chiefest thing in this world". The Queen kept his letter, and in her own hand wrote upon it "HIS LAST LETTER".

Nearby, the Van lead mines were famous until the end of the nineteenth century. Many financiers and diggers made, or lost, a fortune in these hills. The remains of the workings are easily reached. The pleasantest way is to follow the road from Trefeglwys toward Llanidloes, taking the third turn on your right, crossing a footpath, bearing right, crossing a road, and so to the mines within sight of Fan Hill, dominating the Clywedog Reservoir, nearly 1,500 feet above the Severn.

Severn itself winds through a valley of great beauty. On the left the woods of Gorn Hill overlook the road; on the right some farmhouses shine like random mushrooms. But all this is marred by traffic roaring within a few yards of the river. If you do wish to explore, you must follow the footpaths and tracks inland a little on the right bank. These are near enough and sufficiently high to offer a ringside view.

Montgomeryshire, of course, is a border county, and many people will wonder why I have called this part of it the Heart of Cymry. Yet the word 'heart' may be used without reference either to its place in anatomy or to its function in physiology. The truth is, when you reach Caersws, you do enter the Heart of Cymry. If you come here often, and live among the people, and get to know something of all sorts of them, you will agree that these parts are as Welsh as any in Wales. Since Time in Paradwys Cymru marches easily, I doubt that it has noticeably outstripped a census of 1951, which showed that 94 per cent of the population of Llanfighangel yng Ngwynfa spoke Welsh: the exact figures were 431 villagers out of 478.

These linguistics unveil another feature, the Welsh gipsies, who arrived from the Continent during the early fifteenth century; being then a race part, not unlike a modern Jew who practices his orthodoxy in any land. The earliest statute against the gipsies was passed in 1541. Twenty years later, claiming that they were Romish spies, Queen Elizabeth ordered them to leave the kingdom within three months, on pain of death. Her command was widely disregarded. Like the Celts before them, the gipsies withdrew deeper into Wales. As lately as 1942 a tribe of Balkan gipsies settled in Wales, and some of them observed the custom of arranging their children's marriages. Despite this custom, or perhaps because of it, divorce and abortion are almost unknown among the Welsh gipsies.

In 1926 the Oxford University Press published *The Dialect of the Gipsies*, a grammar and vocabulary of the older forms of British Romani as it was spoken by the clan of Abram Wood. Since that book appeared the number of gipsies who speak their ancient language has dwindled steeply, but is not yet nought. I have seen what Owain Glyn Dwyr saw, a gipsy encampment at night, swarthy men and women around a fire that glinted their ear-rings . . . fine-feathered dancers swirling to the tune of a fiddle . . . and dogs chained to trees half a mile away, to warn against an approaching stranger. These are the true gispies. They scorn the travellers who act as ticket-collectors at a fun fair. The menfolk deal in ponies, grind knives, make and mend baskets, work seasonally to harvest corn, hops, hay, potatoes (and it may be that one of them has found a hare or a pheasant by the way). The women tell fortunes, and sometimes sell mops made from fleece gleaned from barbed wire, hedges, gateposts. The conduct of such people is a rebuke to the misconduct per head of the population elsewhere. Bookless, unhygienic, superstitious, guilty of not keeping office hours: these things the gipsies are: but gipsies are also exponents of the philosophy which Borrow attributed to them: "There's night and day, brother, both sweet things; sun, moon, and stars, brother, all sweet things; there's likewise a wind on the heath. Life is very sweet, brother; who would wish to die?" For a few more years, until they are compounded or otherwise confiscated, the gipsies will add twopennorth of colour to a plainly penny world.

But something is happening. These hills are rising higher with every mile, and ever closer. This is more than a steep land. The Severn is lapping the mountains; and before it climbs them, we must pause, even at risk of seeming to lag, in order to admire a new feature of the portrait, the harp, which is also very old—old as the Pharaohs, from whom, after many centuries, it reached Britain via Scandinavia.

The three-stringed *telyn* or Welsh harp—an invention of the fourteenth century—was common throughout Wales until the Industrial Revolution. According to the *Triads*, a handbook of early Welsh culture: "A man needs three things in his house . . . a loyal wife, a cushion for his chair, and a harp." The laws of Hywel Dda cited three kinds of harp; the king's, a music-master's, a nobleman's. Only an acknowledged virtuoso was permitted to play the best kind of harp. Unknown performers were confined to a horse-hair instrument; and if they wished to advance to a higher kind, they had to pay twenty-four pence to the chief bard.

> The harp that once through Tara's halls
> The soul of music shed,
> Now hangs as mute on Tara's walls
> As if that soul were fled.

That Irish lament by Thomas Moore has been defied by the Welsh. In 1934 a Welsh Harp Society was formed (*Cymdeithas Cerdd Dant*) to foster harp-playing and to buy harps that are borrowed by promising players under the age of eighteen. So, the harp still plucks the heart-strings on the Welsh river.

The English Severn, too, loved its harp. Indeed, harps were the favourite musical instrument of the English nobility during the fifteenth century. The *Liber Niger* of King Edward IV required every royal henchman to be a harpist. King Henry V and his French Queen were skilled on the instrument. Thereafter, however, it was ousted by the lute. Richard More—"blynde Dick" they called him—was the chief harpist to four Sovereigns; and when he visited the Severn, in 1520, the corporation of Shrewsbury feasted this "minstrel of our Lord King, the man who is blind and the principal harper in England".

If you come here at Christmas you may find news of *Plygain*, a carol service resembling those of the Celtic peoples in Cornwall, in Brittany, and in the Isle of Man. *Plygain* or 'first light' began as an aftermath of midnight Mass on Christmas Eve, but was later held at dawn on Christmas morning. The Welsh, in fact, stayed awake until *Plygain*, and afterwards the younger carollers assembled at a farmhouse, there to eat *cyflaith* or treacle toffee. In 1968 *Plygain* was held at several Welsh churches.

Unlike Cornwall—whose Women's Institutes published a book of Cornish recipes—Wales neglects its national dishes. From Montgomery to Llanidloes I have sought in vain any hotel serving Welsh food; by which I mean, for example, Snowdon Pudding, a blend of raisins, lemons, eggs, brown sugar, wine sauce. Yet a cookery book of 1845 reported that Snowdon Pudding was ". . . constantly served to travellers at the hotel at the foot of the mountain from which it derives its name". Welsh Rarebit or Rabbit is at least as old as the first known reference to it in 1725. *The Oxford Dictionary* whets the appetite: ". . . cheese and a little butter", it says, "melted and mixed together, with seasoning, the whole being stirred until it is creamy, and then poured over buttered toast". It is true that the Welsh eat leeks, but nowhere on the Welsh river have I found a hotel serving Meslin bread (*Bara Brith*), Welsh cheese-cakes (*Bara Tenau*), girdle cakes (*Slapan*), oat pancakes (*Crempog Surgeich*).

We may seem to have been talking for a long time, yet the Severn all this while has travelled little more than a mile beyond the woods of Gorn Hill, which is far enough to bring it within sight of Llanidloes, the last town on its banks.

Llanidloes has saved its soul, though the body is beginning to be encrusted with factories and housing estates, as out of place in the mountains as a pig in Piccadilly. However, these lie on the outskirts of Llanidloes, leaving the true town intact. In any event, it is wrong to regard industry as a recent blemish on Wales. In 1851 nearly 40 per cent of the working population was employed in occupations not connected with farming; and about one-third of the people worked either in mines or in quarries. During the nineteenth century 100,000 Welshfolk emigrated; some to North America (the passage then cost £4); others to the coal, gold, or copper mines of Brazil, Russia, Australia, New Zealand. In 1865 many families left the Welsh river to join Dan Jones, the Moron missionary, in a Kingdom of the Saints beside the Great Salt Lake. Britain had put so many eggs into one industrial basket that she could not feed her own hens. Cheaply imported food—fodder for the manufacturing masses—starved even the hardy Welsh hill farmer. R. S. Thomas's poem, "The Hill Farmer Speaks", echoes the mood of those years:

> The wind goes over the hill pastures
> Year after year, and the ewes starve
> Milkless for want of the new grass,
> And I starve, too . . .

As a result of that exodus the population of rural Wales in 1968 was smaller than it had been in 1868.

Nor was this plight confined to the farming community. Many of the lesser Welsh gentry were relatively as poor as their tenants. Few could afford to send their sons to Oxford or Cambridge; none to stand for Parliament. So continued a state of affairs which King James II had found when, summoning the Welsh gentry to Ludlow, to discuss religious toleration, he was informed that half of them declined to come; poverty having sapped their interest in service. Few indeed followed the Tudor example of Sir John Wynne when he sent his boys to Westminster and Bedford, but made their English wives learn the Welsh language.

Llanidloes has weathered those withering storms. It is a lively little town. The hub is a half-timbered Tudor market hall, raised on oak arches, offering a cobbled shelter against rough weather. At this hall, which contains a museum, John Wesley thrice preached; the stone on which he stood has been moved to the rear wall. During one of his visits Wesley was entertained by the Bowens of Tydden Hall. In 1968 the Hall was a farmhouse, still occupied by the Bowens, who had preserved the bed in which Wesley slept.

On another visit Wesley conducted the marriage of his brother to Sally, daughter of Squire Gwynne, at Llanlleonfel church. He remembered the day in his *Journal*: "Not a cloud from morning till night. I rose at four, spent three hours in prayer . . . At eight o'clock I led my Sally to church." His entry in the register was simple: "Charles Wesley and Sarah Gwynne were lawfully married, April 8, 1749."

Llanidloes church—the church, that is, of St. Idloes, a sixth-century missionary—is impressively spacious; suggesting that Llanidloes was formerly a large town; but it never was so. The parish church added several cubits to its stature when the Abbey of Cwm Hir transcended the Dissolution by bequeathing some of its masonry to St. Idloes. In 1542 the thirteenth-century arcade of the abbey was rebuilt at St. Idloes; the main timbers of the roof came from the abbey; the stone tracery of the east window is a modern copy of the original at Cwm Hir.

In 1282 the great Prince Llywelyn was invited to help the mid-Welsh against the English. On 1st December he encountered an English army led by Sir Edmund Mortimer and Sir John Giffard. During the skirmish he was killed by a Shropshire infantry officer named Stephen Frankton. His body was found next day, and the head was sent to the English King; the rest was taken to Abbey Cwm Hir.

Like Welshpool and Newtown, Llanidloes stands athwart a summer speedway to Aberystwyth; out of season, however, it is a leisurely place. Sheep are driven through it. Larks are heard above it. Mountains are seen around it. The Welsh language is heard in it. About the year 1280 King Edward I granted to Owain of Arwysth, Prince of Powys, the right to hold a weekly market and two annual fairs at "Thlanydleys infra Wallium". Soon afterwards the town became a borough.

Llanidloes is, or ought to be, a godly place; partly because it was named after a saint; partly because (so they claim) a Cardiganshire man, Jenkin Morgan, anticipated Robert Raikes of Gloucester by founding a Sunday School near the town in 1796; and partly because of the two chapels dissenting from each other across a street near the bridge (in 1905 the seating arrangements in Welsh nonconformist chapels could have accommodated 74 per cent of the total population).

However, godliness sometimes forsook Llanidloes; or vice-versa. Thus, in 1839 the town was seized by a gang of Chartists who maintained mob rule for a week. Yet this lawlessness was an ancient feature of the portrait. In 1284 Archbishop Pecham, troubled by the immorality of Welshfolk, reminded himself of Aristotle's dictum that nobody above the age of ten can feel certain of achieving civic regeneration. The Archbishop therefore wished all Welsh parents to send their children to be educated in England. The parents, he urged, must live in boroughs, where their misbehaviour could be more effectively controlled. He cited a precedent from the Roman Emperors who had compelled certain unruly Gauls to move from the countryside into boroughs—*habiter en borgs*—whence their name, Burgundians.

Llanidloes today is so orderly that one or two of its people resemble the Oxfordshire folk of Richard Braithwaite's jingle:

> To Banbury came I, O profane one,
> Where I met a Puritane one
> Hanging of his cat on Monday
> For killing of a mouse on Sunday.

Yet, as I say, Llanidloes is a pleasant place ... intimate, friendly, weekday-lively, off-peak-leisurely, endeared to me by old acquaintance. Here, more than anywhere else along the Severn, I have seen and continue to meet those twinkle-eye farmers who tally with Coventry Patmore's observation: "All the love and joy that a man has received in perception is laid up in him as the sunshine of a hundred years is laid up in the bole of an oak."

Perfection, alas, is not of this world; if it were, Llanidloes would have made better use of its river. Instead, the banks are marred by a builder's bric-à-brac yard and the relics of rusted charabancs. But this modernity soon falls astern. Glancing over your shoulder, you see only the roofs of a little town among hills. After a few hundred yards you notice something else. The Severn is a river no longer. It has become a stream. And in order to reach its source, you must climb a mountain.

# IN THE MOUNTAINS:
## LLANIDLOES TO PLYNLIMON

"A MOUNTAIN and a river are good neighbours." So said the *Outlandish Proverbs* which George Herbert published in 1639. As the Severn approaches its own mountain, so the hinterland changes. There are no riverside abbeys above Llanidloes, no famous birthplace, no imposing manor house. If a traveller has been here before, he makes the most of what remains of humanity; notably a farm and a watermill in a wooded dell near Mount Severn, a mile above Llanidloes. Here a lane leads south to Llangurig, a village worth visiting for its own sake and also because it is the last that will be seen before the Severn turns its back upon mankind.

Llangurig bestrides the road to the coast, and is therefore loud in summer. It has a church, a commendable Black Lion Hotel, a shop, and a few houses. The stripling Wye flows nearby, scarcely an hour's walk from the Severn. An old Welsh proverb says *Hafren a Wy* etc. or "The Severn and the Wye glide agreeably".

Llangurig had a brace of self-helping brothers, William and Edward Owen, who in the eighteenth century became respectively a sea captain and rector of Warrington in Lancashire.

The church is dedicated to St. Curig, a sixth-century missionary from Ireland, who founded several churches in these parts; five centuries after his death the friars were still carrying his image as a wonder-worker. The stained glass—illustrating *inter alia* the alleged adventures of St. Curig, which were extremely Celtic—was designed by J. Y. W. Lloyd, sometime curate of Llanidnam, who submitted to Rome, served with the Pontifical Zouaves, and in 1875 returned to the Church of England. This eclectic cleric spent a fortune restoring and enlarging Llangurig church.

There is a lonely farm beyond Llangurig, called Eisteddfa Curig or 'Curig's resting place'. Tradition says that the saint landed at Aberystwyth, and then halted here, after twenty-five mountainous miles. Knowingly or not, he had chosen to relax at the foot of the path to Plynlimon.

It is a steep and airy walk back to the Severn . . . or, rather, to the Hafren, for the river has changed its name. Indeed, the etymology is altogether vague. Tacitus and Bede called it Sabrina. In A.D. 800 the *Historia Britonnum* called it Saefern, which Domesday spelled as Sauerne. The poet Layamon preferred Seuerne. The relation between Severn and Hafren can be explained by the Celtic habit of interchanging *S* and *H* as the initial letter of a word.

Hafren or Severn, the stream now enters a steeply pastoral valley, and then a steeper and treeless valley, and then a precipice of Forestry Commission conifers, and then for a while it becomes pastoral again, flowing sometimes as an open brook, sometimes among elms and willows, followed by a lane hundreds of feet up on the right. This lane passes an ancient schoolhouse for children from the remote farms. I never see it without recalling the wisdom of Thomas Bewick, that self-taught artist, who did not regard education as the key to a car and a collar. "If children," he said, "were sent to the edge of some moor, to scamper among its whins and heather, under the care of some good old man who would teach them a little every day, . . . they could there, in this kind of preparatory school, lay the foundations of health, as well as of education."

Here, by the way, you notice what may be called the living ghosts of a departed feature of the portrait, the elms that were used by the Welsh archers. Giraldus described the bows as "crude and unpolished", but they more than held their own until the English—preferring yew—perfected the craft of archery. King Edward I's statute of Winchester confirmed the Anglo-Saxon rule that every man between fifteen and fifty must serve, with his weapons, in the militia or *posse comitatus*. The English longbow had to be bent by pressure of the whole body. Its arrows were a cloth-yard long. Bishop Latimer learned archery as a boy: "for men," he said, "shall never shoot well unless they be brought up to it."

*My favourite Severn bridge*

Presently the lane passes my favourite Severn Bridge—two planks and a wire handrail, slung across the foaming water—and all this while the scene grows wilder, the farms fewer, the air keener. It is not only that the summits are taller; their nightly shapes blot-out half a constellation. Few men have followed every yard of this reach, for that would mean burrowing through copses, clambering over rocks, scaling the waterfalls. Even so, I have scaled, clambered, and burrowed awhile, for this is the reach I love best. It is secluded but not isolated; populated companionably because sparsely. Instead of passing like strangers in a scurrying street, the farmfolk and foresters linger and are pleased to meet one another. Here you are not simply a number on a computed card. You are a human being; and you will be accepted or shunned according as you respect your neighbour, and his wife, and his ox, and, above all, his sheep.

Now a Forestry Commission track appears on the left of the lane, signposted "To the Source of the Severn". There is no right-of-way for vehicles, but the Commission does allow walkers to use the tracks, on the understanding that the walkers do not light bonfires or in any other way make a nuisance of themselves. The tracks are not suitable for private cars. In wet weather—which is to say, for most of the year—only tractors can vanquish the mud.

The track passes Severn Falls, pleasantly sign-posted by the River Authority. Here the Hafren is no more than a beck, scalding downhill, lithe as a salmon.

Soon another sign appears, saying that the source of the Severn is one mile away. Maybe it is one mile away, but the mile itself is the longest in Wales; longer even than the length which Celia Fiennes noted during her own journey through the Marches: ". . . the miles here very long so that at least it may be esteemed the last 20 mile as long as the 30 mile gone in the morning". Over a bare mountain it goes, through a silence so profound that only the wind raises its voice. There are no trees up here, neither paths nor hedges nor walls. If it were not for some footprints in the mud, made by a shepherd, you might rate yourself the man before Adam. Soon even the footprints disappear, for the summit does not welcome sheep. As Wordsworth remarked of a Cumbrian fell: "This situation is not favourable to gaiety."

Defoe's visit here so overawed him that he set Plynlimon above

13

*The source of the Severn*

Snowdon: ". . . tho' 'tis hard to say which is the highest hill in Wales, yet I think this bids fair for it". Another eighteenth-century climber, Sir William Pennant, complained that the ascent was a bog, and the summit hidden by mist. The Augustans were landscape gardeners: anything above five hundred feet daunted them. Even Gilbert White regarded the South Downs as ". . . that chain of majestic mountains".

In 1813 *The Beauties Of Wales* quoted some creaking lines by Philips:

> . . . that cloud-piercing hill
> Plinlimmon from afar the traveller kens,
> Astonishment how the goats their shrubby browse
> Gnaw pendent . . .

The "shrubby browse" remains, but pendent goats no longer gnaw it.

As you will have noticed, Plynlimon bears several names. The latest Ordnance Survey calls it Plumlummon, but down at Llangurig they spell it according to the day of the week.

George Borrow knew what the name meant: "The mountain of Plynlimmon", he wrote, "is the third in Wales for altitude, being inferior only to Snowdon and Cader Idris. Its proper name is Plum, or Pump, Lummon, signifying the five points, because towards the upper parts it is divided into five hills or points." The highest of the five is approximately 2,500 feet above the sea. If you climb here alone, and break a leg, you may die before they find you. A botanist will commune with his algae, the zoologist with a universe of creeping things, but during five ascents I never saw an animal on the summit, and only once a human being.

At last a signpost marks journey's end. Borrow described it precisely: "The source of the Severn," he reported, "is a little pool of water some twenty-five inches long, six inches wide, and about three deep. It is covered at the bottom with small stones, from between which the water gushes up." Borrow ought to have known, because he came here with a local guide; yet some shepherds still doubt that he ever reached the source. A few people doubt that the source is reachable, arguing that several pools confuse the issue. It is a matter for geologists. I am content to know that somewhere very near to this place the Severn does rise and shine.

"The child," said Wordsworth, "is father to the man." Likewise a stream begets the river. Of the physics of water I know next to nothing, yet the Lucretian *nil ad nilum* suggests that the sea itself swallows some particles of the beck which here trickles among boulders and moss. Certainly the beginning fits the end. The Thames is chiefly a sociable river; the Tyne, too, becomes a meeting place for motorists; and Duddon flows accompanied through most of its short life. But Sabrina went her own ways, and they were sequestered.

On my last ascent the sun shone, and Cader crouched like a lion in the north. The ground was streaked with snow. The world below seemed vague. Only the treeless summits were precise, falling away like skins from an onion. It was difficult to believe in the existence of traffic jams, cinemas, Moon probes, and betting offices.

For a moment I shared Edward Gibbon's sadness when he, too, reached a long journey's end: "I had taken leave," he sighed, "of an old and agreeable companion, and whatsoever might be the future of my *History*, the life of the historian must be short and precarious." Plynlimon, however, tends to purge a personal nostalgia, it takes the larger view.

Mapped therefore on my mind, the Severn from *alpha* to *omega* outspread itself before me on the mountain, so that Montgomery arose from a wind-worried solitude, seeming warmly companionable . . . and Buildwas arose, the ghost of an abbey that did not die . . . and Mary Webb arose, from the dead to the Marches . . . and Arley's lovers, handclasped beside sunlit water . . . Elgar at Broadheath, with a cheap violin under his arm, and in his head the notes that will remain beyond price . . . the May morning on Malvern Hills when Langland dreamed of Peter the Ploughman and his heavy yoke . . . a countryman's calendar carved at Ripple church . . . the old men of Awre, listening with Mother in a deep and summer stillness . . . Gatcombe's bearded sea-captain, bespeaking timber against the Armada . . . W. G. Grace, learning to play a straight bat in his Downend orchard . . . Jenner of Berkeley, weighing one life against millions . . . William Tyndale, in a prison cell, dreaming of the Severn as he knew it long ago . . . the pilots of the lower estuary, and the little English ship that sailed therefrom "unto the costes colde of Yseland".

Some of those visions are Welsh, some are English; and together they form links in a chain not only of bilingual destiny but also of every life that is lived beside flowing water. Life itself flows, and its other name is change. Change therefore had been the password as I travelled from the estuary to the source; yet the reply to that password was an *Adsumus* from the ghosts of men and women who had lived beside the Severn. The portrait changes indeed, and will continue to change, more rapidly than ever before, but not yet beyond recognition. Wales is still Wales; and England still is England.

No matter how you choose to define eternity, all things ought always to be viewed through its eyes, for that is the ultimate perspective. But rivers live longer than men. Thomas Fuller understood as much when he jotted down the old English proverb: "A thousand years hence the river will flow as it always did."

# INDEX

# INDEX

## A

Abercrombie, Lascelles, 60
Abermule, 172
Acton, Lord, 93, 111
Afon Ceirist, 183
Afon Garno, 180
Afon Trannion, 183
Alberbury, 159
Aldenham Park, 111
Alveley, 105
Apley Park, 111
ap Gruffydd, Llewelyn, 131
ap Gwilym, Daffydd, 152, 177, 181
Arley, 83, 103-4, 195
Arnold, Matthew, 152
Arthur, King, 164-6
Arthur, Prince, 101
Ashleworth, 56, 57
Astley, 93
Astley Abbots, 111
Atcham, 136
Attingham Hall, 136
Auden, W. H., 120
Aust, 12, 25, 29, 58
Avonmouth, 21, 22, 30, 83
Awre, 46-7, 58, 156, 195

## B

Bacon, Francis, 94
Baldwin, Earl, 13, 101, 125
Ball, Hannah, 53-4
Baker, Thomas, 51
Battlefield, 156
Baynham, John, 50

Baxter, Richard, 128-9
Beachley, 26, 28, 29
Bede, Venerable, 27, 136, 192
Beerbohm, Max, 88
Beirion, 183
Belloc, Hilaire, 70, 155
Benbow, Vice-Admiral, 145, 157
Bergson, Henri, 96
Berkeley, 15, 34, 37-40, 49, 61
Berriew, 164
Berrington, 127
Bevere Island, 91
Bewdley, 13, 43, 99, 101
Bewick, Thomas, 192
Birrell, Augustine, 71
Birtsmorton Court, 78
Bishop's Castle Railway, 135
Blount, Sir George, 103
Bonner, Bishop, 78, 92
Borrow, George, 138, 181, 194
Boscobel, 13, 89
Boswell, James, 110, 129
Bourne, Bishop, 92
Braithwaite, Richard, 189
Bray, Thomas, 167
Bredon, 68, 72
Breidden Hills, 147, 157
Bridges, Robert, 13, 64, 91
Bridgnorth, 108-11, 128
Brindley, James, 97
Bristol, 15, 17, 22, 30, 33, 40, 41, 99
Britten, Benjamin, 29
Bromley, family, 92, 111
Brooke, Rupert, 60

Broseley, 17, 112
Brown, T. E., 11, 53
Buckland, William, 26
Buildwas, 115–18, 195
Bushley, 69
Butler, Samuel, 84, 85
Byng, Hon. John, 146

C

Cabot, John, 18
Caersws, 174, 179, 180, 182, 184
Caldicot, 23
Cam, 40
Camden, William, 47, 103, 139
Campion, Edmund, 41
Canute, King, 32, 63
Cardiff, 17, 21, 30
Careless, Colonel, 89
Carlyle, Thomas, 13
Caxton, William, 37
Chaceley, 63
Charles I, King, 101, 160, 174
Charles II, King, 13, 88–9, 107, 128, 139
Charles V, Emperor, 41
Chateaubrian, 17
Chelmarsh, 104
Chepstow, 23, 29, 30
Cherbury, Lord Herbert of, 129–30, 168, 170, 182
Chipping Sodbury, 38, 40
Chirbury, 167
Church Stretton, 124
Churchyard, Thomas, 157–8
Cinderford, 32
Clareland, 93
Clarendon, Lord, 101
Clevedon, 15, 53
Clevelode, 81
Clywedog, 183
Clifford family, 42–3
Clifton, 82

Clutterbuck, Richard, 42
Coalbrookdale, 100, 112, 113
Coalport, 112
Cobbett, William, 80, 84, 91
Colchester, family, 50
Coleford, 32
Coleridge, S. T., 19, 115, 129, 142–3
Condover, 127
Conrad, Joseph, 23, 52–3, 68
Constable, John, 95
Coombe Hill Canal, 61
Cotswold Hills, 12, 49, 57, 71, 77
Cound, 127
Craik, Mrs., 67
Cressage, 126
Cromwell, Oliver, 26, 85, 88, 94
Cromwell, Thomas, 117, 132

D

Darby, Abraham, 113, 114
Darrell, Sir William, Bt., 43
Darwin, Charles, 83, 141–2
Daudet, Alfred, 95
Davies, David, 182–3
Davies, John, 170
Davies, the Misses, 179, 183
Davies, W. H., 19–20
Dawley, 113
Davenport, family, 111
Dda, Hywel, 185
Dean, Forest of, 30, 32, 34, 45–6, 49, 60
de Barri, Gerald, 173–4, 181, 192
de la Mare, Walter, 60, 125
de Nerval, 74
Deerhurst, 56, 62–3
Defoe, Daniel, 17, 22, 30, 37, 48, 52, 58, 59, 66, 77, 139, 162, 193
Dickens, Charles, 68, 82
Donne, John, 169, 170
Downend, 128
Down Hatherley, 55

Drake, Sir Francis, 45, 46, 105
Drinkwater, John, 12, 60
Droitwich, 17
Dryden, John, 42
Dymock, 60

E

Eardington, 105
Easton-in-Gordano, 22
Eaton Constantine, 128
Edward I, King, 188, 192
Edward II, King, 36, 37
Edward III, King, 50
Edward IV, King, 63, 64, 66, 99, 131, 186
Edward VI, King, 140, 162
Eistedda Curig, 192
Elizabeth I, Queen, 17, 40, 70, 78, 94, 124, 127, 136, 140, 150, 183, 184
Elizabeth II, Queen, 132
Elgar, Sir Edward, Bt., 13, 89–91, 100
Elmore, 51
Epney, 44
Evans, Caradoc, 151
Evans, Grace, 163
Evelyn, John, 146
Eyton, 129

F

Fan Hill, 183
Farquhar, George, 144–5
Fiennes, Celia, 17, 29, 35, 58, 59, 77, 143, 154, 193
FitzHardinge, family, 36
FitzWalter, Milo, 23
Fletcher, John, 114
Ford, 159
Forden, 164
Forthampton, 63
Framilode, 44, 48
Frampton, 42, 49
Fretherne, 43, 48, 49

Frost, Robert, 13, 60
Froude, J. A., 79
Fuller, Thomas, 143, 196

G

Gatcombe, 45, 46, 195
George I, King, 67
George IV, King, 60, 159
George, Lloyd, 162
Gibbon, Edward, 117, 195
Gibson, Wilfred, 60
Giffard, Charles, 88–9
Glen Hafren, 164, 174
Gloucester, 15, 23, 24, 31, 35, 40, 43, 44, 47, 48, 49, 50, 51, 55, 56, 58, 60, 63, 68, 100
Gloucester and Berkeley Canal, 42
Glyn, 159
Glyn Dwr, Owain, 21, 149, 150, 168, 184
Godwin, Bishop, 25
Gorn Hill, 184
Gosse, Edmund, 133
Great Woollaston, 159
Griffiths, Robert, 162
Groves, John, 105–6
Gully, James, 82
Gully, John, 44
Guise family, 51
Gwinnett, Button, 56

H

Hafren, River, 192, 193
Hallows, 91
Hampshill, 93
Hampton Lode, 106
Hakluyt, Richard, 78–9
Hanley Castle, 78, 79
Hardy, Thomas, 74, 124, 133
Hartlebury, 94
Hartlibb, Samuel, 46
Harvey, William, 160

Hazlitt, William, 142, 143
Hawkshaw, Sir John, 24
Hengwydd, 183
Henley, W. E., 52
Henrietta Maria, Queen, 33, 34
Henry I, King, 158
Henry II, King, 155, 173, 181
Henry III, King, 43, 81, 85
Henry IV, King, 156
Henry VI, King, 33
Henry VII, King, 131, 149
Henry VIII, King, 30, 36, 50, 78, 85, 124, 132, 149
Herrick, Robert, 33
Hewlett, Maurice, 176
Highley, 103
Holt, 92
Hone, J. F., 60
Hoskins, W. G., 95
Housman, A. E., 12, 72, 133-4
Hough, Bishop, 94
Hughes, John, 180
Hurd, Bishop, 94
Huskisson, William, 79-80

I
Ingram, family, 99
Ironbridge, 17, 114
Isle of Rossall, 156, 161
Islwyn, 12

J
Jackson, Sir Barry, 83
James I, King, 45, 132, 170
James II, King, 37, 187
Jenner, Edward, 38-9, 47
John, King, 35, 49, 85
Johnson, Samuel, 31, 129, 138, 141, 142, 151, 152
Jones, family, 162
Jones, Ronyon, 49
Jonson, Ben, 128

K
Kemeys, family, 23
Kennet and Avon Canal, 17
Kerry, 172
Keyes, Sidney, 117
Kilvert, Francis, 118
Kinlet, 103
Kipling, Rudyard, 52, 75

L
La Gallienne, Richard, 177
Landor, W. S., 39, 144
Langland, William, 13, 83-4
Latimer, Bishop, 192
Laud, Archbishop, 151
Lawrence, Robert, 145
Lechmere, family, 80
Leicester, Earl of, 183
Leigh, 61
Leighton, 123-4
Leland, John, 100, 101, 106, 138, 172, 180
Lewis, C. D., 75
Linchcomb, 93
Llangurig, 191
Llanidloes, 13, 58, 181, 183, 187-90
Llanidnam, 182
Llanwog, 180, 182
Llanymynech, 133, 159
Llyfnant Brook, 179
Lloyd, J. Y. W., 191
Longmynd, 115, 124
Longdon, 62
Loton Park, 159
Louis XVIII, King, 17
Lower Mitton, 97
Lydney, 30, 33, 34-5
Lyn Ebyr, 183

M
Macaulay, Lord, 42, 172
Madeley, 114

Maisemore, 55
Malory, Sir Thomas, 166
Malvern, Great, 82–4, 90
Malvern Hills, 12, 49, 77
Malvern, Little, 90
Margaret, Queen, 66, 70, 78
Marshall, Bishop, 25
Mary, Queen of Scots, 92, 111
Mary Tudor, 36, 72, 78, 92, 101
Marx, Karl, 142
Masefield, John, 13, 18, 20, 31, 60, 64,
   84, 104, 107, 147, 166
Mathern, 24
Matilda, Empress, 23
Maurice, Prince, 34
Meredith, George, 75
Minehead, 22, 92
Minsterworth, 50
Monmouth, Geoffrey of, 173
Monmouth, Humphrey of, 41
Monmouthshire, 15, 23, 25
Montgomery, 168–70
Moore, Thomas, 186
More, Richard, 186
More, Sir Thomas, 41, 137
Morfe, Forest, 106, 108
Morgan, Jenkin, 189
Moritz, Pastor, 63
Moryson, F., 81
Mount Severn, 191
Mythe, 69

N

Nailsworth, 20
Nass, 49, 170
Nelmes, Sarah, 38
Newburgh, William of, 67
Newnham, 49
Newport, 15, 19, 20, 21, 30
Newtown, 174–5, 179
Nibley, 31
Nithsdale, family, 163

O

Occam, William of, 13
Offa's Dyke, 161, 168
Oglethorpe, Bishop, 40
Oldbury, 30, 31
Ombersley, 91
Ormerod, Eleanor, 25
Oswald, Bishop, 85
Owen, Brothers, 191
Owen, Robert, 175
Owen, Robert Dale, 175–6
Over, 55, 77, 179

P

Parr, Thomas, 59, 159–60
Parry, family, 136–7
Patmore, Coventry, 189
Pecham, Archbishop, 189
Pegwyn-bach, 183
Pelagius, 151
Penderel, Richard, 89
Pennant, Sir William, 194
Pepys, Samuel, 45, 89, 121
Perceval family, 21–2
Percy, Bishop, 110
Philips, John, 64, 82, 194
Phipps, James, 38
Playfair, Lord, 27
Plygain, 186
Plynlimon, 19, 193
Pollock, Sir John, 93
Pool Quay, 161
Potter, Gillie, 142
Potter, Beatrix, 154
Portishead, 21, 22
Portskewett, 23
Powick Bridge, 85
Powis Castle, 163
Powis, Earls of, 163–4
Pryce, family, 174, 176
Purton, 44–5

## Q

Quantock Hills, 15, 18
Quatford, 105
Quatt, 106
Quay, 58
Quiller-Couch, Sir Arthur, 53

## R

Raikes, Robert, 53–4, 189
Raleigh, Sir Walter, 45
Reade, Charles, 82
Reade, family, 182
Rhiw, River, 164
Ribbesford, 99
Richard III, King, 67
Richard's Castle, 147
Richardson, John, 24
Ripple, 70
Rhys, Sir John, 148
Roberts, family, 90
Rodney, Admiral Sir George, 157
Rose, John, 112
Ross, Anne, 148
Royal Navy, 27–8, 45
Rudder, Samuel, 49
Ruskin, John, 88, 152, 182

## S

Sandford, family, 156
Sandhurst, 55
Saul, 43
Saxon's Lode, 70
Scott, Sir Walter, 169
Severn Bore, 47–8
Severn End, 80
Severn Falls, 193
Severn River Authority, 44, 83
Severn Stoke, 80
Shakespeare, 67, 81, 149, 151, 152, 156
Sharpness, 31, 35, 40
Shaw, G. B., 19

Sheperdine, 30, 31
Shrewsbury, 13, 100, 124, 138, 139–147, 186
Shrawardine, 158–9
Shrawley, 92, 93
Shropshire and Montgomeryshire Railway, 135
Shropshire Union Canal, 174
Sidney, Sir Philip, 111, 140–1, 143
Slimbridge, 15, 40
Smalman, John, 108
Smart, Christopher, 82
Smiles, Samuel, 81
Smith, Francis, 103
Spender, Stephen, 52
Spenser, Edmund, 158
Squire, Sir John, 20, 133
St. Alphege, 63
St. Augustine, 27, 126, 151
St. Curig, 191
St. Cuthbert, 136
St. Eata, 136
St. Tecla, 25, 31
St. Tewdric, 24
St. Theoc, 66
St. Woolos, 21
St. Wulfstan, 90
Staffordshire and Worcestershire Canal, 97
Stephen, King, 23
Stephens, Colonel, 136
Sternhold, Thomas, 46–7
Stevenson, R. L., 52
Stokesley, Bishop, 40
Stonebench, 48
Stourport, 51, 97–8, 99
Strata Marcella, 161
Strickland, family, 60
Strongbow, Richard, 49
Sturmy, Samuel, 22
Sudbrook, 24
Swift, Jonathan, 22

Swinburne, A. C., 15
Synge, J. M., 121

T

Talbot, family, 144
Tarlton, Richard, 127
Taylor, John, 52, 160
Tennyson, Lord, 82, 96, 167
Telford, Thomas, 55, 69, 100, 114, 115
Tern Hall, 136
Tern, River, 135
Tewkesbury, 13, 52, 59, 62, 63, 66–9, 83, 100
Thames and Severn Canal, 17, 43
Thomas, Edward, 60, 119
Thomas, R. S., 187
Thompson, Francis, 105
Tiddenham, 30
Tinley, 60
Tintern, 24
Traherne, Thomas, 119
Tredington, 63
Trefeglwys, 183
Tregynon, 179
Trevelyan, G. M., 12, 158
Trevisa, John de, 37–8
Trewern, River, 161
Tyndale, William, 31, 40–2, 195

U

Upper Broadheath, 89, 195
Upton, 71, 77–8
Upton Cressett, 105
Usk, River, 20

V

Van, 183
Victoria, Queen, 78, 85, 150
Vrynwy, River, 159, 161

W

Wakeman, John, 63
Walpole, Horace, 129, 130

Walsh, Sir John, 40
Walton, Izaak, 81, 103, 171
Wansdyke, 21
Warham, Archbishop, 50
Watson, Sir William, 155
Webb, Mary, 13, 73, 75, 122, 124–6, 135
Webb, Matthew, 113
Welshpool, 162–3, 169
Welsh Harp Society, 186
Wen, Daffydd y Garreg, 181
Wesley, John, 54, 88, 114, 188
Westbury, 49
Weston-in-Gordano, 21
White, Gilbert, 194
Whittington, Richard, 61
Wick, 44
Wickenden, William, 47
Wigwydr Brook, 183
Wilkinson, John, 112, 123
William I, 62, 130
Winter, family, 33–4, 45, 46
Wolryche, family, 106–8
Wolsey, Cardinal, 78
Wood, Anthony à, 43
Woodward, family, 70
Worcester, 13, 17, 48, 51, 70, 85–9
Wordsworth, Dorothy, 126
Wordsworth, William, 68, 110, 126, 139, 193, 195
Worfield, III
Worth, Thomas, 150
Wrekin, 12, 126, 131–2, 147, 157
Wroxeter, 133, 134–5
Wyatt, Sir Thomas, 11, 158
Wye, River, 17, 19, 30
Wynne, Sir John, 187
Wyre, Forest, 102

Y

Yarranton, Andrew, 93
Young, Francis B., 82, 158